THE SUMMER OF LIES

LOUISE DOUGLAS

Boldwood

First published in Great Britain in 2024 by Boldwood Books Ltd.

Cover Design by Alice Moore Design

Cover Imagery: Shutterstock

A CIP catalogue record for this book is available from the British Library.

Paperback ISBN 978-1-80048-617-1

Large Print ISBN 978-1-80048-618-8

Hardback ISBN 978-1-83561-909-4

Ebook ISBN 978-1-80048-620-1

Kindle ISBN 978-1-80048-619-5

Audio CD ISBN 978-1-80048-612-6

MP3 CD ISBN 978-1-80048-613-3

Digital audio download ISBN 978-1-80048-614-0

Boldwood Books Ltd
23 Bowerdean Street
London SW6 3TN
www.boldwoodbooks.com

For Lil and Lola. I miss you, my lovely girls. xxx

1

It had been the hottest summer that anyone could remember. Across Europe, heatwave records were broken. Trees started shedding their leaves in August and the surfaces of the roads melted. There were hosepipe restrictions and droughts. Vendors couldn't keep up with the demand for chilled drinks, ice and ice cream. Climate change protestors occupied capital cities. Deniers, for the most part, fell silent.

In the Finistère region of Brittany, in France, the seaside town of Morannez, on the Atlantic Coast, recorded its first ever breach of 40 degrees Celsius. There had been a number of uncontrolled fires. The worst had devastated 600 hectares of land in the ancient Forêt de Paimpont in the department of Morbihan. Everywhere, there were signs warning people not to throw cigarette ends from car windows; not to light fires or barbecues; to take care.

Still the wildfires burned; the flames fanned by the winds, for which that area was known. Summer breezes should have been a welcome respite from the heat, but they only made things worse.

Mila Shepherd lived in Morannez, but once a month she returned to England for a long weekend. She caught the Thursday night ferry from St Malo to Portsmouth, travelled by bus to Bristol and stayed with her fiancé, Luke Hogg, until Saturday morning, when she went to Maidenhead by train. She spent most of Saturday and Sunday with her mother, Lydia Shepherd, at Lydia's house: a gloomy villa on the banks of the Thames.

Mila did not look forward to visiting her mother, but as these weekends always followed a more-or-less identical routine, at least she knew what to expect. And as each visit progressed through its component parts, Mila knew she was drawing closer to it being over. Soon she would be freed of her daughterly obligations until the third weekend of the subsequent month when she would make her next visit from Morannez, where she had lived for the past two years.

This weekend was panning out exactly like those that had gone before – only hotter. Luke's apartment had been unbearably warm, so Friday night's sleep had been fragmented and sweaty. Luke had dropped Mila at Parkway railway station early on Saturday morning and she'd caught the train to Maidenhead, changing at Reading. Both trains had been stifling.

When she reached her destination, Mila had walked through the strengthening glare of the sun from the station to her mother's house, one of a number of individual Victorian properties backing onto the river. The soupiness of the air made her miss the ozone-dry atmosphere off the coast of Brittany, the brisk breeze that freshened Finistère, the blues and whites and greens of the place she now regarded as 'home'.

Most of the houses on the road where Mila's mother lived had been sold in recent years and purchased by the kind of people for whom money was no object. They had either been knocked down to make way for modern replacements – out with the old stone gable ends and sash windows and in with acres of glass and wrap-around balconies, turned into exclusive flats, or 'done up', with landscaped gardens, electronic gates, swimming pools and the like. The house that Lydia Shepherd had taken over after her mother's committal, with its lack of improvements, stood out like an ascetic at a beach party.

It was a turn-of-the-century brick-built pile, severe in aspect, with windows that appeared to be frowning out beneath angry gable-brows over the top of a straggly leylandii hedge that was three quarters dead. Weeds had sprouted in the gutter and the exterior woodwork was peeling and rotten. There was nothing to stop Lydia employing someone to come and make good the damage caused by time and weather, but she wouldn't do this on a matter of principle because, according to her, maintenance was not a woman's responsibility. She blamed Mila's father, her ex-husband Patrick Shepherd, for the state of the house, because he wasn't there to fix it. It was one of the many reasons she felt hard done by on account of his desertion.

Mila didn't know Lydia's exact financial situation, but she did know that Patrick helped her mother out and, in Mila's experience, Patrick was a reliably generous man. Mila felt guilty for doubting Lydia when Lydia complained about her financial struggles, but she couldn't help but be slightly suspicious about their veracity. She knew that Lydia had no outstanding mortgage to pay and still received a substantial income from her own parents' investments. In any case, if the house was too much for her, which it clearly was, she was at liberty to sell it.

'Why should I?' Lydia retorted, whenever Mila – gently and tactfully – pointed this out. 'This is the only home I've ever known. I don't want strangers crawling all over it, changing things.'

'If you're not here to see the changes, what would it matter?'

'My mother *loved* this house!' Lydia would cry. 'What would it do to her if she found out the rose garden was being dug up to make way for a... a jacuzzi!'

'Jacuzzi' was Lydia-speak for the worst in tastelessness.

Behind the words was the self-pity that was Lydia's constant companion. She had never, and would never, recover from Patrick's abandonment. She would never be happy and – according to her – it was all down to him.

Lydia's self-imposed martyrdom was her tragedy. It was obvious to everyone that she would be happier away from the Maidenhead villa and the memories it held. Lydia was not stupid, she must have, deep down, known this too. Mila sometimes wondered if Lydia enjoyed her situation, relished it even in some perverse way, or if she'd simply been enmired in it for so long that she couldn't picture herself anywhere else.

The house at 124 Acacia Road could have been lovely – and perhaps, in a time before Mila could remember, it had been, but now the endemic lack of care, combined with Lydia's bitterness, had tainted the property and its gardens and nothing was lovely any more. Inside, the house was moth-infested, dark and dank; outside, the garden was narrow, the soil was poor, and few plants survived. The garden ran down to a derelict boathouse looking out over the Thames. Some quirk in the way the river flowed meant that rubbish washed up and became trapped in the shallow inlet directly beside the old boathouse, along with grey foam, caused by some kind of effluent whose source had never been identified. The foam, together with the greasy sheen on the water's surface and the fact that there was almost always either a dead fish, a dead bird, and once even a dead sheep bumping against the rotten tyres bound to the planks at the entrance to the boathouse, meant Mila had never been tempted to try to swim there, nor even to cool her feet in the water as a teenager.

She hadn't lived at 124 Acacia Road since she left home to start work with the NHS when she was nineteen, but Mila still felt the same old discomfort when she returned, as if she didn't belong; as if she was in the wrong place, in the wrong time, in the wrong body. It was weird that she'd never missed her childhood home anywhere near as much as she missed the sea house, where she lived in Brittany, when she was away from it for more than a few hours. This weekend was no different. It had barely started and already Mila longed for it to be over.

Mila arrived at her mother's house just before noon on Saturday. The front door was wooden, with a stained glass insert in the shape of a semicircle divided into three segments on the top. The middle segment was cracked. All three were dusty with cobwebs and insect detritus. Mila rang the bell and, after some time, the door opened.

Lydia Shepherd was a tall, big-boned woman, with greying gingery hair that always made Mila think of Valerie in the Amy Winehouse song. She was pale as ever, a sheen of sweat on the surface of her skin. She was dressed in a skirt, blouse, tights and slip-on shoes like a vicar's wife in an Agatha Christie novel. Her hair was back-combed into a bun and she was wearing pink lipstick; her eyebrows drawn on with a pencil; rouge on her cheeks. Behind her, the hallway was dark, sombre as a church; the woodwork polished, the air thick with the smell of furniture wax, dust heated by the old vacuum cleaner, and fly-killer spray which hadn't been completely effective.

She managed one of her weak smiles when she saw Mila. 'Hello, darling.'

'Hi!' Mila stepped forward, took hold of Lydia – God, she was thin – and kissed her on her cheek. 'How are you?'

'Oh... you know,' said Lydia, the three words being shorthand for a litany of physical, emotional and practical complaints with which she wasn't yet ready to burden Mila – she'd save them for later tonight, after she'd exhausted her repertoire of uncomplimentary stories about people she knew.

'Good!' Mila said, as cheerfully as she could. She couldn't think of anything to add to this. She could have done with a prompt from her stepsister, Sophie.

Sophie had died two years previously in a boating accident, yet Mila still heard her voice in her mind and, most of the time, it was a comfort to her; it lifted her spirits. But Sophie's life was rooted in Morannez.

She had never been to Maidenhead; she had never met Lydia or Lydia's mother, Constance, and at times like this, when Mila would have appreciated some irreverent Sophie input, Sophie was absent.

'I'll make the tea, shall I?' said Lydia. 'Earl Grey all right?'

'Coffee for me if that's okay.'

'Coffee?'

Mila always drank coffee. Like her father, she preferred it to tea. In Lydia's eyes, this was another betrayal and one which seemed to catch her out each time Mila visited.

'Yes please. Without milk.'

Without milk was also like Patrick.

Lydia sighed in a put-upon manner, and went off to busy herself in the kitchen.

Mila, meanwhile, wandered out through the French doors at the back of the conservatory. Lydia, who had fallen out with her old gardener, must have found someone else to mow the lawn – perhaps it was the nice neighbour, Mr Singh – because it was tidier than the last time Mila had visited.

Mila found a spot where she knew Lydia couldn't see her through the kitchen window, took out her phone and checked her messages. There was a missed call from Sophie's mother, Mila's stepmother, Cecille Toussaint. Cecille, or Ceci, had married Patrick after he left Lydia, becoming the second Mrs Shepherd. Ceci was, in personality, optimistic and cheerful, the antithesis to Lydia. Although they were no longer together, Ceci and Patrick remained good friends and she and Mila had always been close. She had sent a message saying:

Call me when you have a moment – it's work.

Ceci ran a small agency, Toussaints, based in Morannez, that specialised in tracking down missing people, and took on other investigative commissions. After Sophie's death, Mila had taken her stepsister's place in the agency. She didn't officially work there any more, but she still got involved from time to time.

She glanced over her shoulder: the windows at the back of the house were open and she couldn't risk talking to Ceci and Lydia overhearing. Ceci was, according to Lydia, the reason for Patrick's desertion and the root cause of all Lydia's unhappiness; her *nemesis*. Lydia couldn't bear to even hear Ceci's name. To call her stepmother from Lydia's house would be the most disloyal thing Mila could do.

Also in her messages was a photograph from Sophie's daughter Anaïs, more usually known as Ani. She was the number one reason why Mila now lived in France. Ani's father, Charlie, was missing after the accident that had claimed Sophie's life. Her only other direct relative was Cecille, who suffered from heart trouble. Of necessity, Mila had stepped forward to look after Ani. There was nobody else and it was only ever intended to be a temporary measure, but now, after all this time, Mila was committed to bringing Ani up.

Ani had sent a selfie of herself and her best friend, Pernille Sohar, sunbathing beside the pool at the back of the Sohars' house. The water glowed blue, reflecting the tall trees that surrounded the property. Mila enlarged the photo and scrutinised it, but found no evidence of smoke, or wildfires, in the background. She was reassured: Ani was safe, and having a great time.

Mila tried to remember how she used to feel when she was fifteen – the age Ani was now. Patrick had left the family home by then, he was married to Cecille, and Mila had been living here, in this house, with Lydia, but her memories were vague. During her teenage years, Mila had lived for the summers she spent in Morannez with Sophie. There, she had felt truly alive. The rest of the time – at school, and here with Lydia – she was merely existing. She'd blanked the Maidenhead memories of her past away, not deliberately, but they were gone.

Mila followed the parched lawn's gentle incline downhill to the boathouse and leaned one hand against the old handrail, originally built to stop anyone from falling into the water, but now so rotten as to be useless. The wood, beneath the sun's glare, was hot to the touch. In the gloom beneath what remained of the roof, Mila could see several large planks half submerged. She suspected that if there was heavy rain in the coming winter, much of what was left of the structure would be washed away.

Treading carefully, pushing aside brambles, nettles and stalks of the ubiquitous, invasive Himalayan Balsam, she made her way along the rotting boards at the side of the derelict building. At last, she reached the river's edge and looked down into the scummy surface of the water in the inlet.

And suddenly she was blindsided by a flashback.

She saw the body of a woman, face-down in the water, her arms extended on either side, her fingers splayed as if she were playing the piano, the body moving gently in rhythm with the river.

3

Mila gasped and grabbed hold of the nearest upright post. It lurched, but supported her weight as she squeezed her eyes shut, and tried to calm her breathing.

'Oh God,' she whispered, as the panic engulfed her. 'Oh my God!'

The woman in the water had seemed so real. Mila had seen every detail: the whorl of the hair on top of her head, the dirty sole of her bare left foot, the weed caught around her fingers.

Mila was frozen with shock, but was immediately comforted by Sophie's voice, in her head.

It's okay, said Sophie. *You're okay. It's not real. You know it's not real, Mila! There's nothing there. Look!*

Mila made herself open her eyes and gaze into the water. Sophie was right – nothing was there, save a discarded juice carton caught amongst the weeds, and a dead pigeon; an assembly of insects hovering above it. A little black moorhen darted into the reeds.

I told you, said Sophie. *I told you it was nothing.*

Mila had had flashbacks before but nothing like this. It was by far the strongest and the most realistic and it had had the most profound effect on her body.

What was that all about? she wondered.

It's stress, Sophie replied. *Lydia makes you stressed. She's not good for you.*

She's my mother, Sophie.

Not all mothers are good.

'Mila? What are you doing down there? Are you all right?'

Mila straightened and turned to see Lydia standing on the lawn a little way distant and higher than Mila. The sun was above and behind her, Mila couldn't make out her mother's expression.

'I'm fine, I just came over a bit dizzy,' Mila said. Despite her best efforts, her voice sounded weak.

'What do you mean?'

Mila laughed, and tried to shrug away the icy sensation in her veins. She tentatively let go of the post and began to make her way back along the length of the boathouse. As a rule, Mila avoided mentioning Sophie and Ani to Lydia, because – although they weren't as reviled as Cecille, even a mention of their names was enough to upset her. On this occasion, she had no choice but tell the truth.

'It's ridiculous,' she said, 'and absolutely nothing to worry about, Mum, but since Sophie drowned, once or twice, when I've been looking down into water, any water, I've had fake flashbacks, where I imagine I see her body.'

Lydia's face, already pallid, became whiter still. Her lips made a line. The sun shone through the frizz of her greying hair.

'That's horrific!' said Lydia. 'You *see* Sophie's body?'

'I don't *really* see it,' said Mila. 'They're not real memories. I never saw Sophie in the sea after the accident. Nobody even described the scene to me; I imagined it. It's my brain tormenting me. You mustn't worry about it. False flashbacks can be symptoms of shock. I hadn't had one for months before today. It took me by surprise, that's all.'

She jumped over the last clump of brambles and found herself back on the lawn. She walked up to Lydia and took her arm; soft flesh wrinkled around the big bones.

Lydia looked dreadful. 'Mila, I can't bear to think of you experiencing these kinds of awful visions.'

'I told you, it's nothing. I shouldn't have looked in the water.'

'It's not "nothing",' Lydia said in a trembly voice. 'You shouldn't be suffering like this. You shouldn't be living in France looking after Sophie's daughter. You should be here, in England, with your real family, where you belong, with me, where we can look after one another!'

Ani is my real family, Mila thought, although she would not dream of saying as much to Lydia.

'Mum, I'm fine,' she said.

'But obviously you're not! I saw your face just now, Mila, you looked like you'd seen a ghost. And you have to be careful, darling. Our family is fragile, emotionally. You know that.'

Lydia had a tendency to hint darkly at psychological trouble buried deep within the family genes. Her own mother, Constance, had been committed to a psychiatric hospital after a violent psychotic episode when Mila was a small child. She had never recovered sufficiently to come back out into the community, moving around a host of facilities before she settled in the home where she now resided. Lydia's sister, Ava, had also undergone electroconvulsive therapy as a young woman to treat episodes of mania. There were others, relatives who Mila had never met who had suffered too.

'The flashbacks don't mean there's anything wrong,' Mila said, sounding more convinced than she felt. 'In fact, they're the opposite. They're waking dreams: aspects of grief, and proof that I'm working my way through the trauma of losing Sophie.'

'Who told you that?'

It had been Cecille; the woman Lydia blamed for breaking up her marriage and condemning her to a life of bitter loneliness.

'I don't remember,' Mila said. She struggled to find a way to change the subject. 'Is the coffee ready, Mum? I'm parched.'

4

Every Saturday that Mila spent with her mother, they lunched at a depressing restaurant called the Rookery.

'Why don't we try somewhere different?' Mila had once asked, bored by the unimaginative menu; tired of the restaurant's dark, oppressive décor; and irritated by the obsequiousness of the head-waiter who haunted the place like a resident ghost.

'Because this is where your father used to take me when we were courting,' Lydia had replied and her face had taken on the hurt expression it always assumed when she thought of her ex-husband, Patrick.

Lydia's observation had surprised Mila, because Patrick was a foodie; the kind of person who would always, given the choice, plump for the least conventional option and The Rookery continued to serve up fare that couldn't have been ground-breaking in the 1950s, when it first opened as a hotel.

On this occasion, Mila ate pumpkin risotto, which was traditionally stodgy and unappetising, and obliged her mother by choosing a slice of treacle tart with custard for dessert. Then, feeling as if she had a cannonball in her stomach, she and Lydia walked to the institution where Grandma Constance lived.

Scrivingers was a grand old building, set in extensive gardens, every-thing secured behind a thick wall, with security cameras and various systems installed to stop intruders getting in and patients getting out. It had been purpose built as an asylum in the Victorian era, and was unashamed of its history – the letters ASYLUM were carved into the façade of the building, and various vestiges of the past remained inside. Since the 1970s, it had become a facility that cared for elderly and infirm psychiatric patients.

Mila and Lydia, fanning her face with her hand, announced their arrival via an intercom at the gate, which opened automatically, and they went through a kind of airlock system into the grounds. A gardener was moving the sprinkler to a different set of flowerbeds and a care assistant was pushing an old man in a wheelchair, the man's head nodding against his shoulder. Mila and Lydia crossed to the entrance and were admitted via another intercom.

Inside, the décor was tired. Efforts had been made to make the place appear homely, rather than institutional, but there was no getting away from the fact that it was dark, cavernous and full of straight corridors with locked doors at either end. It was also very warm.

'It's too much, this heat,' said the receptionist, who had set up a fan on the desk. Her cheeks were rosy red. 'I know we shouldn't complain, but I don't know how much more of this I can take. We're not set up for it in England, are we? Our buildings are designed to keep warmth in, not let it out. Anyway, remind me who you have come to see?'

'Mrs Banks,' said Lydia. 'Constance Banks.'

'Of course.' The receptionist checked her laptop screen. 'Connie is in her room,' she said. 'She's on good form. She's been behaving herself, eating well, taking part in group activities and therapy sessions. There've been no problems since your last visit; nothing you need to know about.'

'That's good,' said Lydia. 'Thank you.'

* * *

Constance Banks was eighty-nine years old. She was sitting in a chair by the open windows in her room on the ground floor, her hands, wizened and roped with blue veins, on the armrests, her legs, swollen and bruised, crossed at the ankles. She was thin as a bird. She had been dozing, but she lifted her head when Lydia put a hand on her shoulder and her eyes snapped open.

'Oh,' she said, 'it's you.'

Lydia stiffened but smiled. 'It's always me, isn't it, Mother? Nobody else ever comes to see you, do they? Look who I've brought with me.'

Mila stepped forward into Constance's line of vision. 'Hello, Grandma!' she said brightly, raising the hand that held the bunch of freesias they'd bought from the Waitrose en route.

The old woman leaned forward to see better. 'Where are my glasses?'

'Here,' said Lydia.

Mila's grandmother put the spectacles on, and peered at Mila. 'Is it you?'

'Yes, it's me,' Mila said cheerfully.

'I haven't seen you in years. Years and years. Not since you were a slip of a girl.'

'I came last month, Grandma.'

'Lydia?'

'Not Lydia, no. I'm Mila.'

'Mila?' asked Constance, looking at Lydia. 'What kind of name is that?'

'It's the name I chose for my daughter,' Lydia said.

'Well, it's a ridiculous name. And she's not *your* daughter. She's Lydia's!'

It was the same every time. They went through this same rigmarole; Constance mistaking Mila for Lydia; sometimes refusing to acknowledge Lydia at all, and then grumbling about Mila's 'silly' name. Often, she accused Lydia and Mila of trying to trick her, or of treating her like an imbecile. Sometimes, she became so confused that the visit would have to be curtailed. Occasionally, Lydia and Mila never even got to sit down.

Today, Lydia shook her head, put her fingertips to her forehead and went to stand in the corner of the room, behind Constance's chair, out of her line of vision. Immediately, the old lady became a little calmer. There was only one visitor to contend with now. The thumb of her right hand worried at the arm of the chair, a tic so often repeated that the upholstery in that spot was almost completely worn away.

'I'm Mila, Grandma,' Mila repeated gently, taking hold of the old woman's hand. It was light as a feather and covered in dry, papery skin. The nails were too long, ridged and yellow. Mila had attempted to cut them once; it hadn't ended well, so now she tried to ignore them. 'Remember me? The little girl you used to make biscuits with in the kitchen of the house in Acacia Road? I used to stand on a chair by the counter and cut out the dough with a cutter in the shape of daisy. You used to keep the cutters in an old biscuit tin with a picture of Princess Margaret and Antony Armstrong-Jones on the lid. And when we'd made the biscuits, we'd put a chocolate button in the middle of each flower.'

This was her single, clear, defining memory of herself as a child with her grandmother and consequently it was brought out regularly for an airing when she was here. Still, on this occasion, it took a great deal of energy to prompt the memory in Constance. Eventually, it seemed, the penny did drop.

'I remember you,' Constance said. 'Of course, I do! You were a greedy little monkey. You were always trying to pinch the chocolate buttons!'

'That's right,' said Mila.

'I used to smack your hands but you wouldn't stop. You were a wilful little bugger.'

Constance sat back in the chair, arms folded across her bosom, looking pleased with herself.

Mila was not convinced that her grandmother really had remembered. Constance always appeared to be paying attention, although she rarely retained information for longer than the duration of the visit. Lydia, on the other hand, appeared not to be listening, but had a habit of later asking in forensic detail about some apparently throwaway comment of Mila's – especially if the comment in question made even the most tenuous reference to Patrick.

The whole rigmarole was as familiar as it was exhausting. Mila fought to stop her eyes flicking up to the clock on the wall. She shouldn't wish her life away, but she couldn't wait for the next hour to be over.

5

It didn't seem to matter how much energy Mila expended during the weekends she spent with her mother. Afterwards, she always felt guilty, as if she should have stayed longer, and tried harder; been kinder; more entertaining; a better, more dutiful, more attentive daughter. When, at last, a dreary, overcooked Sunday lunch had been eaten and the dishes cleared away, it was time for Mila to say goodbye. Lydia's eyes filmed over with tears, as they always did. Her cold hands trembled as she embraced Mila.

'Don't leave it so long before you come next time,' she said.

'I'll come next month – same as I always do,' said Mila brightly.

'If you lived in England, I could see you more often.'

'Mum, when I did live in England, we didn't see each other any more regularly than we do now.'

'I'm not sure about that,' said Lydia. 'I think you might be misremembering the facts there, Mila.'

'It's your big birthday next month,' Mila said. 'I'll be here for that. I'll bring a cake. We can take it round to Scrivingers and celebrate with Grandma. Maybe I'll put chocolate buttons on top!'

'She won't appreciate it,' said Lydia; Mila's attempt to lift her spirits falling on barren ground. 'Don't you think she's got worse since the last time you saw her?'

'The confusion over who we are certainly isn't getting any better.'

'She doesn't see you often enough,' said Lydia. 'That's the problem. If she saw you more regularly, she'd stop confusing the two of us. Why don't you just stay one more night, and then you can pop in to have another chat with Grandma tomorrow? It would mean the world to her.'

'I can't,' said Mila. 'I have to get back to Brittany. There's nobody else to look after Ani.'

Lydia sniffed. She muttered something about priorities.

Mila did not react and, after a beat, when it became clear that she wasn't going to leap to her own defence and initiate an argument that would end in Lydia's tears, Lydia said stiffly: 'I can see that your mind's made up. I'll call you a taxi to the station.'

'I'm walking,' said Mila.

'But if you miss this train, Luke will be upset with you.'

'I won't miss the train, Mum. And even if I did, Luke would understand.'

'It seems silly to risk it when I'm more than happy to treat you to a taxi.'

'It's okay, thank you,' Mila said. She kissed Lydia's cheek. 'I'm off! See you next month.'

Mila wanted to walk because she needed a little time entirely alone, so that her brain could process everything that had happened during the visit, and begin to reset itself. It was the same every time she came. Mila arrived feeling as if something awful might happen – it never did, but the feeling persisted. When she left, she always felt troubled, as if something really had gone badly wrong. Every single time the pattern repeated. As she walked to the station, she wracked her brain, wondering if she'd said something unkind, or inadvertently told a lie, or done something she shouldn't have done. She could never pinpoint the cause of her discomfort, but it was always there.

Mila had never had counselling, but she had read books about mindfulness and analysed her own emotions and, when it came to her mother and grandmother, she'd found a toxic mixture of pity, affection, resentment and guilt. Nothing ever seemed to change for the better; not Lydia's bitterness, not Constance's confusion, and the house continued its process of sullen deterioration as if it, too, was determined to be miserable. The brief exercise Mila took walking to the railway station didn't make the feelings go away but helped to tamp them down.

At the station, Mila bought a chilled can of gin and tonic and went to sit on a bench at the end of the platform, in the sunshine. The air was still baking hot. She popped the lid of the can and drank, enjoying the buzz as the alcohol travelled through her veins. She watched a sparrow darting amongst the branches of a hawthorn tree at the side of the track and tried to push away the feelings the visit to her family had awoken inside her.

* * *

The train, when it came, was air-conditioned and mercifully uncrowded. Mila found a seat by the window and settled herself down, waiting until it was moving before she called Ceci, who answered with her usual brisk cheerfulness.

'Hello, darling girl. How are you?'

'I'm good. On the train. Sorry I took so long getting back to you.'

'It's no problem. I knew you'd be busy. How is Lydia? And how's your grandmother?'

'They're fine,' Mila replied. It would have felt disloyal to tell Ceci about Lydia, even though Ceci had an immense capacity for empathy. Mila would have liked to ask Ceci's advice as to the best way to cope with Lydia, but she'd never do it; she simply couldn't betray her mother like that. As a result, Ceci had no idea how dismal the situation in Maidenhead was. 'How are things in France?' Mila asked, to move the conversation forward.

'Good,' Ceci replied. 'I spoke to Madame Sohar earlier and she told me Ani and Pernille are going to the cinema in Bloemel to meet up with some friends and watch the Crawdad film.'

'Oh good! And everything's okay with the agency?'

'Busy.'

'What's Carter up to?'

'He's been talking to the authorities in Rennes about strategies to combat the recruitment of young people into drug gangs.'

Carter Jackson was an old friend of Sophie and Mila's. He had moved to Canada as a young man, and worked his way through the ranks of the police force, finishing that part of his career as a high-ranking detective in the drugs squad. He had given up the role when he returned to Brittany following his divorce and taken over Sophie's former position at Toussaints. His expertise, skill, and wide-ranging connections had done wonders for the agency. Largely thanks to him, it now had a glowing reputation, was achieving record profits, and had the capacity to take on more complex and interesting commissions than before.

Ceci was still talking. 'And I've been trying to track down the family of an old chap who died intestate but with a small fortune in cash hidden around his house. He had more than 20,000 euros in shoeboxes under his bed.'

'That sounds intriguing!' said Mila. 'Was that what you wanted to talk to me about?'

'Oh goodness no, not that! An enquiry has come into the agency from a Welsh woman who is missing a daughter and who doesn't do Zoom. It's a troubling case. The young girl has absconded with an ex-addict whose long-term goal, I suspect, is to extort money from the family. The daughter is chronically sick and very vulnerable. Could you go and speak to the parents tomorrow? It would mean you staying away an extra twenty-four hours.'

'Of course,' said Mila, 'only what about Ani?'

'I'll look after her until you get back.'

'Okay. And will you email over the details of the job?'

'I will. Tell me...' Ceci began, but the train went into a tunnel and the signal was lost.

Mila put the phone down and rested her head back against the seat, suddenly full of weariness and guilt. Ceci had only had to ask once and

Mila had agreed to extend her visit. Earlier, Lydia had used her full arsenal of emotional blackmail to try to persuade Mila to spend more time in Maidenhead, and Mila had insisted she had to get back to Brittany on the Monday ferry.

What kind of daughter was she?

6

At Bath station, Mila went into the Ladies', splashed water on her face and changed out of her T-shirt, shorts and deck shoes into a navy-blue linen dress and sandals. She sprayed perfume on every available piece of skin, put on a little mascara and lipstick, threaded some funky drop earrings into her ears, then went down the steps from the elevated platform and outside to meet Luke. He was freshly showered, wearing beautifully ironed clothes and was gratifyingly pleased to see her. They dropped her rucksack off in Luke's car, then went to the tapas restaurant on Barton Street for something to eat before the theatre.

In the walled garden, dipping into little pots of deliciously oily, garlicky, salty food, with South American music playing and the chatter of other diners around them, Mila offloaded the experiences of the previous thirty-six hours to her fiancé.

'Basically,' she said, dipping a piece of soda bread into the patatas bravas sauce, 'it was the most depressing visit in a series of depressing visits and both Lydia and Connie were in a worse state when I left than they were when I arrived, so I feel really awful. I don't know what to do for the best, or what to do at all.'

Luke frowned. He picked the wine bottle from the chiller and topped up Mila's glass.

'Thanks,' she said and, Ceci not being there to scold her for disrespecting good wine, drank it back as if it was lemonade.

Luke filled the glass again.

'And the worst thing is that it's only going to keep getting worse, isn't it? Connie's not going to get any better and Lydia's not getting any younger. The house is disintegrating round her, she only leaves it to go to the shops and to visit Connie. She has no friends that I know of and it's all just...' she threw her hands in the air in an Ani-esque gesture of frustration, '...hopeless!'

'Lydia needs some kind of hobby or interest,' said Luke.

'Yep. I have mentioned that to her about a million times.'

'Why don't you invite her to visit you in France?' Luke suggested. 'It might at least broaden her outlook.'

'Seriously? Invite her to Morannez? When she can't say a single nice thing about Ani, and she believes Ceci is the Devil's spawn?'

'But if she actually met Ceci, and Ceci had the chance to charm her...'

'No,' Mila shook her head. 'It absolutely wouldn't work.'

'And there's no other family you can ask for help?'

'Only my aunt, Ava, who disappeared decades ago and hasn't been heard from since. Not that I blame her. I'd've done a bunk too if I was her.'

Luke sighed. 'Then you need to have a word with your father.'

'Patrick? What's he going to do?'

'I don't know, but it is kind of his fault that Lydia's like this.' Luke spoke this last sentence carefully. Mila was not blind to her father's shortcomings but remained fiercely protective of him. 'What I mean,' Luke continued, 'is that Patrick wouldn't want all the responsibility for your mother and grandmother to be on your shoulders. He'd want to help you.'

Mila considered this for a moment and concluded that it was a fair comment. When Patrick asked how things were with Lydia, Mila had always, but especially lately, painted a picture of what Patrick wanted to hear, rather than telling him the truth. It wasn't as if Patrick needed protecting; nor had he asked for the situation to be sugar-coated, it was simply that, since childhood, Mila had always tried to please her father, as he had always tried to please her. Making him happy was her default position. It probably had something to do with love.

'Telling the truth…' she murmured. 'There's a novel concept.'

'Shall I order some more wine?' Luke asked.

'Is there time for another bottle?'

'I meant a glass, for you. I can't have any more if I'm driving.'

'Is there time for a glass?'

Luke looked at his watch – he still wore the watch that Mila had given him twelve years earlier for his birthday, the autumn after they first got together, a small loyalty that always made her feel tenderly towards him. 'The play starts in fifteen minutes.'

'No more wine then,' Mila said sadly. 'The play had better be worth it.'

They had seats to see the Deborah Warner directed version of *The Tempest* at the Ustinov Studio, part of the Bath Theatre Royal complex. Patrick had recommended it to Mila as a must-see, he said the performance by the actor playing Ariel was out of this world. He'd even organised the tickets for them. Mila had read a review in the *Guardian* that had mentioned shit being thrown around the stage. Theatrical faeces was the last thing she wanted to see.

She stood up reluctantly and they made their way to the bar to settle the bill.

'I'm really not in the mood for Shakespeare,' Mila said, thinking of the review; taking Luke's hand. 'We could just go and drink wine somewhere instead.'

'Give it a chance,' said Luke. 'You might enjoy it.'

7

Patrick had been right about the play. It was challenging, exhilarating and brilliantly acted, directed and staged. When Mila and Luke emerged into the muggy warmth of the Bath evening, Mila had forgotten that a couple of hours earlier she'd been mentally and physically exhausted. Now, she was buzzing.

She persuaded Luke to take her for a cocktail and then they bought a bottle of chilled Sancerre with a screw top and found a bench beside the wall that overlooked Pulteney Weir and sat together, Mila drinking wine from the bottle and Luke sipping the water he'd brought from home. Despite the lateness of the hour, the air was still oppressively warm. Mila texted her father and Patrick called her back at once and they had an emotional video call during which Mila said a great deal about _The Tempest_ and the weirdness and brilliance of the staging in the tiny theatre and not a single word about Lydia's unhappiness.

After that, Luke and Mila went back to the car, he holding her hand, she singing 'American Pie', which took a long time as each time she forgot a lyric she had to return to the beginning. She still hadn't got beyond the jester stealing the thorny crown by the time they were back at Luke's flat just off the Bath Road in Bristol.

'Shh,' Luke said, as Mila leaned against him as he opened the door to the communal staircase.

'Don't you like my singing?'

'I love it, baby, but it's an acquired taste and not everyone's as fond of you as I am.'

Mila giggled.

She stumbled upstairs and into Luke's apartment. While he made peppermint tea, she washed and brushed her teeth and then Luke brought in the tea and made love to Mila, who was struggling to stay awake but managed to stay conscious long enough for Luke to come. As soon as he did, she fell asleep without drinking the tea, which was a mistake because she was dehydrated when she stirred in the night. She drank the tea cold and went back to sleep and when she woke it was Monday morning and she was saturated with tiredness.

Luke had left a note to say he'd gone to work – he was a detective with the Avon and Somerset Police – and that he loved her. Mila made coffee and took it into the living room with the big picture window looking out over the gentrified industrial estate known as The Paint-works. She curled up in a corner of the sofa, opened the window to let in some air – the air did not want to come in, although several flies accepted the invitation – lifted the lid of her laptop and read the email that Ceci had sent.

We've had an enquiry from Gwyneth Moorcroft (Mrs) of 63 Thornbury Drive, Wentloof Estate, Carnarth, on the outskirts of Cardiff. Her daughter Briony, aged 19, left home eight days ago with a woman called Billie Dexter, who's in her mid-twenties. Billie is a convicted criminal with a history of drug abuse. Billie verbally and physically assaulted Mrs Moorcroft, whose wrist was broken when she tried to stop the two girls leaving in a van belonging to the Moorcrofts' cleaning company. Subsequently, the Moorcrofts discovered that money, bank cards and other items were also missing.

Briony has a number of complex medical conditions and is likely to become severely ill if she doesn't receive appropriate care.

The Moorcrofts know that Billie and Briony are in Brittany

because money has been withdrawn from cashpoints in Morannez and Lorient and the cards have also been used in supermarkets and clothes shops. The cards have now been blocked – the Moorcrofts are concerned that otherwise their accounts will be emptied.

I spoke to Mrs Moorcroft at length on the telephone, but she and her husband, Briony's father, want to talk to someone (you) in person. Mrs M. sounds as if she's only just managing to hold herself together. She's – understandably – terribly anxious about her daughter. Her contact details are below.

I told her that unless she heard otherwise, you'd be with her at 12 noon tomorrow (Monday) – I checked the train times from Bristol and that should give you plenty of choices. I've changed your ferry ticket to the Tuesday morning crossing, link attached.

Hope that's all okay. I love you.

8

It was sweltering outside, but the interior of the Moorcroft family's home was air-conditioned and cool.

Mrs Gwyneth Moorcroft, mother of the missing Briony, was sitting on the edge of the beige-coloured sofa, the ditsy, floral fabric of her dress stretched tightly over her knees. She had a tic, the corner of her eyelid twitching relentlessly; her anxiety crackling like static. As well as the broken wrist, she had the remnants of a black eye sustained during the altercation with Billie Dexter when she'd tried to stop Billie and Briony from leaving. She took off the sling to show Mila her wrist, which was in a lightweight cast with Velcro fastenings. Mrs Moorcroft explained about the bone that was broken, the ulna, and the complex nature of the fracture. She was from a nursing background, she said. She had worked for some time in the orthopaedic clinic at Llinas Powys Hospital. She knew about these things.

'Is it painful?' Mila asked.

'The bruises are worse,' said Mrs Moorcroft, 'but not being able to use my wrist makes everything awkward. As if life wasn't difficult enough at the moment anyway.'

When she got up to make coffee, refusing Mila's offer to help, Mrs Moorcroft walked awkwardly, favouring her right leg. She was keeping herself as calm and controlled as she could, but she had the vibe of a ticking bomb that might explode, or implode, at any moment. Mila felt desperately sorry for her.

'You don't expect something like this to happen,' Mrs Moorcroft said to Mila, when she returned with the refreshments. 'You don't expect your precious daughter to be brainwashed by a... a...' She struggled to find a word to describe Billie, 'A *monster*. You don't expect that *monster* to steal from you and drive off with your daughter with no care in the world about what she was doing or who she was hurting. And now we don't know where they are, or if Briony's okay, or if we're ever going to see her again!'

At this point, David Moorcroft, husband to Gwyneth and father to Briony, came into the living room. He told Mila not to get up, shook her hand, apologised for not being present sooner, but explained he'd had to make an important work call.

'Try to stay positive,' Mila said, to both Moorcrofts. 'In the majority of cases, when the missing person is a young person, like Briony, they're soon back home none the worse for their experience.'

'But Briony isn't a *normal* young person,' said Mrs Moorcroft. 'And Billie Dexter isn't normal either, is she, David?'

'No,' said Mr Moorcroft. 'She's certainly not normal.'

'Evil,' said Mrs Moorcroft bitterly. 'She's evil.'

'That's a strong word,' Mila said gently.

'How else am I supposed to describe her, this woman who's abused our kindness and made off with our daughter?'

They were sitting in the living room of the Moorcrofts' home, an executive-style house on an executive estate. The houses were new, fancy, superficially different, but essentially the same. They'd had air conditioning installed, Mrs Moorcroft told Mila, because Briony's fragile body couldn't cope with extremes of heat or cold. It had been a godsend during this summer's heatwave. She dreaded to think how Briony must be suffering in France, with the mercury rising relentlessly, and wildfires burning.

'Her lungs are weak,' she said. 'She'll struggle to breathe if the air's full of smoke. Is it as bad as it looks on the television?'

'The firefighters are doing an amazing job,' Mila answered. She didn't tell Mrs Moorcroft that the situation was at least as bad as the newscasters described; that several forest enclaves of exclusive holiday homes had burned to the ground and that vast swathes of the Brittany countryside had been turned into ashy wastelands.

She sipped her coffee and looked about her.

The exterior of the house had been picture-perfect and the interior was immaculately tidy too; like a show home. As she'd walked through the estate a little earlier, Mila had noticed that the gardens were oddly kempt, not a rogue weed, nor a discarded toy anywhere. Some of the lawns had been almost violently green, in marked contrast to the parched, patchy yellowness of the heat-baked grass in the rest of the country. It was only when she bent to touch it, that Mila had realised the turf was made of plastic. The whole estate had an air of artificiality about it, as if the land on which it was built was trying to pretend it hadn't once been a rough old sheep field, but wasn't entirely succeeding in the deception.

Mila put down her coffee cup on the coaster on the occasional table that had been placed beside her chair. Everything in the room was in a shade of beige or brown, with teal highlights. Large vases contained tasteful silk flowers. The sofa cushion covers were all the same mocha colour, but differently textured; one sequinned, one velour, one fluffy. The room had the aura of a Wayfair catalogue. 'Do you mind if I ask you a few more questions, Mrs Moorcroft?' Mila said.

'Ask whatever you want. I'll tell you anything I can that will help. *We* will, won't we, David?'

'Of course.'

David Moorcroft was standing by the windows. He was a good-looking man in early middle-age; younger than Mrs Moorcroft, Mila would have guessed. His energy was in contradiction to his wife's. He seemed calm and thoughtful, as if, while she verbally careered between her ideas and memories, he was trying to plot the most rational way through his own.

Mila checked her notes. 'You said, Mrs Moorcroft, that this is the first time Briony has left home?'

'Yes.'

'But she must have had days away before now?'

'She's never so much as gone to the shops without me before.'

'Never?'

'All her life, Briony has been sick. She was born prematurely and was in the neonatal intensive care unit for the first twelve weeks of her life. She had to be resuscitated three times. She was in and out of hospital as a toddler. Then, when she was six and first diagnosed with cancer, we were told it would be a miracle if she lived until her seventh birthday.'

Inside Mila's head, Sophie whistled. *That's awful!*

'How frightening for you,' said Mila.

'It was terrifying and it's still terrifying now.' Mrs Moorcroft glanced at her husband. 'With treatment, Briony got over that particular illness, eventually, but cancer has recurred periodically, it won't leave her alone. And there have been other problems. Briony's conditions are complex.'

'I understand.'

Mrs Moorcroft continued: 'If she doesn't take the correct medication in the correct dosage every day, Briony will soon become critically ill. And even if she does take the drugs, nobody else knows how to look after her except me. She literally depends on me to keep her alive, doesn't she, David?'

'Yes,' said Mr Moorcroft. 'She does.'

'Presumably Briony knows what drugs she needs to take?'

'Yes, but she only took a week's supply with her. She'll have run out by now. If she doesn't get new supplies soon then...' She trailed off, unwilling to say the words.

'She might die,' said Mr Moorcroft. 'I'm sorry to be so blunt, but that's how it is.'

'Okay,' said Mila, feeling the urgency of the situation shift up several gears. 'Let's hope Billie is looking after Briony.'

Mrs Moorcroft's expression became bitter. 'Billie Dexter wouldn't know what to do if Briony were to have a seizure,' she said, almost spitting the words. 'She wouldn't know how to help Briony if she was struggling to breathe. She'd be useless in an emergency.'

'I can see why you're so concerned.'

'With respect, Ms Shepherd, I don't think you can have any idea how distressing this situation is for us,' said Mr Moorcroft.

'You're right. I can't.' Mila turned the page on her notebook. 'Can I ask, how did Billie and Briony meet if Briony never goes out?'

Mrs Moorcroft shot a furtive glance to her husband.

'Billie was an employee,' said Mr Moorcroft.

'We own a cleaning business,' said Mrs Moorcroft. 'David runs it, while I care for Briony.' She looked to her husband again. He did not acknowledge her and she carried on speaking. 'A few months ago, we were desperate for staff, we'd lost several workers to the new Tesco superstore and then Billie tipped up looking for a job.'

'She wasn't the kind of applicant I'd have taken on, if I'd had a choice,' said Mr Moorcroft.

'Why not?'

'All kinds of reasons. The most significant being that she had a criminal record.'

Mrs Moorcroft interjected. 'But she told him straight off she'd been in prison, didn't she, David? And because she was honest with him, about her background, he thought he could trust her.'

'Do you know why Billie was in prison?' Mila asked.

'Drug-related crime,' said Mrs Moorcroft. 'Theft. But she told David she'd been to rehab, that she was clean now, and that her criminal days were behind her. She said she was trying to turn her life around.'

'It was foolish, in retrospect, to trust her,' said Mr Moorcroft, 'but she seemed genuine. I wanted to give her a chance.'

'David is good like that.'

'No, I won't be praised for altruism. It was a selfish move. It's tough, these days, finding employees,' said Mr Moorcroft. 'I used to have people queuing up to work for me. Now I sometimes have to join the cleaning teams myself.' He gave a loose shrug. 'I don't mind getting my hands dirty, it's not that. It's just there's so much else to do when you run your own business. You have to meet so many criteria, tick so many boxes, look after so many people. And the clients expect you to respond to them whenever they want you, any time, day or night. It's hard keeping all the balls in the air.'

'He works all hours,' Mrs Moorcroft confirmed. 'He has to, to keep the roof over our heads. That's why Briony and I are so close. We spend every minute of every day together. Her not being here is like I'm missing part of me.'

'Have you reported Briony as missing to the police?'

'It was the first thing we did. When we told them the circumstances of Billie and Briony's departure, they said the assault on me was a crime, and also the thefts, obviously. They're happy to investigate, but we have to be sure we want them to because Briony might be implicated – which is rubbish. We have video from our security camera which shows the van driving off, and it's clear who is responsible.'

Mrs Moorcroft paused for breath, then continued, 'According to them, Briony is nineteen, and she left home of her own free will, which she's entitled to do as a consenting adult. But it *wasn't* her own free will because she never would have gone if Billie Dexter hadn't brainwashed her into leaving, would she, David?'

'No.'

'Okay,' said Mila. 'We need to move quickly on this. Would it be possible for me to see the video you mentioned?'

'Sure,' said Mr Moorcroft. 'The app's on my phone.'

9

The video was good quality. It began with a still picture of a small van, liveried in the blue-and-white colours of *Moorcroft's Maid Services,* with a logo of two perky, cartoon women dressed in aprons and rubber gloves holding an assortment of mops, brushes and dusters. The van was parked on the sloping drive outside the Moorcrofts' house; Mila recognised the faux-wooden planters beside it. On the other side was a BMW, registration MM5 DAV. Mila had walked past that very car a little earlier.

After a few moments, someone appeared from beneath the camera above the front door. It was a woman, a tall, broad-shouldered, boyish character, wearing football shorts and a polo shirt, workmen's boots and sports socks. She was carrying a holdall-style bag, which she put on the drive. Her muscular arms were covered in tattoos and her hair was shaven around the neck and ears, floppy on top.

'That's Billie,' said Mr Moorcroft, 'with Briony's bag.'

The woman looked around, and behind her, then opened the passenger door of the van. She went back into the house, and returned with a wheelchair, which she collapsed and loaded into the back along with the bag. Then she beckoned to someone standing in the house doorway, her movements were urgent.

'There's no audio,' said Mrs Moorcroft, 'but you can see she's saying:

"Come on, hurry up." Effectively bullying Briony.'

Mr Moorcroft covered his eyes with his hand.

A tiny, hobbling figure emerged, clutching onto the handrail that had been installed next to the ramp that led up to the front door. This girl was so thin and frail that it was almost painful to watch her. Swaddled in a huge jumper and tracksuit bottoms, she could have been an old woman. Her long hair was fastened on either side of her head into bunches. She made her way down the ramp, took hold of the hand that Billie was extending and allowed herself to be helped into the passenger seat of the van. Billie pushed the door shut, ran round to the driver's side, got in and started the engine. The next moment, Mrs Moorcroft came running out of the house and down the ramp. She was dishevelled, bleeding from the cut above her eye. She grabbed hold of the handle on the passenger side, trying to open the door, but it was locked.

As the van began to move, Mila caught a glimpse of Briony's pale, horrified face looking through the window. Mrs Moorcroft was clinging on for dear life, but it was evident Billie had no intention of stopping. As the van turned into the road, Mrs Moorcroft was dragged forward, and then let go of the handle. She hit the ground, which sloped steeply, hard. The violence of the episode explained the severity of her injuries.

The video ended with one of the neighbours rushing out of her front door to tend to Mrs Moorcroft, leaning over her, helping her to her feet.

'Where were you while this was going on?' Mila asked Mr Moorcroft.

'I was at work in Cardiff. I didn't find out what had happened until I got a phone call from Mrs Latif. She had driven Gwyneth to the local medical centre.'

'Mrs Latif's the lady in the video?'

'Yes. She witnessed the whole thing. She said she'd be happy to speak to you if that would be helpful.'

'It's not necessary. The video shows exactly what took place.'

Mrs Moorcroft touched her injured wrist. Mila felt another pang of sympathy for the woman.

'Have either of you spoken to Briony or Billie since they left?' she asked.

'No,' said Mr Moorcroft. 'I left messages on Billie's phone, telling her how absolutely vital it was that Briony keeps up with her medication, but she never responded, and after twenty-four hours, the number didn't work any more.'

'She probably bought a new SIM when they arrived in France. Have you been round to her address?'

Mr Moorcroft looked embarrassed. 'I don't know where Billie lives.'

'No?'

'There was a form for personal details that she was supposed to fill in and return to me when I took her on, but she never did.'

'Okay. What about Briony's phone? I guess you've tried that?'

'She doesn't have one.'

Seriously? cried Sophie. *A nineteen-year-old girl without a phone?*

'Okay.' Mila passed Mr Moorcroft's phone back to him. 'Would you forward that video to me, please? And any other good-quality pictures you have of Billie and Briony.'

'There's a photo of Billie on the business website. You can take it from there.'

'Okay.'

Mila scanned back through her notes.

'So we know from the cash withdrawals that Billie and Briony are somewhere close to the town of Lorient in Brittany. Does Briony have any connection with France?'

'No.'

'She never went there on a school trip?'

'She was home-schooled.'

'What about holidays?'

'Briony was too poorly for normal holidays. We only ever went to a special hotel in Devon that catered for Briony's needs.'

'And Disney...' Mr Moorcroft interjected. 'Once we were given a trip to Disney World in Florida by a charity that fulfils dreams for chronically ill children.'

'It must have been Billie's idea to go to Brittany,' said Mrs Moorcroft.

'Though God knows why she chose there.'

'Right. And I'm guessing there's no tracker on the van?'

'We never thought we'd need one. It's a distinctive van. It shouldn't be that hard to find it in France, should it?'

'Let's hope not.'

Despite Mrs Moorcroft's evident distress, she had taken trouble with her appearance. Her hair was neatly styled, and she was wearing make-up and jewellery. Mr Moorcroft was also pulled together. They were the kind of people who would always make the effort to keep up a good show, no matter what was going on in their lives, or that they were exhausted. There was something admirable in their stoicism, but their determination to present such a respectable and united front in these circumstances was unusual.

Mila could feel the couple's desperation and did not doubt the depth of their concern for the safety of their daughter, nor their desire for her to be brought home. But she couldn't shake off the feeling that there was something else; something she hadn't been told. And it was this conviction that some important detail was being withheld that niggled as she put her phone back into her bag and gathered up her reading glasses, notebook and pens.

What had she missed? What question had she omitted to ask?

'If you think of anything later, that might help us track Briony down, you can always give me or one of my colleagues a call,' said Mila. 'You've spoken to the boss, Cecille Toussaint, already. And the third member of our team is Carter Jackson. He used to be a detective with the Canadian police. He knows everything about surveillance and tracking and getting people out of sticky situations. He's very good at what he does. As soon as I leave here, I'm going to call Brittany and tell them what you've told me. They'll start looking for Briony straight away and I'll join the search myself when I get back.'

'What about *her*?' Mrs Moorcroft asked. 'Billie Dexter?'

'We don't have any authority over Ms Dexter.'

'She will try to persuade Briony to stay with her. We know that she will. That's the only way she'll be able to keep getting money out of us.'

'You need to get Briony out of Billie's clutches,' said Mr Moorcroft. 'That's the bottom line.'

'We'll do everything we can to get your daughter safely back home to you,' said Mila. 'Try not to worry.'

10

As Mila stood, she observed details of the room. It had been adapted to make it suitable for use by a person using a wheelchair and there was other evidence of Briony's infirmity. On top of the largest of the occasional tables was an oxygen machine, narrow plastic hoses wrapped about it, and a wicker basket contained a selection of folded shawls and blankets, perfect for wrapping around shoulders and knees. Tucked unobtrusively behind the waste paper bin was a little yellow bucket, of the kind used by hospitals to dispose of needles and other sharps.

An old golden Labrador was stretched on his side beneath the extruder of the air-conditioning unit. He'd lain so still, Mila hadn't noticed him before.

'Is there anything else?' Mrs Moorcroft asked. 'Anything else at all that we can help you with?'

'Would you mind if I had a quick look in Briony's bedroom?' asked Mila.

'Of course we don't mind,' said Mrs Moorcroft. 'Come with me.'

Mila followed Mrs Moorcroft out of the living room, through a hallway, one part of which had been given over to a glass-walled wheelchair access lift, and up a wooden staircase, carpeted in beige. The dog yawned, stretched, and followed them. Mila spotted a framed photograph of Briony on the wall beside the stairs, a picture taken in a hospital. Briony in jolly Christmas pyjamas was sitting in a chair, a drip attached to her arm and an oxygen tube under her nose. Her mother, in full festive regalia, was standing behind her, with her hands resting on the back of the chair. The Labrador was there too, patiently sporting a pair of reindeer horns on his head and a jacket that said: *Therapy dog, sponsored by Moorcroft's Maid Services.* The company logo featured on the side of what appeared to be a sack of Christmas presents. Smiling nurses were photobombing the picture, giving the thumbs-up and wide grins. Briony had a wizened little face. She looked far younger than her years, yet at the same time, older too; like a character from a fairy tale.

'That was last Christmas,' said Mrs Moorcroft, 'at St Anne's. Briony was terribly poorly. We were worried for a time that she wouldn't pull through.'

'What exactly is the matter with Briony?' Mila asked.

'A complex array of illness,' said Mrs Moorcroft. 'Recurring cancer compounded by an autoimmune condition: ERGA.'

'I've never heard of that.'

'It's terribly rare.'

'It sounds as if your daughter has been unlucky.'

Mrs Moorcroft nodded. 'Poor child. The staff at A and E say she ought to have a season ticket, she's there so often.'

They reached the top of the stairs and walked past the upper section of the lift.

'This is Briony's room,' said Mrs Moorcroft, pausing outside a door decorated with a porcelain plaque that spelled the letters of her daughter's name. 'Go on in.'

Mila stepped into a large, square bedroom, a riot of violet and pink, the bed covered by a fluffy throw, the walls draped with fairy lights. The dog padded in after her. To one side, a door-shaped gap revealed an en-suite bathroom; there were handles on the walls, a shower with a seat in place beneath it and a red emergency cord.

Inside the bedroom, dolls were lined up on a large chest that looked like a toybox. Beside it was an elaborate dolls' house, almost as tall as Mila. Amongst the plethora of fairy lights and glow-in-the-dark stickers, little wooden plaques hung on the walls, in the shape of hearts and flowers. Ani was years younger than Briony, and her room was less childish than this.

'Briony's condition means she's young for her age,' Mrs Moorcroft said, as if reading Mila's mind. 'Outwardly, she's a woman. She's small and underweight. Her body has developed...' She made a vague gesture in the region of her own breasts, 'but emotionally and intellectually, she's still a little girl. That's why David and I are finding this so difficult. You can't imagine what goes through our heads every evening. Briony's such a sweet girl, so eager to please. If Billie Dexter is taking advantage of her, she wouldn't know she was being used. And every day without her drugs, her condition is becoming more unstable and she'll be experiencing more pain...' She trailed off, shaking her head in despair.

'I'm sorry,' said Mila. 'I can see how difficult this is for you.'

'Thank you,' said Mrs Moorcroft. 'You've been so understanding.'

Mila tilted her head to read some of the spines of the books on Briony's bookshelves; they were mostly ballet stories and girls' boarding school adventures. None of the Jackie Collins novels or Jilly Cooper-style romances that she and Sophie used to read as teenagers. Ani was addicted to classic sci-fi. She was currently reading her way through John Wyndham's catalogue. Even she had outgrown these kinds of books.

'Does Briony have a computer?' Mila asked.

'We have a family computer downstairs, but she only uses it with my supervision.'

'And she doesn't have a phone. She doesn't go out. How does she stay in touch with her friends?'

'She doesn't have friends. She doesn't need them. I'm her best friend. We have one another.'

Poor kid must have been lonely as fuck, said Sophie.

As if concurring, the dog pushed his nose into the palm of Mila's hand. Absent-mindedly, she stroked his soft ear.

She crossed to the window and looked down. Briony's bedroom was at the back of the house, on the other side to the living room. From this spot, Mila had a good view of the garden, with the leaves on the miniature trees and shrubs browning after the long, hot summer. Beyond, on the other side of the main road which marked the perimeter of the estate, was a park, with its pathways and flowerbeds; the huge war memorial plinth in the centre. If she turned to the left, and leaned forwards, the grey expanse of the Bristol Channel gleamed pewter.

Mrs Moorcroft came to stand beside Mila. 'This is where it started with Billie and Briony,' she said. 'The entrance to the park is just down there. Briony used to enjoy waving to people coming out of the gates. She had her regulars, people who used to look out for her. She started waving to Billie' – she spoke the name as if it had a foul taste – 'when Billie had finished her cleaning shift at the tennis club.'

'Where is the tennis club?'

'There, in the park. You can just see the courts.'

Mila peered through the foliage of the trees. 'Oh yes.' It was easy to picture Briony standing here, lonely and friendless. It must have been a boost to have a new person wave back at her; a young woman with a rebellious air, who perhaps, to Briony, represented freedom. 'When did your husband take Billie on as an employee?' Mila asked.

'At the beginning of the year. Normally, he would never even have considered someone like Billie, but Briony had been particularly poorly over winter, so I had to care for her twenty-four/seven, which meant I couldn't help out. David had to manage the big clients in Cardiff, save his best workers for them. We needed someone for the local jobs: the tennis club, the public toilets on the seafront and the two pubs. Billie came along. She said she lived nearby. She was evidently strong. She was frank about her history. And she seemed keen.'

'Did your husband ask for references?'

'No. He should have, but, to be fair, Billie wasn't that much of a risk. She wasn't going to be driving a company van. She would only be cleaning in places where she'd be supervised. It seemed as if she really did want to make a new start and put the past behind her, and David thought it would be good to help her.'

Plus, he was desperate, Sophie pointed out.

'He said to me, "Gwyneth, what's the worst that could happen?" and we thought about it, we honestly did, and we thought the worst was that

Billie might be slapdash in her work, and a poor timekeeper. Or that she'd be overfamiliar with the clients, because she was a bit much, you know? She wasn't always appropriate in her conversation. She didn't know when to stop; there was quite a bit of effing and blinding, and she had a strong accent. But the places she was going to clean, it wouldn't really matter if there was the odd verbal lapse or if she called someone "my lovely". David asked her to mind her language while she was wearing a Moorcroft's Maid Services apron and to be respectful to the clients and she seemed to take that on board.' Mrs Moorcroft sighed and leaned her hands against the windowsill. 'It seemed to be working out. Billie was always punctual, she was polite with us – as polite as she knew how to be – and she was a grafter, I'll give her that.'

'Did she clean the tennis club every day?'

'Wednesdays through Sundays. She'd pick the cleaning kit up at ten to eight and walk across the park. She'd do the changing rooms, sort out the bar, sweep and mop the floors. Then, when she was done, she'd bring the kit back and David would tell her where to go next, or, if David was out, I'd tell her.'

'And when did Briony and Billie's relationship move on from just waving to one another?'

'Briony started coming downstairs at the same time as Billie was sorting out her cleaning kit ready for the next job. They chatted, joked about a bit. I should have heard alarm bells but I never thought anything of it! I mean, they are so different. They couldn't be more different.'

It occurred to Mila that both young women were misfits; both lonely.

Mrs Moorcroft continued: 'It progressed from Billie and Briony chatting, to Billie staying for a cup of tea. She was from a different world, Ms Shepherd. She had five sugars in her tea. Five! I used to give her a particular mug. I didn't like any of us to drink out of it afterwards. Even when it had gone through the dishwasher.'

She shuddered, then leaned closer to Mila.

'Can I tell you something in confidence?'

'Of course.'

Mrs Moorcroft lowered her voice. 'Sometimes, I used to leave them unsupervised, Briony and Billie. It gave me a little respite when they were together. I'd go and sit in the garden and call my sister, or take a shower. I couldn't see any harm in it. I've never admitted to David that I left them alone. I would never have done so if I'd realised that Billie was already grooming Briony. That's how it happens, you see, you take your eye off the ball for a few moments and everything goes to pot.' She wrapped her arms about herself. 'I can't bear it!' she said. 'Really, I cannot bear the thought of the two of them together, and knowing that it's all my fault; that I wasn't careful enough!'

Mila murmured a few words of reassurance, then, as they turned to leave the room, she paused by the dolls' house. 'I always wanted one of these. May I look inside.'

'Help yourself. I don't think Briony's touched it in years.'

Mila found the catch that opened up the front of the house. As the façade swung open, the rooms lit up, illuminated by tiny bulbs in tiny lamps. She drew in her breath.

'Oh, it's wonderful!'

Mila crouched down to get a good look inside. There were four storeys: an attic in the eaves of the roof and beneath that three sets of two rooms on each floor, with a staircase going through the centre. Each room was decorated with exquisite, miniature pieces of furniture and accessories. Mila's eyes followed the stairs upwards. On the top floor beneath the attic was a bedroom decorated in a similar style and colours to Briony Moorcroft's real-life bedroom. A little toy golden Labrador was standing in the hallway, as if guarding the door. Two dolls were on the bed, lying together, facing one another. One doll had its original long hair. The other's hair had been crudely cut short and someone had painted tattoos on its arms with felt pen.

There was no doubt at all in Mila's mind that the dolls represented Briony and Billie.

And Briony had put them to bed.

11

Mila left the Moorcroft household clutching a plastic bag containing several days' worth of Briony Moorcroft's drugs to give to the teenager when she was found and walked across the road into the park. She found a spot where she had a good signal for her phone and sat on the bench beside a tear-shaped rose bed, wondering how many times Billie Dexter might have sat in this exact spot, perhaps having a roll-up to break up the short journey between the Moorcrofts' house and the tennis club. She didn't know that Billie smoked; but she had a feeling that she might.

Mila took a couple of deep breaths and rolled her shoulders, trying to make herself relax. She was stressed. Partly it was because she now understood how imperative it was to find Briony quickly: literally a matter of life and death. But there was something else too.

The interview with Mr and Mrs Moorcroft hadn't gone badly; what was bothering Mila was her visceral reaction to the situation. She had not met the Moorcrofts before: she had not even spoken to them on the telephone. Yet she had the strongest sense that she'd been here, or somewhere similar, at some time in the past. She had heard the same answers given to the same questions. She remembered a distraught woman trying to stay composed, and a man, standing at the window, exactly as Mr Moorcroft had stood. Worst of all, was the sense of absolute dread that Mila herself was experiencing. It was a cold, lump of fear deep inside her. And it made no sense.

Mila tried to shake off the mood. Perhaps she was recalling a scene from a film, or a book she'd once read. She had to snap out of it. She took out her phone and called Toussaints agency. Carter answered in his usual cheerful manner. He hadn't yet lost the habit he'd formed when he worked for the Canadian police, of shouting when he was on the telephone. It was because, he said, he was used to having to make himself heard in a room full of noisy colleagues.

'Toussaints Agence des Perdus – the agency for the lost, Carter Jackson speaking! How can I help you?' he bellowed.

'It's me,' said Mila, holding the phone away from her ear.

'Hey, you,' said Carter, enthusiastic as a puppy. 'How's South Wales?'

'Hot,' answered Mila. From where she was sitting, she could catch glimpses of the gunmetal grey Bristol Channel between the roofs of the houses and the treetops going down the hill. 'Sweltering. Listen, I just left the Moorcrofts. We need to start searching for their daughter straight away. Can you get on to it this afternoon?'

'I certainly can. What's the story?'

'The missing girl is Briony Moorcroft, age nineteen, but looks and acts younger. She has a multitude of health issues – including cancer and a crippling autoimmune disease. She's run away with a woman called Billie with an "I" and an "E" Dexter. Billie's mid-twenties, ex-addict, ex-con, employee of Briony's parents' cleaning company.'

'Okay.'

'Briony's life depends on her taking medication, but she didn't take much with her and she'll have run out by now. At some point, sooner rather than later, she's going to need emergency medical attention.'

'Will Billie take care of her?'

'Unlikely, given her background, but if she doesn't get Briony to a hospital quickly when the crisis comes, there's a very real chance that she will die.'

Carter whistled.

'The police aren't interested,' said Mila, 'because, legally, Briony is a consenting adult who's left of her own free will. But Briony has hardly any life experience, she's been shielded from the real world since she was a baby. She's never had a romantic relationship; she doesn't even have any friends. I get the impression – although this wasn't spelled out to me in so many words – that Briony's mother thinks Briony might have interpreted Billie's friendship as love when, in truth, it's barely disguised abuse.' She paused. 'I'm certain Mrs Moorcroft thinks Billie couldn't make a friend in the normal way, so she preyed on someone who wouldn't judge her by the usual parameters.'

'Right,' said Carter. 'So, Ceci's already told me that Billie and Briony have used her parents' bank cards in a supermarket in Lorient.'

'That's right. There was various activity both in Morannez and Lorient, but now they know where the couple are, Mr and Mrs Moorcroft have stopped the cards.'

'Was that a good idea?'

'I don't know,' said Mila. 'If they don't have access to money, it's going to put a lot of pressure on Billie.'

'Does Briony have her own bank account?'

'She's never needed money of her own. Either she or Billie took £250 cash from Mrs Moorcroft's handbag on the way out. Billie was paid cash weekly. She'd received £80 the day before they ran away.' She paused. 'I don't think Mr Moorcroft was paying her through the books. Not that that's relevant to what's happened but...' Perhaps it was relevant. Perhaps it was indicative of the fact that the Moorcrofts weren't quite the sticklers for propriety that they made themselves out to be. Also, £80 seemed a miserly payment for the amount of work Billie had been doing. 'Mrs Moorcroft doesn't think Billie's the sort to have any savings or anything.'

'Not if she's an ex-junkie, no. What about phones?'

'Briony doesn't have one. Billie's number is non-responsive.'

'And their transport?'

'It's one of the Moorcrofts' work vans. I'll text you the registration, although it's quite clear on the video.'

'Is there a connection with Brittany?'

'Not on Briony's side. I've no idea about Billie.'

'Okay,' said Carter. 'Do you know which supermarket they were in?'

'The Intermarché Super on Rue Général de Bollardièr.'

'That's great. I'll make a start on this now.'

'Thanks, Carter.'

Mila watched a pigeon with its chest puffed up, strutting around after another that was searching for crumbs by the bench. 'Is everything all right there?' she asked.

'Yep. Ceci said to tell you if you called that Ani is good.'

'Isn't Ceci at work?'

'She's gone home.'

'Is she okay?'

'She's fine.'

'Carter?'

'She'll be mad at me for telling you...'

'Tell me anyway.'

'She was supposed to meet Monique Girard at the Grand Hotel in Bloemel for lunch and she clean forgot.'

'Forgot? That's not like Ceci.'

'She's mortified; blaming a migraine. She's gone to lie in a dark room with a flannel on her forehead until she feels better.'

'When she checks in, will you tell her I called.'

'Sure. When are you coming back?'

'Tomorrow. I'll find out as much about Billie as I can here today, then head back to Bristol tonight.'

'That's worked out well then. You have a bit of together time with Luke while you've got the chance,' said Carter.

If anyone else – Sophie, for example – had used the phrase 'together time', Mila would have bristled at the perceived sarcasm, but sarcasm was something of which Carter was incapable. He was the most emotionally transparent person she'd ever known.

'Have you been to the sea house every day like you promised?' she asked him.

'Yes, and Berthaud's fine. She said to say "hi" if you called.'

'You put down some water for her?'

'I put down some water, I filled up her kibble bowl, I gave her some tuna flakes; we sat on the swing seat in the sunshine, I rubbed her cheek and she did that weird cat-paddling thing that freaks me out. Then she climbed up on my shoulder, purred for a while, and fell asleep. She told me to tell you that I'm her favourite now. She doesn't love you any more, Mila. As far as she's concerned, you're *pain grillé*. Toast.'

12

When she'd finished the phone call, Mila walked through Carnarth Park, through a formal garden area where the great trees were drooping, as if they'd lost the will to live; their mantles yellow and browning. The leaves they had shed lay motionless on the surface of a large, rectangular pond, tips curled upwards like fingers. The level of the pond water was low and it was stagnant; smelling foul. If there had once been fish in the murky depths, Mila doubted they would have survived.

Wales hadn't had fires, like Finistère, but everywhere it was evident that nature was suffering.

She walked past a grand, bleak war memorial, and on to the tennis club, demarcated from the leisure areas by a small, half-dead hedge and a wooden gate, latched and painted green. There were six hard courts. Despite the heat, two of the courts were being used by adults, on a third, two young boys were being coached by a muscular, tanned man in his forties, with his greying hair pulled back into a ponytail. Mila stood and watched until the lesson was over.

The boys, sweating so much they looked as if they'd been caught in a downpour, ran around collecting the balls and putting them into buckets. Then the coach called: 'See you next week, lads!' He collected his racquet and water bottle, dabbed his face with a towel and headed into the clubhouse. Mila followed him into a thin, gloomy room with wooden floorboards and walls painted a shade of mustard, or perhaps they'd been stained that colour by decades of cigarette smoke.

The coach perched on a stool beside a bar, behind which was a full-figured woman with black hair and striking blue eyes. A fan was circulating warm air which smelled of sweat and spilled beer.

The bar woman poured lime cordial and scooped ice into a glass and then used a dispensing hose to top up the glass with what Mila assumed was soda water. '*Dyna ti*,' she said, passing the glass to the coach. She wiped her forehead with the back of her wrist and spotted Mila, hovering by the door. 'Can I help you?' she asked in English. The coach watched Mila over the rim of his glass.

'Hi,' said Mila. She walked further into the room. The furniture, tables and chairs were old and chipped. Boards on the walls listed the names of former club champions and there was a glass-fronted trophy cabinet full of silver-plated cups. Mila put on her most personable smile. 'I'm looking for information about Billie Dexter.'

The bar woman's expression became less friendly. 'Well, she's not here, is she?'

'She works here though, doesn't she? As a cleaner?'

'*Used* to work here. Haven't seen hide nor hair of her since the week before last.'

'No?'

'No.'

'I don't suppose you have her address?'

The woman narrowed her eyes. 'You don't suppose right. What are you after Billie Dexter for, then? Did the Moorcrofts send you?'

'Not directly, but they have employed me to help find their daughter.'

'I thought as much,' said the bar woman. 'Gwyneth Moorcroft was in here the other day; going on about her precious Briony and how Billie Moorcroft had sodded off with her. I told her never mind her bloody daughter, what about me?'

She pointed to herself with the expression of someone who had experienced grave injustice.

'I don't understand,' said Mila.

The woman leaned across the bar, speaking slowly and bitterly.

'Mrs Moorcroft's not the only one Billie-bloody-Dexter has ripped off. I told Billie where I kept the key to the staff locker, more fool me, and she only went and made off with my handbag. My house keys were in it. And when I got home, guess what? She'd got there first, hadn't she?'

'What did she take?' Mila asked.

'Cash. My passport. Bottle of gin. I told Mrs Moorcroft she and her husband ought to pay me compensation but she didn't want to know. So I'll tell you what I told her. I don't *know* where Billie Dexter is, I don't *care* where she is, I never want to hear another word about that waste-of-space, cheating, lezzer smack-head again. Is that clear?'

'Don't hold back, Ffion,' said the coach.

The woman picked up a terry cloth, squeezed it and furiously wiped the top of the bar, which was already perfectly clean. She looked again at Mila. 'And just so as you know, lady, this bar is for club members only. There's a sign above the door, see!' She flicked the cloth. '"Strictly members only." So, if you want to come in again, you'll need to join the club.'

'Okay,' Mila said, taken aback by the vehemence of Ffion's outburst. She moved away. 'Sorry. I missed the sign.'

'Yes, well you want to be more observant, don't you? You're trespassing. I'd be within my rights to call the police.'

Inside Mila's head, Sophie whistled. *Not exactly a welcome in the valleys.*

* * *

Mila was on the way out of the club, walking past the courts, when the ponytailed coach caught up with her.

'Hey,' he said, 'don't mind Ffion. She's at the end of her tether having to do everything here herself.'

'I'm not offended,' said Mila. She paused, then asked: 'What did she mean by "cheating"? Were she and Billie in a relationship?'

'Not like you mean, no. But Ffion liked Billie. She told Billie all her problems, and Billie listened. You wouldn't have thought it to look at her, but she's a good listener.'

'Really?'

'Yeah. Gobby as hell, with a mouth like a sewer, but Ffion didn't mind that. She said it wasn't what Billie sounded like, it what was *inside* that counted. Ffion thought that underneath all the swearing and the swagger Billie Dexter was a rough diamond. She tried to help her. That's why she was so hurt when Billie let her down like she did.'

It seemed to Mila that Billie Dexter must have perfected some trick to enable her to overcome the natural reticence of strangers. Firstly, she'd convinced David Moorcroft to take her on as a cleaner against his better judgement, and then she'd won the friendship of the volatile Ffion – someone who didn't seem the kind of woman to tolerate fools.

The coach continued: 'Ffi doesn't trust most people, she's had a bad time with men, see, but she trusted Billie. She thought Billie cared about her. Then Billie buggered off with Ffion's passport and a kid half her age and left her in the lurch. She's having to do all the catering, run the bar, answer the phone and clean the toilets herself, all the while working overtime to recoup her losses and pay the rent.'

'I can understand why she's annoyed,' said Mila.

'Hurt, more like. She hasn't had much luck lately; her last partner left her with a stack of debt and now her trust has taken another battering.'

Mila winced in sympathy.

'I keep telling Ffion,' said the coach, 'that she needs to choose her friends more carefully. Losers like Billie Dexter are ten a penny. Look under any rock and you'll find one.'

'Could you point me in the direction of Billie's rock?'

'Splott Terrace. Billie lives in her granddad's flat. You can't miss it; it's the one with the gnomes.'

* * *

It took Mila fifteen minutes to walk from the tennis club to Splott Terrace, following the directions of the map app on her phone. She found it easily enough, a small cul-de-sac on an estate of local-authority flats and maisonettes. It was a grey, depressing place, with rubbish in the gutters, dead or dying shrubs in the beds and the buildings in a poor state of repair. Plastic bags of dog poo hung from the branches of a scrubby tree. The windows to the upper flats were all open and it appeared as if some people had simply been chucking their rubbish out onto the paths.

Mila followed the pavement until she spotted a particular ground-floor flat. The entire base of the wall was lined with plaster gnomes, the paint chipped or faded on most of them. The ornaments appeared to be the only occupants of the place. The door and windows had been boarded over and someone had sprayed a picture of a graffiti tag in the shape of a lizard on the pebbledash wall.

The gnomes, several holding fishing rods, others gardening imple-ments, wore sinister expressions. Their eyes seemed to follow Mila as she walked around the building. At the back was a concrete yard with a couple of heavily loaded rotary clothes driers. A small boy was pedalling a tricycle around; a woman was sitting on the wall, in front of the recy-cling bins, half staring at her phone screen, half watching the child.

Mila went up to the woman. 'Hi,' she said.

'Alright?'

'Yeah. I'm looking for information about Billie Dexter. Do you know her?'

The woman pulled a face which Mila took to mean the woman did know Billie but didn't think much of her. 'I haven't seen her for weeks. Last I heard, she was sleeping rough.' She eyed Mila cautiously.

'I was told she lived here, with her grandfather?' Mila persisted.

'Well, she did, but not lately. He's lost it, hasn't he?' The woman made a twirling motion with her finger and held it up against the side of her head. 'Gone into a care home, he has. We could all see it coming. He was wandering round in his underpants shouting abuse at the neighbours.'

'So the grandfather is in care and Billie was kicked out of the flat?'

'That's right. And there wasn't a soul on the estate sorry to see the back of her.'

'Why's that?' Mila asked.

'She's a psycho,' said the woman. 'Always has been. Right from when her dad used to bring her round here when she was a little kid, you could see there was something wrong with her. She was feral. A little terrorist.'

Mila's state of anxiety ramped up several notches. The more she heard about Billie Dexter, the more concerned she felt for Briony Moorcroft's safety.

'She's been in trouble all her useless life,' the woman continued. 'She broke my brother's finger once, bending it backwards to hurt him, and my dad went round to see her granddad and told him that if he didn't sort her out, he'd teach her a lesson himself. The grandfather, miserable bugger that he was, beat her with a golf club right there on the grass so that everyone could see. Knocked seven bells out of her, but Billie didn't care. Laughed in his face, she did. She's missing some part of her brain. The part that makes her human.'

13

This is going well, said Sophie. *We started out thinking Billie was a bit dodgy, and now we find we're dealing with a sociopath.*

Mila was thinking about the public thrashing meted out to Billie by her grandfather. No matter what Billie had done, no child should be hurt and humiliated that way. And also, if that was how Billie had been treated by someone who was supposed to love and care for her, if her role model had taught her that it was okay to thrash the person you were supposed to protect, it didn't bode well for her behaviour in future relationships. Most pressingly, it wasn't a good omen as far as Briony's welfare was concerned.

'Do you think the timing of Billie and Briony's disappearance is a coincidence?' Mila wondered.

I'd say not, Sophie replied. *I'd say Billie had reached a point in her life where she had nothing left to lose. Her granddad had gone into care, she had nowhere to live. She was looking for an opportunity to escape. Briony was that opportunity.*

It made sense. Briony, trapped in her parents' house like a princess in a fairy tale, would have represented a fresh start to Billie, and Billie, unlikely fantasy that she was, probably fulfilled the same role to Briony.

The younger woman couldn't have known anything about Billie's past: as far as Briony was concerned, Billie was a clean slate. She could present herself to Briony in any way she wished. And over the course of the last hours, it had become apparent to Mila that Billie had a talent for assuring people that her intentions were good, even when they blatantly were not.

Mila thought of herself, and Sophie. She recalled how, when she first used to visit Morannez with her father, she had put on an act, making out that she was bolder, cleverer, more popular than she really was. She was a long way from home; nobody knew her. Sophie was evidently one of those girls who everybody wanted to befriend, and Mila was worried that her vivacious stepsister would find her dull and boring. But Sophie had never made Mila feel like an outsider and soon Mila had given up the charade and just been herself. Sophie made her realise that she was enough as she was. She didn't have to pretend.

Sophie could be infuriatingly selfish. She could be deceitful. She wasn't always honest, not even with Ceci, but she had always been loyal to Mila. She was the best friend Mila had ever had. It was because of Sophie that Mila could look back at the summers the two of them had spent on the beach at Morannez as the happiest times of her life. It was one of the reasons why, two years after Sophie's death, the hurt of losing her was as sharp as ever.

* * *

Mila had time to kill before she caught the train back to Bristol. She walked downhill to the seafront, following the cawing of the gulls and the smell of ozone, and bought a slice of cold pizza and a can of lemonade from a small bakery. Beyond, the tide was coming up the Bristol Channel; millions of gallons of grey water, heavy with sediment, pushing up the ancient waterway just as it had done for millennia. Scandals came and went. People left one another and came back, or didn't come back, children grew up, adults fell in love and broke up and fell in love again, but the tide kept on doing its thing regardless. In and out, up and down, a movement so immense that, like infinity, it was almost beyond the scope of human comprehension, even though it happened every single day.

There was something hugely soothing about it.

Mila took her snack and walked on, past the pier, thinking about what the woman by the bins had told her about Billie, how the community had turned against her.

She remembered a story from years earlier, when she and Sophie used to spend their school summer holidays together in Brittany. There'd been some trouble with a certain family in the town of Morannez, one of the sons had taken to robbing tourists to pay off the debts accrued on account of a cocaine habit; this was having a detrimental effect on the town's reputation. The problem had been 'sorted' by the Girards, the most powerful and influential family within the local community, a family rumoured to be involved in everything from protection rackets to people smuggling. They had delivered a swift, brutal punishment to the young man – nothing permanent, he hadn't lost a hand or anything – but immediately the tourists stopped having their cameras stolen. Nothing more had been said about the matter and the fact that nobody knew exactly *what* had been done to the culprit made the deterrent even more effective. The man's mother had been employed by the Girards in some capacity and was said to be grateful for their intervention and for the fact that her son hadn't been burdened with a criminal record, as he would have been had the matter been referred to the police.

At the time, Mila and Sophie were friends with the Girard sons, Guillaume, who was their age, and Arnaud, who was a couple of years older. They'd all been part of the same gang, the *Bande Sauvage*, or Wild Bunch, who spent their summers on the beaches around Morannez. It was Guillaume who had told the others the story about the one-man crime wave and how he had been 'fixed'. Arnaud, if Mila's memory was correct, had been embarrassed by his brother's pride in blurting out what had happened. Arnaud felt uncomfortable about his family having the power and prestige to act like gods.

Arnaud's unease was justified. Whatever punishment it was that had been dealt to the young thief that summer was morally and legally wrong. But it was the old way of maintaining the status quo, and in any community, especially close-knit, relatively isolated communities, there would always be people who believed the old ways were best.

Mila looked around her as she walked along Carnarth seafront. The seaside town had once attracted tourists in some number, but now it was faded and old-fashioned. The amusement arcade was still open, albeit with few punters playing the slot machines, and inflatable toys, buckets and spades were still tied outside what Sophie would have called the 'tat' shop, but the colours of the plastic had faded so badly they must have been out in the sun for more than one season. Strange how some places fell out of favour. Sad how nothing ever stayed the same.

The air was muggy; humid and sticky. Everything from the brick-work to the metal railings to the exposed concrete in the derelict paddling pool had warmed to the same temperature.

Mila went through an archway in the sea wall that opened onto the beach; a beach remarkable for the huge, awkward-to-walk-on grey-black pebbles that covered the space between the sea wall and the water itself. Mila perched on a concrete bollard and pulled the paper back from her pizza. Murky waves were breaking a few metres in front of her; the sea, close up, almost black in colour. Gulls hunted for scraps amongst the stones. Out in the estuary, she could see the squat shape of Flat Holm island; its lighthouse pointing skyward like a finger, with the Somerset coastline on the other side hazy in the distance beyond.

While Mila ate, she balanced her phone on her knees and forwarded the various images and documents she'd copied at the Moorcrofts' house to Carter Jackson. She summarised the facts she'd found out about Billie Dexter and suggested Carter search for social media accounts belonging to Briony Moorcroft, perhaps using a different name. Her mother might have believed Briony incapable of deception, or complicit in the running away, but the dolls in the dolls' house told a different story and Briony and Billie must have had some way of keeping in touch while they were planning to abscond. Mrs Moorcroft couldn't have been supervising her daughter every minute, of every day.

That should keep you busy,

she texted.

Carter replied with a thumbs-up. Ani had told Mila that was one of the emojis – along with the red heart that Mila used to use all the time, and the gritted-teeth face – that 'only old people' used these days.

'Hey, old man,' Mila murmured, feeling rather pleased with herself for knowing something that Carter didn't. 'You're showing your age.'

14

Luke was waiting for Mila in his car on the ramp outside Bristol's Temple Meads station when she emerged from the grand Victorian concourse into the cool evening air. The sky was darkening; black, purple, yellow – the colours of a bruise – and a flock of pigeons was circling above the station; the evening traffic lit up the road beyond.

It seemed ages, to Mila, since she'd lived in this city; since she'd worked in the communications department of the NHS Trust; since she'd bought bread from the bakery built into one of the arches beneath the station forecourt; since she'd known the best places to buy a snack, or a birthday card, a skein of wool, or a craft beer. Ages since she'd been a member of the St George's potters' collective, ages since she'd spent her free time going to gigs and exhibitions, talks, protests, taking part in climate change activism, lazing about in Ashton Court watching the hot-air balloons go up on summer evenings, drinking wine in courtyard pub gardens, jogging around the docks in the winter, the route run so often that she knew every weed that grew through the cracks in the paving, every dent in the tarmac, the plants in the pots on the roofs of the houseboats. At one time, she had recognised the individual Southville runners who were going in the opposite direction; and was familiar with the smells of cooking from the kitchens of the restaurants, chilli frying, meat searing, the warming scent of fat heating in the fryers of the chip shops.

All of this felt lost to her now.

She walked past a woman begging for change and slipped her a ten-pound note, knowing she should stop to talk to her, to check if she was safe. But Luke was waiting and she owed him every second of her attention.

Mila had moved to France to look after Ani literally days after Luke had proposed. At the exact point in time when the two of them should have been spending more time together, looking for a home, planning their future, Mila had gone to live in a different country. Instead of supporting Luke's career, and forging her own path in writing the novels she wanted to write, Mila had stepped out of her life and into Sophie's; not only caring for Ani, but also taking over Sophie's job.

Mila and Luke had no choice but to turn their relationship into a long-distance one, she returning to Bristol when she could, and, less frequently, he coming to Brittany. For a while, Mila had felt as if the enforced absence was good for them; she and Luke had appreciated one another so much more when they were together. Lately, though, it was evident that Luke was growing tired of the arrangement and Mila, feeling responsible, was defensive. What little time they did spend in one another's company, time that should have been happy and fun, was, more often than not, both tense and intense. Mila found herself walking on eggshells; trying not to talk too much about her life in France, or, at least, trying not to sound as if she was enjoying it. And Luke was under huge stress at work. He wanted to offload when Mila was with him, and she did her best to be supportive, but she didn't recognise the names of the colleagues he talked about any more – people had been promoted or had retired; she wasn't familiar with the cases he was working on; she was always one step removed. And, if she was honest, she had lost interest.

The previous evening, after Mila had come back from Maidenhead, had been fine. Luke knew she'd be stressed after a weekend spent with her mother, they'd had the theatre and she'd been giddy with relief at being back with him.

But Mila knew this evening would be more difficult. She felt almost permanently guilty when she was with Luke; knowing that he never had the best of her; conscious that she wouldn't have been so patient if their situations had been reversed.

As she walked through the gloaming towards his car, she tried to fan those flames of affection that still burned in her heart. She tried to be more enthusiastic than she felt. What she really wanted to do was talk about her day; what she'd found out about Briony Moorcroft and Billie Dexter, to let her imagination run riot as she tried to map out their relationship. What were they? Friends? Accomplices? Lovers? But she knew the trivia of the lives of two young women from South Wales would be of no interest to Detective Inspector Luke Hogg. Compared to the county lines-related homicide he was working on, Briony Moorcroft voluntarily leaving home with an allegedly reformed heroin addict, even if there'd been some ABH involved in their getaway, was of no importance.

Luke jumped out of the car as Mila approached and came forward to greet her, wrapping her in his arms. 'Hey,' he said.

'Hey.'

He kissed the top of her head. 'It's good to see you.'

'It's only a few hours since we were last together.'

'Still good to see you.' Luke opened the passenger door for her.

Mila managed not to snap at him; didn't he remember that she hated having things done for her? That she found this kind of behaviour patronising? She slid into the seat and fastened the seat belt. He closed the door. 'Thanks,' she murmured, too quietly for him to hear.

Luke's favourite Pink Floyd album was playing, 'Wish You Were Here' was the track. The volume was turned up loud. Music to slit your wrists by was how Sophie used to describe this album. Mila used to think Pink Floyd's music was emotionless; recently, for some reason – maybe it was simply that she was getting older – it had started to make her feel sad.

She reached out and turned the volume down while Luke came round to the driver's side. He got in, started the engine and turned the volume up again. Then he drove down the long ramp that took vehicles in and out of the station's parking area, joining the queue at the traffic lights at the bottom. Mila pressed the button to let her window down and stared out at the people walking towards the city.

'You okay?' Luke asked.

'Yes,' Mila replied. 'No. I'm not sure. Can we stop at a pub, Luke? I really fancy a drink.'

'There's plenty of wine at home.'

'I'm in the mood for a pub.'

'I'm halfway through making dinner. Thought it made more sense than going out.' He turned to smile at her. 'You used to love it when I cooked for you.'

This was true. She did.

'Oh,' said Mila. 'Okay.'

* * *

The table had already been laid at Luke's apartment. There was sliced focaccia and a green salad that had been tipped out of a bag into a bowl, and a candle on a saucer waiting to be lit. In one corner of the tiny kitchen, Luke's washing was drying over a rack. His wallet and car keys were on the window ledge; his sports bag on the floor beside the washing machine. You couldn't cross the room without negotiating a domestic assault course. It was like being in a student house, albeit an upmarket student house, and one that didn't smell of weed.

Mila reminded herself, Luke was living a single man's life, not through choice but circumstance. She had no right to be irritated by his solo domestic arrangements when, if they'd stuck to Plan A, they'd be married and sharing a house by now. And yes, she'd have been happy with a takeaway, but it was good of him to think to prepare something for dinner. Even if it felt slightly uncomfortable. Even if she'd have preferred them to be out somewhere neutral, somewhere Luke wasn't doing things for her.

And why was that? She used to regard him preparing food for them both as the ultimate romantic gesture. He, who had spent all day being stressed, sworn at, physically threatened, having to deal with police force politics; this man, this *important* man who did a great job protecting society, was still willing to wash his hands, roll up his sleeves and stand in the kitchen part of his flat pressing garlic with the side of a knife, wiping the soil from the cups of mushrooms, sizzling butter in a pan to make a meal for her.

She used to love him for it.

Mila tried to resurrect that love.

'Can I do anything to help?' she asked.

'No.' He put a large glass of rosé into her hand and kissed her cheek. 'You go and relax. I'll call you when dinner's ready. We'll have an early night tonight and then tomorrow we'll drive up to Slimbridge. We could stop and have brunch on the way; go to that place in Wotton-under-Edge we found last time. You kept saying you wanted to go back there – best coffee in England, you said.'

Mila caught her breath.

'How does that sound?' Luke asked. 'A good plan?'

'Luke, I told you, I'm going back to Brittany tomorrow. I'm catching the morning ferry.'

She had told him. She knew she had. They had talked about it while they were in Bath, the previous evening, sitting beside the river.

'But,' Luke said slowly, his tone a mixture of hurt and irritation, the kind of tone that might easily tip over into anger, 'I've taken the day off to be with you. I told you I was going to and you said that'd be great.'

This was also true. He had told her he would *try* to take a day's leave, and she had been enthusiastic about the idea, but she hadn't thought it would actually happen. Luke was hardly ever able to go officially awol in the middle of difficult cases like the one he was working on now. When Mila had said that spending the random Tuesday together would be wonderful, it had been because she had assumed it was a pipe dream. She hadn't thought for a minute there was any chance of it actually happening, and she'd assumed that Luke's understanding of the situation was the same as hers.

Shit. How would she wriggle out of this one?

Luke's hair was ruffled and his glasses were on his forehead. He was holding a tea towel in one hand, his shirt had come untucked from his trousers. Mila used to find him sexy. There had been a time – not that long ago – when, if he had stood in front of her like this, she'd have thrown her arms around his neck and her legs around his waist and they'd have had sex on the settee. It would have been passionate and erotic and fun and never mind if the dinner was burned.

Now, she found it less easy to be interested in Luke in that way. It wasn't his fault. It was something to do with guilt; something to do with resentment; everything to do with circumstances.

Things had changed since Sophie had died. Mila and Luke were in a different place and she didn't know how to get them back to where they were before.

'I have to go back,' Mila said. 'I know what I said last night, but I was a bit drunk and I wasn't thinking straight. I'm really, really sorry, Luke, but this girl who's missing is vulnerable and I—'

Luke flipped the tea towel onto the work surface. It wasn't a violent act, merely a gesture of frustration, but Mila winced. 'Sometimes,' he said, 'most of the time, in fact, I feel like I'm at the very bottom of your list of priorities.'

Mila shook her head. 'No,' she said, 'that's not true.'

But, deep down, she knew that it was.

15

Mila drank most of the wine in her glass, topped it up and went into the living room of Luke's apartment. She curled up in the same corner of the sofa where she'd sat, alone, that morning and gazed out of the window, watching the lights and movements of the city at night; it was such a contrast to the darkness and quiet at the sea house. Even in the short time she'd been away, new buildings had grown up in this part of Bristol; the road layouts had changed. You didn't notice places changing when you lived there; you absorbed the changes into your own DNA, so that as soon as a new building was erected, it was impossible to remember how the place used to look before. But when you lived away and came back, the differences were disconcerting. They made Mila feel as if she didn't belong.

Beyond the city lights, the sky was dark and heavy. There wasn't a whisper of breeze. God, she was tired of this heat.

In the kitchen, Luke put the radio on, loudly. This felt like a small act of aggression because Luke knew noise got on Mila's nerves. But Mila also knew that music stopped Luke from dwelling on the forensics of murder; the psychology of killers; the grimy, filthy, distressing business of untangling other people's lives and crimes that was his work. She had no right to resent him listening to music in his own home. She was the one with the problem.

No, it's Luke that's the problem, said Sophie. *He's stressing you out.*

You never liked him, Mila reminded her stepsister. *You were jealous. You were so used to having 100 per cent of my attention, all the time. You couldn't bear that I was interested in someone else besides you.*

I wasn't jealous, don't be ridiculous. I just thought you could do better than him.

No disrespect, Sophie, but you were hardly in a position to judge my romantic decisions.

In her mind, Mila heard Sophie make the sarcastic, crescendoing: *Oooooh!* sound she always made when she wanted to pooh-pooh some comment of Mila's. This made Mila recall the combination of hurt and irritation that Sophie had always been uniquely capable of provoking when it came to matters of the heart.

Mila had loved Sophie most of the time. She'd confided in her step-sister, sought her advice, poured out her soul to her. There'd been no secrets between them, until one particular summer when everything changed.

It was because of Carter. He had been part of the *Bande Sauvage* too. Mila, Sophie and Carter, and the others had been friends when they were young teenagers, and for a few summers their friendship had been so easy, so... magical, almost. They'd been like siblings; having fun, looking out for each other. And then the years had turned and they'd become older and sex and love had muddied the clean waters of their friendships. In Mila's case, the transitioning between child and adult-hood had been especially painful. She had fallen in love with Carter when she was sixteen; she'd been hopelessly attracted to him; all she wanted was to be close to him. She pined for him when they were apart; blushing when he looked at her and becoming tongue-tied in his presence. She disguised her true feelings behind a mask of ambivalence. Carter was oblivious, and continued treating her as he always had; in a teasingly affectionate way. Mila hadn't breathed a word of her feelings to anyone; not even Sophie. She had been afraid that Sophie would say something to Carter; that her fragile heart would be exposed, and tossed about between the members of the *Bande Sauvage* like a ball. Mila had seen the same thing happen to Arnaud Girard. His younger brother, Guillaume, had found an unfinished love letter in Arnaud's bedroom, and brought it to the beach. For the rest of that summer, the boys, and Sophie, had teased Arnaud relentlessly, quoting the more purple passages of the letter which, Guillaume said, had been written to a friend of the boys' mother on whom Arnaud had a crush.

Mila didn't want to risk being similarly humiliated, neither did she know how to handle her feelings. She was naïve and inexperienced; all she knew about love, she'd learned from the pages of novels and the lyrics of pop songs. Convinced by these unreliable sources that if she waited faithfully, Carter would, eventually, recognise that she was the one for him, Mila bided her time. When, the following summer, he started following Sophie round like a puppy, it was a shock. Mila tried not to care. She believed the infatuation would come to nothing because she knew that Sophie wasn't interested in Carter in that way – Sophie had told her as much. But Sophie could be cruel. Carter didn't know that Sophie didn't want to be his girlfriend, because sometimes Sophie led Carter on; it was how Sophie was. She couldn't help herself any more than Ceci's cat, Fifi, could refrain from pouncing on spiders.

One time, when they were camping overnight something had happened between Sophie and Carter. Even now, all these years later, Mila could hardly bear to think of it.

The next summer was the summer of Lydia's breakdown. Mila had to stay in Maidenhead to look after her mother and the year after that Sophie was going out with Charlie Cooper. Still Mila waited for Carter; but the plan had backfired catastrophically. He and Sophie had begun an affair. Mila had left it too late to make her feelings clear. How could she tell the truth to Sophie now without sounding petty, spiteful or jealous?

It was an unbearable situation.

Sophie was living in Paris, studying at the Sorbonne, when the affair between her and Carter reached the peak of its intensity. Mila recalled walking with Carter through the Bois de Boulogne one winter's day; a thick frost on the grass and the plants all turned to ice; the path rock-hard and slippery beneath the soles of her boots, and their breath hanging so heavy in the air that the condensation froze on their eyelashes. Carter, head held low, wrapped in a padded coat, gloves and a scarf, was talking about Sophie, telling Mila how much he loved her; how he really, truly, didn't think he could live without her; how he couldn't understand why she was so reluctant to end it with Charlie Cooper; how this situation was killing him – killing him!

Mila remembered how she had assimilated Carter's pain; added it to the stack of her own. And she'd known it was a weight too heavy for her to carry; she had known that at some point she'd have to let go. She should have left Paris, removed herself from the situation, but she hadn't.

Later – not the same day, a different day – she and Carter had gone to a dark, mirrored bar, tucked away in the back streets of the city. Sophie was with Charlie back in her flat, with the bars of the electric radiator turned up high; when Carter and Mila had left, the two of them had been playing music and dancing, Sophie's body pressed against Charlie's. In the bar, Mila had drunk tiny glass after tiny glass of Chartreuse, and later, the city twinkling and sparkling like a city in a movie, she and Carter had gone back to his room and she had bared her soul to him; told him what she truly felt. She'd been hoping the scales would fall from his eyes, that he would see Sophie's 'love' for the sham it truly was and realise that the person who loved him, really loved him as he deserved to be loved, was she, Mila. But she was too inexperienced then to understand that life doesn't work like that. Nobody can switch one love off and another on.

It was still too humiliating for Mila to remember in any detail the shock on Carter's face when she'd said the words: *I love you*, and then, witnessing his reaction, her subsequent drunken attempts to remedy the situation; trying to take back something that could not be revoked because it was the truth.

It didn't matter now, she told herself, all those years later. Sophie was dead; Mila was engaged to Luke, who was, right now, making dinner for her and Carter had married and then divorced Emmanuelle Aubert. He would have forgotten that encounter. He didn't care enough to remember. Mila's feelings had meant nothing to him; never had, never would.

She picked up her rucksack from where it was slumped against the wall, took out her laptop, opened it and booted it up, blinking hard to push away the residual shame. She stared at the screen, feeling the light burning her eyes, concentrating on what she was doing as she typed in her password, forbidding herself to dwell on matters of the heart; too messy; too painful; impossible now to resolve. She should focus her attention on something she could affect: the finding of Briony Moorcroft.

When the MacBook was awake, she typed the young woman's name into the search bar. A slew of news stories immediately appeared. The hospital picture that Mila had seen on the wall by the stairs at the Moorcrofts' house was reproduced in a newspaper article headlined: *Brave Briony is our Christmas Cracker*. Tens of thousands of pounds had been raised for a new MRI scanner for Cardiff's St Anne's Oncology Hospital following an appeal launched in Briony's name.

Mila read that not only was Briony 'battling an extremely rare' autoimmune disease, that she'd also undergone treatment for cancer several times over the last few years and, on top of all that, she had heart troubles. Had Mrs Moorcroft even mentioned the heart problems? Mila thought not.

Briony, or at least Briony's image, was obviously well known in South Wales – she was a poster girl for the therapies and treatments being pioneered by a charity based at the hospital. Moorcrofts' Maid Services' logo featured prominently in their branding.

With a growing sense of unease, Mila realised that it was entirely feasible that Billie Dexter had first come across Briony Moorcroft via social media, or through some item in the press or on TV. It was possible that their friendship had not been the result of fate bringing them together, as she had supposed, but rather that Billie had read about Briony and sought her out. Less meet-cute; more meet-sinister.

Mila flicked through the articles until she found a quote from Briony. *'I don't meet many people because I have to be careful to avoid infection, but I like to wave to people from my bedroom window,'* the brave teenager said. *'I have a lot of friends, even if we don't know each other's names.'*

There it was, in black and white. If Billie Dexter had read this article, she might well have orchestrated the whole relationship with Briony; taking the time to find out where she lived; what her parents did; applying for the job; waving to Briony; building her trust. Had her intention all along been to abduct Briony? Did she care about the sick young woman at all, or was this whole thing a ploy to extract money from the Moorcrofts?

The family weren't in the mega-wealthy bracket, but they had a flashy car with a personalised registration parked outside the house and they ran their own business. To someone like Billie, the Moorcrofts would appear to be rolling in money.

Mila drank some more wine and searched the internet for Billie Dexter. Google thought she meant an American professional basketball player of that name who accounted for most of the hits. It took her ages to find anything about the Carnarth Billie Dexter, and when she did, it was the picture that David Moorcroft had mentioned, on the Moorcrofts' Maid Services website, where she was described as a 'Hygiene Operative'. There was a decent photograph of Billie wearing a company-branded sweatshirt which covered most of her top half, but her hands, one holding a dustpan and brush, the other a bottle of spray detergent, were raw and scarred, the knuckles covered in home-made tattoos.

Compared to tiny, delicate Briony Moorcroft, thought Mila, Billie was like a giant.

Billie didn't have any social media accounts – at least none that Mila could find. There seemed to be literally nothing about her on the internet, save that single image and each time Mila looked at it, Billie Dexter's expression appeared more brutal.

She sent the link to Carter Jackson.

He pinged back another thumbs-up emoji.

There was no point telling Carter what Ani had said about the emojis because he wouldn't give a damn. And he was right not to care. Mila wondered why she'd taken any notice herself, over a matter so utterly trivial.

It's because you care what Ani thinks about you, Sophie said.

And she was right, it was partly that – but there was something else too. Was she afraid of growing older?

Are we getting old? Sophie asked quietly.

Not you, replied Mila. *Dying when you're in your thirties makes you forever young.*

Sophie was silent. Mila had a pang of missing her terribly.

You had so many secrets, Sophie, she said. *Why did you always make everything so complicated?*

16

Mila had set the alarm on her phone for 5 a.m. the following morning, but Luke woke her before then with a mug of black coffee and a hand between her legs.

Mila had always disliked being woken in this way; it put her in an instant bad mood. But after everything that had transpired the previous evening, she going to bed while he stayed up to watch some political debate on TV, she felt obliged to turn towards him. They kissed as he pulled down her pyjama shorts, and then they had quick, unsatisfying sex, during which Mila had to fight herself to keep her mind on Luke, rather than on the other thoughts vying for attention inside her head.

Afterwards, in the shower, listening to Luke on the phone in the bedroom barking orders to some subordinate, she felt both sad and irritated. Annoyed that he was making a work call on his day off, even though she knew he wouldn't be doing this if she and he were going to spend the day together, as he'd planned and she'd promised. The very fact he was doing it was a reprimand to her. And sad because... well, she didn't really know why. It was to do with the sex and the situation they were in. Which wasn't, she reminded herself for the hundredth time, Luke's fault.

Shampoo suds streamed down her face, down her body. Foam

bubbled around the plughole. The shower was monochrome; bachelor-esque. Mila heard the chorus of 'Wish You Were Here' playing on a loop inside her head. What she was feeling wasn't unusual. She almost always felt melancholic after sex these days. She and Luke weren't in tune any longer. It was as if Luke was trying too hard to keep their relationship on track, and she wasn't trying hard enough – and no matter how she berated herself for this inertia, she found it difficult, sometimes impossible, to fake an enthusiasm she didn't feel.

Perhaps she was simply grieving for the relationship they used to have. Perhaps this happened to every couple as they grew older. Perhaps, one day, she and Luke would readjust to their changed lives and different plans and they'd find some new level where things would be easier between them again.

She rinsed the last of Luke's sports shampoo from her hair. Caffeine in shampoo. What was the logic of that? She remembered how, in the old days, it used to give her a feeling of pride to smell Luke's scent on her skin, or her clothes, or her hair; as if the two of them were becoming interchangeable; real partners. Now she was missing the sweet pear smell of the vegan hair soap that Ani used. She was missing the bath-room in the sea house, with its old tiles, a jar of wildflowers on the rim of the basin; the window open to let out the billowing steam, towels heaped over the old-fashioned radiator; cosmetics, tissues and girl-detritus everywhere.

She leaned back and wrung her hair, her reflection ghostly in the shower panel.

Tiens bon! Sophie whispered.

Chin up!

* * *

Luke insisted on driving Mila to Portsmouth.

'You don't need to do this,' she said. 'I'll be fine on the coach.'

'I want to take you,' said Luke. 'It's the only chance I'll get to actually talk to you. And anyway, I've taken the day off – what else am I going to do with myself?'

'Well, if you're sure,' said Mila, feeling not grateful but resentful because of the self-pity in Luke's question. And also, for selfish reasons. If she was sitting next to Luke, giving him her quality attention, there would be no opportunity to get out her laptop and do some work, or to chat over Messenger with Carter as she would have done if she'd been on the coach, or even to think about Briony Moorcroft and Billie Dexter.

Anxiety about Briony was churning through Mila's mind. It was Billie's motivation that was worrying her. Why had she run off with the younger girl? Was this a kidnapping, or were they actually in love? Did Billie want money? Did she realise how sick Briony was? Did she know that there was a very real possibility that Briony might become critically ill; that she might die? And how would Billie react if Briony's condition suddenly deteriorated? What if she, in her panic, resorted to violence?

Mila knew that sometimes all it took was enough consideration about a seemingly incomprehensible situation for the solution, or resolution, to make itself clear. But for this to happen, Mila needed headspace – which she definitely wouldn't get in Luke's car with the music system blaring as he recounted disquieting details about his murder case.

The journey was as long and tetchy as Mila had feared it would be.

Despite dreadful traffic congestion on the M27 going past Southampton, the cars shining and glimmering in the heat haze, they arrived at Portsmouth early, parked the car and roamed the narrow backstreets of the seaport until they found a little café. They sat at a table by the open window, facing one another while the surfaces of their coffees steamed, trying to think of things to say.

'When do you think you'll next be back?' Luke asked.

'For Mum's birthday next month,' Mila said. 'It's her seventieth. I can't not make a big deal of it.'

'No.'

'You'll come to Maidenhead with me, won't you, Luke? We could take her into London, maybe. Go out for a meal and then see a show.'

'I didn't think Lydia liked the theatre.'

'It's not that she doesn't like it per se, it's just that what with Patrick being an actor...' Mila tailed off. 'You're right. Maybe not the theatre.'

'I don't know if I'll be able to make it anyway,' Luke said. 'It depends what's going on at work, obviously.'

'Obviously,' Mila echoed.

After that, the conversation dried up. Mila sipped her coffee, trying to think of a way to flip the atmosphere between herself and Luke before they said goodbye and it was too late to make things right.

Nothing came to mind.

Things being as they were, Mila was relieved when it was time for her to join the foot passenger queue for the ferry. She and Luke embraced in the car park.

'I do love you, you know,' he said and she murmured, 'I love you, too.'

'It doesn't count unless you say it first,' said Luke.

This was something Mila used to say to him when they were first lovers. It had been a joke, between them, that Luke was emotionally constipated. Now their roles were reversed. It was Mila who struggled most with showing affection.

He kissed the top of her head and then loosened his hold, and she stepped back, almost falling off the kerb. Luke held onto her. They smiled at one another awkwardly. Luke pushed her hair back behind her ear. The gesture felt paternal, possessive, mildly patronising.

Bloody hell, whispered Sophie, *the poor sod can't do anything right.*

Oh? You're sticking up for him now?

'I'd better go,' Mila said.

'I'll see you soon.'

'Yep.'

Mila blew Luke a kiss and she walked away, hitching her rucksack on her back with her head hanging low.

17

Once on board, Mila deposited her rucksack and went on deck to watch the ferry pull out of the port. The thrill of observing the workers untying the enormous ropes that tethered the craft had never left her.

Some odd confluence of sun and water meant the docks were swathed in a kind of mist that morning. Looking down, Mila could barely make out the familiar architecture of the quay and the terminal. When she faced the sky, she was almost blinded by gleaming light. The humid air was sticky on her skin; so heavy that breathing was an effort.

When she was a girl, and Patrick, separated and then divorced from Lydia, was in a relationship with Ceci, the two of them, Patrick and Mila, used to make this crossing, Portsmouth to St Malo, every summer. Patrick always booked the night ferry. He took Mila on deck, no matter what the weather, so they could watch the ropes, thick as a man's thigh, being unhitched; see them splash into the black water before being pulled back up into the body of the ferry; could hear the thrum of the motors starting, see the water begin to churn white while the gulls screamed overhead. At last, a tiny crack would emerge between the side of the ferry and the dock, and soon the gap would widen until it was too far for a person to jump from dry land. A few seconds later and there was a channel between land and ship, and finally the craft would head out to sea, past the other vessels moored in the enormous harbour.

'It's the best feeling,' Patrick would say.

'Leaving somewhere?' young Mila would ask curiously.

'Going somewhere new!'

After a while, when they were in open water, the waves became huge and exciting, great, dangerous hills that swelled and rolled, and the wake of the ferry was wild and tumultuous. Patrick's cigarette smoke was caught by the wind and sucked away and the stars in the sky were always very bright, and if there were clouds, they were dramatic, backlit by the brilliant moon.

Mila loved being at sea in darkness. She loved the feel of the night sea beneath the ferry. She loved the smell of it; different somehow to how it smelled in daylight: blacker, deeper and more mysterious.

Part of the pleasure, always, was the anticipation of being reunited with Sophie. They wrote to one another while they were apart; Mila from her bedroom in the house in Maidenhead, and Sophie from boarding school in Switzerland. Sophie's life had seemed so glamorous to Mila, filled as it was with ponies and parties, weekends in Lausanne, ski trips to Grindelwald. Even the names of the places were exotic; Mila wrote them in the margins of her school exercise books. Sophie had friends from all over Europe, girls who were the daughters of ambassadors and aristocrats and film stars. Mila, who, as a child, had used a combination of her imagination and an insatiable appetite for reading to counter the suffocating atmosphere at home, liked to imagine, all the time, what Sophie was doing. While she was watching *Blankety Blank* with her mother in the drawing room of the Maidenhead house, night falling beyond the grimy windows and the sound of traffic passing on the road, she pictured Sophie running through an Alpine field – an image conjured from a combination of *The Sound of Music* film and the illustrations in the *Heidi* book. Mila thought of her own life as a grim television documentary, filmed in black and white, and Sophie's as a glorious technicolour movie, a musical starring all the most beautiful people.

Sophie didn't talk much about school when she was at home in

Morannez, but Mila had read The Chalet School stories and the Malory Towers series, she had a clear picture of what boarding school was like. She knew all about midnight feasts and having 'pashes' on older pupils and secret corridors hidden behind bookshelves. She knew there were kind teachers, and strict-but-fair pastoral staff. She was envious of Sophie's roommate, because she could think of nothing more perfect than sharing a bedroom with Sophie, the two of them wrapped in their duvets, sipping hot chocolate and gazing through the dormitory window at moonlight reflecting from the slopes of the snow-covered mountains.

It occurred to Mila that this might be the kind of mental scenario Briony Moorcroft had dreamed up when she thought about the future life she would have with Billie: two young women having fun and adventures together – was that what she'd imagined? Mila felt a strong pang of both empathy and pity for the sick young woman.

As for herself, well, the memories were bittersweet. Sophie was gone, and this Channel crossing was in daytime. Nothing was as it had been.

As the ferry made the long journey out of Portsmouth harbour, the fog became thicker and the air temperature dropped. Mila could hear the foghorns of ships she couldn't see: low and mournful blasts, like monstrous sheep calling for their lambs.

It was weird weather.

But then, it had been weird all year.

* * *

Mila stood on the deck as the ferry ploughed through the sea. She didn't look directly down at the water because she didn't want to provoke another false flashback, up here alone.

She thought back to the day that Charlie and Sophie disappeared. While they were heading out to sea, Mila had been at work in Bristol, unaware that her life was about to change in every way.

It was one of those periods in their relationship when Sophie and Mila hadn't been as close as they usually were. There had been times when Mila had known every last detail about Sophie's life and what was in her heart and mind. But in the year leading up to Sophie's death, their step-sisterhood had entered a fallow period.

That evening, Ceci had called Mila, and Mila had known at once, from the tone of Ceci's voice, that something was wrong. Ceci told Mila that Sophie and Charlie had gone out in Charlie's boat, *Moonfleet*, and that there had been a storm. They hadn't come back.

'I'm sure it's nothing,' Ceci said, 'but I thought I should let you know.'

To her shame, Mila's initial response had been irritation. Why had they gone out, knowing the forecast was for bad weather? Why were they always so selfish? So foolhardy? So thoughtless?

Why did Ceci have to ruin her evening by calling? What did she expect Mila to do about it?

At the time of the phone call, the storm was still raging and Mila had assumed that Charlie and Sophie had found a safe spot to see out the rain and the wind. They were probably sitting in a bar, somewhere in Brittany, their phone batteries dead, waiting for the weather to ease. Or perhaps they'd docked at one of the little islands around the Golfe du Morbihan. Perhaps they'd met up with friends, somewhere, and were safe aboard a bigger boat and hadn't thought to let anyone know. There were precedents for these kinds of scenarios. Charlie and Sophie always believed in the best possible outcome in any situation. They assumed everyone else felt the same, so they couldn't understand why there was anxiety if they were late back from a sailing trip, for example. Ceci had always said parenthood would make them more responsible, there'd been no obvious change in the couple's behaviour since Ani had been born.

'You're so stressy,' Sophie used to tell Mila. 'There's no need for it. We're always fine!'

And right up until that last sailing trip, they were.

For all these reasons, it took a while for anxiety to take the place of Mila's irritation; longer still for dread to replace the anxiety.

Eventually, the weather settled. The sea calmed. But there was no word of Sophie and Charlie. When more than twenty-four hours had passed without either of them getting in touch, and it became more likely than not that something bad had happened, Mila travelled to Brittany, to be with Ceci and Anaïs. The three of them tried to keep one another's spirits up in the sea house, treating each other with the utmost kindness, the adults doing their best to protect Ani, and one another, from their worst fears.

Still, it was another few days before Sophie's body had washed up at the foot of the rugged cliffs of Pointe du Raz, a long way from Morannez; a long way from anywhere where it would have been safe for Charlie and Sophie to sail, even if there hadn't been a storm. It was luck that her body was ever found; luck that a dog walker had been out that morning, walking that particular route. A slightly different confluence of wind and tide would have taken Sophie out into the Bay of Biscay, where she would have been lost forever.

Was that what had happened to the missing Charlie?

Mila couldn't imagine how it must have felt to be Sophie, out in the storm on that tiny boat – how it would have been thrown around by the sea like a terrier ragging a mouse. It must have been almost impossible to hold on. Had she been knocked unconscious by the dinghy's boom and fallen into the water? Or had she simply fallen, in which case she might have seen the craft, *Moonfleet*, racing away from her? Was Charlie struggling to turn the boat, or had something happened to him, too? Had Sophie known she was going to die?

Shh, Mila told herself. *Stop it.*

She turned her back on the great sea, calmer today, but no less powerful, went back inside the ferry and queued in the canteen for a proper breakfast – square chunks of fried potato, beans and oily mushrooms, which she ate with toast and a mug of strong coffee. After that, she went to her seat and wrapped herself in her coat. It was cool inside the ferry. Almost chilly.

Briony and Billie might well have travelled on this same craft. They might have been sitting right where Mila was sitting now.

With this thought in her mind, Mila fell asleep, lullabied by the sound of the ship's engines.

18

Carter met Mila at Morannez train station late that evening and gave her a lift to the sea house on the back of his motorbike. When they arrived, the lights were shining in the windows and Ceci's fancy little sports car was parked on the stony track outside. There was a faint smell of smoke in the air; somewhere not too far distant, a forest fire was burning. Mila narrowed her eyes and peered into the darkness. A sinister light followed the curve of the inland horizon.

She climbed off the bike, the rucksack heavy on her shoulders.

'Thanks for the lift,' she said to Carter.

'I've got some stuff to show you,' Carter said, plunging a hand into his leather jacket in search of his phone.

When he met her at the ferry port, he'd briefed her on what he'd done to narrow the search for Briony and Billie. He was buzzing with the desire to find the runaways, but nothing more could be achieved before daybreak.

'Carter, it's...' Mila checked the screen on her phone, 'almost midnight.'

'Is it that late?' Carter looked at his watch. 'Oh yeah, right. Tomorrow then.'

'I'll come into the office early.'

'Sure. Have a good night.'

'You too.'

He saluted her and then turned the bike, opened the throttle and roared off into the darkness. Mila waited until the sound of his engine had faded, then opened the gate and walked through the garden to the house. The insects were noisy; and the air was still blood-warm.

Above her, a dull skein of smoke hung below a sky filled with stars. The smoke stained the air, but it was not dense enough to screen the land from the sun tomorrow. The heatwave hadn't run its course yet.

Mila wondered about Billie and Briony. Where were they staying? Had they found somewhere safe or were they hiding out in the woods somewhere? Did they even know about the encroaching danger from the fires?

Ceci was waiting at the sea house door, immaculately dressed in wide-legged trousers and a silk blouse. Despite the lateness of the hour, she was still fully made-up, with earrings at her lobes and a chic silver bangle at her wrist.

'Welcome back, *ma chère!*' Ceci greeted Mila with a kiss on each cheek, and the cool scent of eau de cologne. 'How was the journey?'

'Oh, it was good.' Mila put the rucksack down and rolled her shoulders to ease the ache out of them. 'Is Ani okay?'

'Perfectly fine. She's in bed.'

The two women walked through into the kitchen.

'Sorry to leave the house in such a mess,' said Mila. 'Ani and I had made a start on clearing out some of Charlie's stuff.'

'Oh?'

'I thought we'd put it off long enough.'

'It's very good of you,' said Ceci. 'Charlie always was a bit of a hoarder.'

'He certainly was.'

'Perhaps one of the stallholders at the market would take his clothes?'

'That's a good idea, thanks, Ceci.' Mila smiled. 'Maybe some of the bric-a-brac too. There was all kinds of junk in the bottom of his wardrobe.'

Ceci had brought supper, prepared by her housekeeper, Madame Abadie; an earthenware bowl on a tray. Mila lifted the plate covering the bowl and found it contained gazpacho. There was a side plate of gougères – one of Madame's specialities – as an accompaniment. Mila gave a small sigh of pleasure.

'Oh, that smells divine!'

'Shall I cut some bread for you?' Ceci asked.

'No, I'll do it. You get going home.'

Ceci hesitated.

'Unless you'd like to stay? You're very welcome,' said Mila. 'You can have my bed, I'll sleep on the sofa.'

'Thank you, but I'll go,' said Ceci. Still she didn't move.

'Is something wrong?'

'There's something I need to tell you, darling. I was going to leave it until tomorrow, but now you're here, I feel you ought to know.'

Mila gave an anxious laugh. 'Oh my goodness, Ceci, I don't like the sound of this.'

'Let's sit down,' said Ceci.

She indicated a chair at the kitchen table. Mila pulled it out, and sat. Ceci sat beside her. She pushed the soup bowl to one side.

Then she began: 'At the weekend, Monsieur Bolloré – you know, the one-handed fisherman...'

'Yes, I know.'

'Wel, he and his daughters were out on their boat fishing around the Quiberon peninsula. They were following a shoal of sardine. The tide was high and the weather was calm, so they followed the fish closer to the land than they'd normally go. Monsieur said the heatwave is affecting all the marine life. Species are behaving unusually. Anyway, the fish went into a rocky inlet and the boat followed and the crew spotted...' She put her hands palm down on the table and then looked up. 'They spotted the wreckage of a small sailing boat. They think it might be Charlie and Sophie's boat. They think it might be *Moonfleet*.'

Mila caught her breath. Sooner or later, news of this kind had been bound to come. She had practised hearing it; thought about how she'd feel and how she'd react. But now, no matter that she'd rehearsed it, it was still a shock.

'The Bollorés couldn't get the boat close enough to be sure,' Ceci continued. 'The wreckage was caught up amongst the rocks; inaccessible from the sea and probably impossible to get to from the land too, but Monsieur knows all the boats from round here, and he wouldn't have said it was *Moonfleet* if he wasn't pretty confident about it.'

'It seems strange nobody's spotted it before now.'

'Monsieur said if we could see where it was, then we wouldn't think it strange at all. It's in such an awkward, hidden little corner of the ocean, it was unlikely ever to be found.'

'What about Ani? Have you said anything to her?'

'I thought it best to wait until we were certain it was Charlie's boat and until we know if he... if he's...' She ran out of steam.

If he's still inside it, Sophie finished for her mother.

'I guess the whole of Morannez is talking about it already,' said Mila.

'Not at all. You know how superstitious the fisher-people are. Neither Monsieur Bolloré nor his daughters will say anything that might bring trouble back to them.'

'Can you be sure, Ceci? I couldn't bear for Ani to find out something like this without one of us present.'

'None of the Bolloré children goes to the International School, and anyway, it's still the holidays. I think we're safe, for a little while at least.'

It's not safe, said Sophie. *Someone will say something. You know what this town is like, everyone knows everyone else's business. You need to break the news to Ani at once. As soon as she wakes.*

19

That night, Mila dreamed of the sea. The dream turned into a nightmare. She was in the water, amongst the gigantic, green waves that she'd watched from the deck of the ferry. She was being lifted and lowered on the shoulders of the waves, and ahead of her, just out of reach, was a body: face down in the water, arms spread-eagled, the body was slowly being carried further away and Mila knew that if she couldn't reach it, it would be gone forever.

'Sophie!' she screamed in her dream, but when she opened her mouth, the saltwater rushed in and it filled her throat. 'Sophie!'

The more she fought to reach her stepsister, the more the water held onto her, and something was restraining her, gripping her by her shoulders, she couldn't breathe, she was drowning too, everything would be lost, Sophie would be lost forever!

'Mila! *Mila!* Wake up!'

Mila opened her eyes. It took a moment for her to recognise that she was back in her room at the sea house; that, beyond the window, thrown wide by Mila before she climbed into bed, dawn was breaking palely across the wide Breton sky. The towel that Mila had wrapped round her hair when she had stepped out of the shower in the early hours was now around her neck – that was what was causing the suffocating sensation.

Distantly, a cock crowed.

She sat up, still not quite in the real world. Her beloved Ani was beside the bed, barefoot, wearing a holey Hugs not Drugs T-shirt – an old one of Charlie's. Mila realised that the girl had woken her, that it had been her hands she had felt on her shoulders.

'You were screaming,' Ani said.

'I was having a nightmare. I'm sorry I woke you.'

''S'okay,' said Ani. She rubbed her eyes. Mila's heart ached with tenderness for her niece. 'My feet are cold.'

The room was so warm that this couldn't possibly be true, but Mila knew what Ani wanted. She budged up across the bed and Ani climbed into the spot her aunt had just vacated. She pulled the single cotton sheet up to her chin.

'Better?' Mila asked.

'Yep.'

Mila put her arm around Ani and kissed the top of her head.

Don't grow any older, she begged silently. *You're perfect as you are. Stay like this, forever.*

'Were you dreaming about Maman?' Ani asked.

'What makes you think that?'

'You were calling her name. You were like: "Sophie! Sophie! Come back to me, Sophie!"'

'You're right, I was dreaming about her.'

'Do you dream about her a lot?'

'I do. How about you?'

'Sometimes. But they're usually nice dreams, where she's alive, and in the dream I think it was all a mistake about her and Papa being lost and I'm so happy to be with them again and they're happy to be with me.' She snuggled down into the pillows. 'The bad thing about my dreams is when I wake up and I realise they weren't true.'

Do you hear that? Mila asked Sophie. *Do you hear how your daughter dreams of you? How she holds you still in her heart?*

Ani yawned.

'Ani,' Mila said, 'there's something I need to tell you.'

'What?'

Mila took a deep breath.

Just tell her, Sophie said. *Don't beat about the bush.*

'Yesterday,' said Mila, 'or it might have been the day before, Monsieur Bolloré, the fisherman, spotted the wreckage of a little yellow boat out on the rocks in a far-off part of the Quiberon peninsula. He thinks it might be *Moonfleet*.'

Ani was silent for a long time.

'It's not definitely *Moonfleet*?' she asked at last.

'No, but I don't think Monsieur would have said anything if he wasn't pretty sure.'

Ani was very still. Mila could barely hear her breathing.

'Is Papa in the boat?' she asked.

'I don't know, Ani. If it is *Moonfleet*, then there's a chance that he might be.'

Ani was quiet again.

Mila said: 'If anyone can get to the wreckage – it might not be possible to reach it because of where it is – but if someone can, and it turns out to be *Moonfleet*, then we'll know more. We might even find out what happened to your parents on the day they went missing. But that's a lot of "ifs", Ani. We mustn't start assuming there will be answers to all of our questions.' Mila kept her voice soft, her words gentle, delivering the news in the least hurtful way possible.

'Perhaps *Moonfleet* was in a collision with a bigger boat,' said Ani. 'Perhaps there'll be evidence on the wreckage. Scratches or something.'

'Perhaps.'

'And if Papa is there, does that mean we can bring him home and bury him with Maman?'

Mila could hardly bear to listen to these questions. There was hope in Ani's voice, but the situation was so sad. 'Yes. If he's there, we can bring him back to Morannez.'

'What if,' Ani continued, 'the wreckage *is Moonfleet*, but Papa's not there?'

'Then we'll have to wait for something else to turn up that might help us understand what happened.'

'If he's not there, then he might still be alive.'

'It's possible,' said Mila gently, 'but, you know, Ani, it's not likely.'

It was only recently that Mila had realised the extent of the trauma Anaïs had endured in the months after Sophie's body was recovered from the sea. What Mila had interpreted as Ani being resilient, had, in truth, been Ani disassociating from the facts. Now she was conscious of this, Mila had vowed to keep a closer eye on her niece. But it was a fine line to tread between encouraging her to express her emotions and risking her becoming engulfed by them.

'Whatever happens next, Ani,' she said softly, 'whatever comes of this, whether it turns out to be something relevant, or nothing, I'll be there with you, and so will Mamie Ceci. We'll be right at your side. Together, the three of us can get through anything.' She hesitated to use the line she'd used before, jokingly, as this situation was not the least funny. And besides, wasn't Ani too old now for platitudes?

Ani rescued her. 'Like the three musketeers,' she said.

'Exactly like that.'

Then, in the half-light, Ani reached out her hand and touched Mila's head. 'You shouldn't have got into bed with your hair wet. It looks like a bird's nest.'

'Really? Is it a disaster?'

'It's a catastrophe. I'll help you sort it out when we get up.'

'Thank you.'

'I'm going to sleep for a bit longer,' said Ani and she turned onto her side.

'You okay?' Mila asked her.

'Yep,' said Ani.

But Mila knew that, although she was putting a brave face on the situation, as she always did, Ani was not okay; not at all.

20

Later, when she was up and her hair fixed by her niece, Mila headed into Morannez, determined to put in a full day's searching for Briony Moorcroft.

When she first came to France, Mila had, temporarily, used Sophie's old office, in the agency headquarters above the pâtisserie in the medieval backstreets of Morannez town centre. Later, she'd moved out to make room for Carter. Now, if Mila wanted to work from Toussaints, she had to find space in either Carter or Ceci's office. Although Carter was always accommodating, Mila found him an impossible stablemate. He was loud, and took up a great deal of space, and he was clumsy: bumping into the corners of the desk; dropping files and knocking over coffee cups. Sitting still was anathema to Carter Jackson; he paced like a cat, always ending up at the window and sometimes, with no warning, banging on the glass to attract the attention of somebody on the street below.

Although Carter, like Mila, only used to come to Morannez for the summer holidays as a teenager, unlike her, he was friends with everyone. He was magnetic. He could draw people towards him and even now it was impossible to walk down the street with Carter without being

constantly interrupted by men and women coming up to him to shake
his hand, pat his back or give him a hug.

'*Salut, mon pote*! You're back!' they used to say at first. 'It's so good to
see you!'

Now they exclaimed: 'You're still here! That's brilliant! Are you
putting down roots?'

And Carter tried but never succeeded in hiding his pleasure at being
reunited with an old friend. He shuffled from foot to foot, shrugged,
smiled broadly and responded ambiguously. 'Oh, you know me, easy
come, easy go.'

'We must meet up for a drink sometime, buddy.'

'Sure, yeah, of course.'

'Man, it's great that you're back!'

Mila tried not to be ungracious about Carter's popularity. It was
largely what made him so successful an investigator – old friends and
acquaintances were always willing to help him. In truth, she enjoyed
working with him; so much so that she sometimes – almost – forgot that
they had history. But if their friendship had been complicated when
they were young; now it was even more so.

And Mila still hadn't got to the bottom of why Carter Jackson had
returned to Morannez. Ostensibly, it was to take up the position at the
agency. Carter's ex, Emmanuelle, had moved back to Finistère with the
couple's son, so it made sense for him to find work nearby. But Mila was
convinced Sophie, or Sophie's death, was the real reason he had come
back.

She didn't believe him when he said he hadn't known that Sophie
had drowned. Neither could she work out if he had come to lay his
ghosts to rest, or to make sure they never settled.

It didn't matter now. Carter was back to stay, and although he drove
Mila mad sometimes, he was a brilliant detective. As well as being tech-
nologically skilled, his contacts within the police, and other agencies,
gave him access to invaluable information.

He was also so irrepressibly good-humoured that even his noise and
untidiness could be forgiven.

That morning, Mila poured herself a cup of coffee from the little machine bubbling on the hob in the kitchenette, went into Carter's office and pulled up a chair beside his in front of the big screen on his desk. She had bought a selection of pastries from the pâtisserie and picked out an exquisite, tiny éclair filled with vanilla-flavoured crème pâtissière and glossed with white chocolate. The coffee cup was balanced on the window ledge at arm's length, wedged between the sill and the iron window boxes, in which the pelargoniums were still flowering beautifully, trailing bright red flowers that stood out against the grey brickwork. Sunshine beamed down between the roofs of the old buildings on either side of the street, although the blue sky visible amongst the rooftops and chimney pots was smeared with a dirty haze: smuts from the fires hanging high up in the stratosphere. The heat lingered still.

'Right,' Mila said to Carter. 'What was it you couldn't wait to show me last night?'

'Give me one minute, and you'll find out.'

Carter opened the pâtisserie box and devoured four pastries, one after the other. It seemed disrespectful of the time and skill that had gone into making the pastries, to consume them so quickly, and with so little thought, but Carter was like a Labrador when it came to food. Now he reached across Mila to the box and grabbed a miniature baba au rhum, without so much as pausing to see what he had chosen. As he withdrew his hand, Mila saw the Celtic triskele tattoo on the inside of his wrist. All the members of the *Bande Sauvage* had the same tattoo except Mila. She hadn't been there when the others had theirs done because that was the summer of Lydia's breakdown, when Mila had stayed behind in England.

Sophie had never thought to let Mila know about the tattoos. She hadn't told her that she and Carter had kissed at Arnaud Girard's birthday party either. Nor that they had practiced diving together off the deck of the Girards' yacht, Sophie wearing the yellow halter-neck bikini that showed off her tan. All the details had come to light later, in dribs and drabs. It had felt, to Mila, stuck at home in Maidenhead with her sick mother, as if she was out of sight, out of mind; not really important to Sophie at all. Seeing the tattoo on Carter's wrist all these years later was a sting. A small sting, but nonetheless a reminder that Mila had never fully belonged to the *Bande Sauvage*.

It wasn't Sophie's fault, she told herself.

And that was true. Mila being obliged to spend the six-week school holiday in Maidenhead, dividing her time between her weeping mother in the riverside villa and her ranting grandmother in the former asylum, had nothing to do with Sophie. Mila had no right to resent the fun that Sophie had been having.

And she should be glad, now, that Sophie had had that blissful summer, knowing how few summers she had ahead of her.

Carter was oblivious to Mila's introspection. He brushed crumbs from his T-shirt with one hand while he brought up some images onto the computer screen with the other.

'Okay,' he said. 'Here we are. This is what I wanted you to see and this is why I think we should start our search for the runaways in Lorient town.'

Mila snapped herself back into the present. On the screen was a video of a tall, muscular woman, Billie Dexter, wearing the exact same outfit she'd been wearing in the Moorcrofts' video. This time, she was in a supermarket. There was something of the panther about her. She prowled through the aisles. She must have exuded some air of repressed violence, or aggression, because the other shoppers made way for her, dodging out of her path as if they felt threatened by her.

'Where did you get the video?' Mila asked.

'From the security guy in the Intermarché in Lorient where the Moorcrofts' bank card was used. There's a better shot of her face here. This time, she's in the pharmacy a few streets over.'

Mila leaned closer to look. The next video had been taken on a different day and depicted Billie wearing a black T-shirt decorated with some kind of heavy-metal artwork. Now Mila could see the tattoos on her arms and the back of her neck. Her face was mostly shielded by a baseball cap, which she took off as she walked towards the exit, using the hat to fan herself. Her eyes were dark and wary; her nose skewed by an old injury, her lips tight.

'And here she is again,' said Carter.

This time, the video clearly showed the Moorcrofts' Maid Services van pull into a parking space outside a supermarket. Billie Dexter opened the driver's door, climbed out and paced across the tarmac towards the entrance, checking the screen on her phone.

'Where's Briony?' Mila asked.

'There's no sign of her.'

'She's not in the van?'

'I can't see the passenger side, but Billie's body language doesn't suggest there's anyone with her.'

'So, what's she done with Briony?'

Carter shrugged. He reached across Mila for the last remaining delicacy in the pastry box, which he picked up and put into his mouth. 'I also did some research on Billie's family,' said Carter. 'It's grim.'

'How grim?'

'Billie's father, Derek, died in prison last year. He died of natural causes but was serving life for the murder of a young female sex worker, twenty-three years old, a mother-of-two. Doing the best she could for her kids before that bastard came along.'

Mila shuddered.

'Prior to that,' Carter continued, 'Derek had been in and out of jail for various offences of the sexual violence kind.'

'What about Billie's mother?'

'Her name's Maura. She left the family home for good when Billie was eight and her little sister was six. Maura was in fear of her life. She took the younger kid with her. Little Billie had three years alone with Derek before Derek committed murder. I'd bet good money that Derek Dexter didn't win any father-of-the-year awards. He was the kind of man who would have felt humiliated by his wife leaving him and redirected his anger towards other women.'

'And Billie too,' said Mila.

'At the very least, she'd have witnessed it.'

It was the kind of upbringing that left marks on a child, one way or another.

'And when Derek went to prison, Billie went to live with her granddad in Carnarth?' Mila asked.

'That's right.'

'I went there,' said Mila. 'That part of Billie's story doesn't have a happy ending either.'

'She also had periods living with foster families when her grandfather couldn't cope. She was described variously as "difficult", "troubled" and "disturbed". She was kicked out of one home after threatening a younger kid with a knife – probably taking a leaf out of Derek's playbook.'

Carter brought up an image of a police record sheet onto the screen.

'By the age of fifteen, Billie was hanging round with one of the Cardiff gangs. She had a reputation for being tough as any lad and she wasn't afraid of scrapping. In the decade between then and now, she's been in trouble with the police countless times, spent more time locked up than she has on the streets and never managed to hold down any kind of job.'

'Until she got the cleaning gig with Mr Moorcroft.'

'Until then.'

'Were any of Billie's convictions for violent crime?'

'Yep. ABH, GBH, possession of an offensive weapon in a public place, threatening somebody with a knife, once... twice... three times. She never actually killed anyone. Not yet.'

Carter tapped his fingers on the table. He reached for the pastry box and then remembered it was empty.

'But,' he said, 'with people like Billie, there's usually an escalation. My professional opinion is that we need to get Briony away from her as quickly as possible.'

Inside Mila's head, Sophie sighed.

No shit, Sherlock, she said.

21

Carter changed the image on his screen. 'I've done a search for Briony Moorcroft too.'

'What did you find?' Mila took a drink of coffee.

'Briony is something of a celebrity in her home town. She and her mother have been special guests at a raft of major community events. Mrs Moorcroft is a high-profile fundraiser and Briony is known for being sick. Her story is tragic. Each time it looks as if she's making progress, she relapses. People feel sorry for her and want to make her life better.'

'Poor kid.'

'Indeed. But look... over the past years, she's had loads of help from local businesses. She's been given free clothes, free accommodation close to the hospital, a new wheelchair, the local car dealership even gave the family a BMW.'

Mila had seen the car, with its personalised plate. Who had reaped the most benefit from the vehicle, she wondered: Briony, or her parents?

Carter continued: 'Right now, there's a crowdfunding appeal in place for Briony to go to New Zealand for some kind of miracle therapy.' He frowned, then asked: 'When you met the Moorcrofts, did you get the impression they had money problems?'

'I didn't, but I never asked about it. Mr Moorcroft said the business had been hit hard over the last few years, but it seemed to be mainly trouble finding and keeping staff.' Mila leaned closer to the TV screen. 'What's that picture?'

'Briony turning on the Carnarth Christmas lights. She's there, in the middle, see, all wrapped up in tinsel like a parcel under the tree?'

Mila scanned the faces in the crowd gathered around the podium on which Briony was sitting in her wheelchair.

'There,' she said, pointing to a figure several rows back. 'Can you zoom in on that face?'

'That guy?'

'In the beanie. It's not a guy. But, yeah; that one.'

'Shit. Is that Billie Dexter?'

'It is,' Mila said. 'I'm sure it is.'

Carter zoomed in even closer, until Billie's face was no more than a blur of pixels. Her eyes were dark squares, fixed on Briony. She reminded Mila of a segment she'd seen on a wildlife documentary about a lion hunting. The lion's body had moved, but its eyes had remained motionless in its head. Everything about Billie's stance in the image was predatory.

'This was last Christmas?' Mila asked.

'Yep.'

'So, Billie's been watching Briony at least since then.'

Carter scratched his forehead.

'She might've been planning this for months,' he said to Mila.

22

There was a gentle rap on the door behind them, and Ceci came into the room; her hair shining in a blonde bob and pearls around her neck. She was wearing a cream-coloured dress with matching shoes.

Mila glanced down at her own biker boots and green linen dress, the bangles on her wrists. She'd thought she looked quite good this morning after Ani had sorted out her hair. Now she felt scruffy.

'Good morning!' said Mila. 'You look very smart.'

'I'm meeting Monique Girard for lunch,' Ceci said. 'I've set a reminder on my phone. Did Carter tell you that I missed my last appointment with her? Monique must think I'm losing my marbles.'

'I'm sure she doesn't.'

Ceci put a hand on Mila's shoulder, leaned down and kissed her cheek. She smelled sweet and fresh and expensive. 'How are you, darling?'

'I'm fine. Carter's been filling me in on Billie Dexter's background.'

'And?'

'It's really not good.'

'No,' said Ceci. 'I thought as much. So, what's the plan? Where do we start looking?'

'I already contacted all the campsites,' said Carter. 'Nobody recognised the descriptions of the two women and nobody's seen the van.'

'Holiday lets?'

'Those too. No joy.'

'They might be sleeping rough somewhere.'

Mila flinched at the thought of fragile Briony Moorcroft bedded down in the back of the van; how hot it would be in the metal box; how little protection there would be from the glare of the sun in the daytime, and from the smoke-polluted air at night.

'Should we put an appeal on social media?' Mila asked. 'Or we could ask the local radio station to broadcast an announcement that we're looking for the van.'

'Nope,' said Carter. 'If Billie gets wind of the fact we're after them, she'll either move on or go to ground.'

'What if Briony's being held somewhere against her will? Shouldn't we try to let her know that help is on the way?'

'I agree with Carter,' said Ceci. 'The last thing we want to do is panic Billie into doing something stupid – or dangerous.'

Carter picked up his feet and spun round on his chair. 'We should go to Lorient and ask around. Lots of people must have seen Billie in the supermarket: someone there might remember her. She might even have given an indication as to where they're staying. I reckon it's our best chance of tracking them down.'

Mila nodded her assent.

23

Carter pulled the Harley-Davidson up in the space reserved for motorbikes outside the Intermarché Super at Lorient and cut off the engine.

The character of Lorient town was very different to that of sleepy Morannez. It was a far bigger place and they'd arrived via the busy ring road, passing high-rise buildings, blocks of flats, commercial centres and shopping districts.

Mila climbed off the back of the bike, unclipped the chin-strap, took off her helmet and shook out her hair. When she first rode on the back of Carter's bike, she used to feel horribly conspicuous because everyone always turned to see the source of the deafening noise. After she dismounted, her ears would ring for ages and her body kept vibrating to the rhythm of the Fat Boy engine. She had the motorbike equivalent of sea legs, wobbling like a foal as she tried to get used to being on terra firma again. These days, she was used to riding pillion. She almost enjoyed it.

Carter took off his jacket and folded it into the pannier. He took Mila's helmet and locked it, with his own, to the bike.

'It's hot,' he said.

Gold medal for stating the obvious, said Sophie.

But it was hot. Mila could feel the heat of the sun on her shoulders and the back of her neck. During the journey between Morannez and Lorient, she'd observed how dry the grass and shrubs and trees had become. She'd noticed the empty riverbed; smooth pebbles heaped together and piles of dead weed where there should have been babbling water, wildlife and flowers. The smell of burning forest had been pervasive. She knew that when she returned to the sea house later, she'd still be able to smell the smoke in her hair.

The sun was almost directly overhead, so there was little shade to be had.

Despite the heat, the supermarket car park was heaving; people pushing laden trolleys back to their vehicles; others negotiating with toddlers; a group of men standing together by the recycling bins, smoking and talking intently.

Mila had spent very little time in this town, and what she knew about Lorient was largely confined to what she'd read on the tourism leaflets: that it had the only museum in Europe entirely dedicated to sailing and that it had five ports, with the second largest fishing harbour in France and a former naval base. She could understand why Billie chose to do her shopping here. She and Briony would be less conspicuous in a large place than a small one. Easier to hide a tree in a forest than on a plain.

The sun beat down above them. Traffic buzzed all round.

Mila and Carter walked to the supermarket doors beneath the huge, black and red Intermarché logo and left the warmth of the outside as they stepped into the chill of the interior. It was a large, modern store, thousands of different products neatly displayed on racks; a massive selection of fruit and vegetables.

'We should begin by talking to the assistants,' said Carter. He considered this for a moment. 'We'll cover more ground if we split up. Why don't I ask round in the supermarket and you wander into the town?'

* * *

Although she'd been involved in searching for missing people on many occasions since she started working for Toussaints, and the work was largely satisfying, Mila did not enjoy the part of the job that involved approaching strangers. She didn't like asking them, most of the time in a language that didn't always come easily to her, if they'd seen the people in the photographs on her phone. It felt intrusive and creepy. Her French still wasn't fluent enough for her to explain proficiently and with the requisite charm that she was neither a stalker, nor a tax official. On this occasion, however, the importance of finding Briony Moorcroft and removing her from the clutches of Billie Dexter as quickly as possible outweighed any misgivings.

Mila set off, heading towards the seafront, because if she were here with Luke and they had time to kill that would be where they'd go and it seemed logical that Billie and Briony would do the same. It would be sheer luck if she happened to find anyone who had noticed the two young women, and remembered them. But sometimes luck happened. The only guarantee was that if you didn't try, you'd never find the person you were looking for.

Mila didn't go into every shop, but picked the kind of establishments that sold snacks, cold drinks and cigarettes. She had two images ready on her phone: one of Billie, one of Briony. She waited until there were no customers, then approached the shop assistant, or manager: '*Vous reconnaissez ces personnes?*'

If people asked for more information, or *why* she was looking for them, Mila told them simply that Briony was sick and they needed to get medication to her.

People tried to be helpful. They wanted to be the one who recognised Briony and told Mila where to find her. They took the phone and studied the pictures on the screen. Sometimes they used their fingers to expand the image, to get a better look at the faces. But the response was always the same: a trawling through their memories, then a regretful shake of the head.

Eventually, Mila found herself beside the river at the Cité de la Voile – the museum dedicated to the sailor, Éric Tabarly. It was a smart building, right on the waterfront. A group of young people was gathered outside preparing to walk across a floating jetty to go on a trip in a boat; they were wearing buoyancy aids and listening to a safety briefing. Their supervisors stood to one side, leaning on the railings, talking amongst themselves.

Almost two hours had elapsed since Mila had left Carter and she was hot and thirsty. In her bag was a bottle of Coca-Cola that she'd purchased from the refrigerated cabinet in the last shop she'd visited. She took it out, held it to her forehead – the cold plastic was wonderfully soothing – and looked around. A man was sitting on one of the permanent metal chairs outside the museum.

'Is it okay if I sit here?' she asked him in French, indicating the seat beside his.

'Be my guest,' he replied in English.

Mila sighed. 'I've been living here for two years now and still every time I speak, everyone knows I'm English.'

'Don't be offended, it's the phrasing,' said the man. 'Most English people can't help talking like they're English even when they're speaking French.' He looked up at Mila and she looked at him properly for the first time and realised that he was a vagrant. He saw the recognition in her eyes and she saw him recognising her realisation and they were both embarrassed. 'I generalise, of course,' the man added, looking away, his demeanour changed. 'Forgive me.'

His clothes were dusty and ill-fitting; he did not have a belt, his trousers were held up with a length of yellow twine. The stubble around his jaw was several days old and the whites of his eyes were bloodshot, their rims crusty. Yet his English was perfect; his manners refined.

Mila sat down and offered him the Coke bottle. 'Would you like a drink?'

He shook his head and raised his hand to show that he had a half-litre of vodka inside a paper bag. Close up, he reeked of alcohol.

'What about something to eat then?' Mila persisted.

Leave him alone, said Sophie. *Why do you always have to be such a goody-two-shoes?*

I'm just being polite!

You're interfering. It's a kind of judging, Mila, you shouldn't do it.

'I'm not hungry,' said the man.

Mila took a drink and narrowed her eyes against the sun's glare to watch the teenagers on the dockside transferring themselves carefully along the pontoon and onto the boat. They were laughing, but the laughter was a little too loud. They were nervous. They must be city students; not used to the water. Mila empathised with their discomfort. It was one thing to cross the sea on an enormous and robust ferry, but small boats offered little protection. She thought of all the news stories she'd seen recently about overcrowded craft capsizing in the Mediterranean and the English Channel; desperate people drowning. And then she couldn't help picturing Charlie's beloved *Moonfleet*, skimming over the waves, and following that image, the thought of that boat capsizing; of Sophie falling into the sea, and Charlie? God only knew what had become of him.

Mila wondered how the supervising adults on the dockside could bear the responsibility of looking after all those young people when it would take so little – a rogue wave, or a discarded fishing net caught around the propeller, to bring tragedy to them all.

The silence between Mila and the man expanded. He glugged back some vodka, wiped his lips with the back of his hand and sighed as the alcohol made its way into his blood.

'Nice day to be going out on a boat,' he said.

Mila pushed away her catastrophic thoughts. He was right. There was no wind; the sea would be flat calm. And it would be cooler offshore than on the land: a respite from the heat.

'Are you a sailor?' she asked.

'Used to be an oceanographer.'

'Oh? What did that entail?'

'The study of physical processes within the oceans.'

'Waves, you mean?'

'And tides and currents.'

'That sounds like it would have been interesting work.'

'It was.'

What happened? Sophie wondered.

The man raised the paper bag to his lips and took another drink.

He got drunk, Sophie answered her own question.

Now who's judging?

I'm observing, Mila. There's a difference.

Mila wondered if the man had endured some trauma or shock that had precipitated the fall into his current situation, or if his addiction had been ongoing.

It wasn't the kind of question one could ask.

She put a hand over her eyes to shield them from the glare and scanned the harbour. 'I like the look of that boat.' She pointed to an elegant ketch moored outside beside a floating quay beneath a raised walkway above the water opposite the museum.

'*Pen Duick*? That was Tabarly's boat. Built for the 1973 Round the World yacht race. She's done 300,000 miles since then and still not ready for retirement.'

'You're very knowledgeable.'

The man shrugged.

The teenagers and their teachers were all on board now. The craft, one which advertised itself as giving tours, was rocking on the surface of the water. A jolly, bearded man was straddling the boat and the pontoon, untying the rope from the bollard that held it in place. A woman with tanned skin and bleached hair was talking to the students, telling them what to look out for while they were at sea. The young people were super-excited and noisy now.

A text came through on Mila's phone. It was Carter, asking where she was. She responded with a link to her location. Then she screwed the lid back onto the Coke bottle and stood up. 'I've got to go,' she said to the man. She hesitated. 'Do you spend a lot of time round here?'

'A fair amount.'

Mila pulled up the pictures of Billie and Briony on her phone. 'I don't suppose you've seen either of these two around, have you?'

The man took the phone and studied the picture. He shook his head slowly. 'I don't recognise them. Are they friends of yours?'

'Not exactly. The young woman on the right is going to be very sick if we don't find her soon and get her to a hospital.' She paused. 'She might already be sick. So, you might just be looking for the one on the left, on her own.'

'I'll keep an eye out.'

'Thank you. And if you do happen to see them, please don't say anything to them, but would you let me know?'

She took one of Toussaints' cards, with her mobile number on it, from her bag and gave it to the man, along with a folded twenty-euro note. 'That's to cover the cost of the call,' she said, in case he thought she was being condescending.

He nodded.

'Thanks,' said Mila. 'I'm Mila Shepherd by the way.'

'Didier,' said the man. 'Didier Désespéré.'

24

Mila met up with Carter back in the town centre.

'Any luck?' he asked.

'Nothing at all. How about you?'

'Billie was in the supermarket yesterday. I spoke to Layla Erdogan, a store supervisor. She is 100 per cent certain it was Billie.'

'But Briony wasn't with her?'

'No.'

Mila had a bad feeling inside. A gnawing anxiety.

'There's more,' said Carter. 'I'll show you.'

They walked a short distance and sat on a bench beneath a line of lime trees in a little park. To their right, teenagers were performing tricks and dares on a skateboard ramp. Women and men were sitting on the benches in the cooler, dark patches of shade; exhausted by the heat.

Carter took his phone out of his pocket and started to play back the interview he'd recorded with Layla Erdogan. She was a thin woman who gesticulated with her hands as she spoke. Behind her, the supermarket was busy.

'There's too much background noise,' said Mila. 'I can't hear anything.'

Carter switched off the phone. 'I'll summarise,' he said. 'Layla said the first time Billie went into the store, she was with a thin young woman, who didn't look well.'

'Briony?'

'Has to be. Layla got the impression she was scared. Layla's sister had been in a coercive relationship and Briony was giving off the same vibes. Layla was concerned, but she doesn't speak any English, so she merely observed the couple. They stocked up with provisions as if they were planning on going away somewhere for a long time.'

'What did they buy?'

'Canned and bottled food, toilet paper, baby wipes, matches, candles and sleeping bags. Dozens of bottles of water. Layla said that, normally, campers buy the essentials but also treats, stuff for the barbecue, beer, crisps. Not these two. She said it was more as if they were preparing for a siege.'

'Like they were getting ready to hide themselves away somewhere?'

'Exactly.'

'All that water means they might be camping miles from anywhere.'

'Yep,' said Carter.

Mila thought of the forest fires; how quickly they moved. A distraught man on the news had described the flames racing towards his woodland holiday home 'faster than a galloping horse'. She imagined Briony, left behind, alone, while Billie came into town for supplies. What could Briony do if the fires threatened her? She couldn't call for help, she couldn't run.

Carter was hunched forward, his forearms resting on his thighs, his face inclined downwards. Mila looked at the curve of his ear; the way the hairline tailed off behind his neck, the tendons in his throat.

'You said Billie was in the supermarket again yesterday?' Mila prompted.

'Yep.'

'That's good news, isn't it? It means she and Briony are still around here, somewhere.'

'Yesterday,' Carter said quietly, 'Billie came into the store on her own.

She looked terrible, like she hadn't slept for a week. Her arms and face were covered in scratches and bruises. Her clothes were filthy. She smelled of vomit, Layla said.' Carter paused. 'I don't know how to tell you the rest, Mila.'

'Tell me what?' She gave a small laugh. 'Billie was in a supermarket. How bad can it be?'

'She bought bleach,' said Carter. 'Five litres of bleach, a roll of heavy-duty binbags and a spade.'

'A spade?'

'Yep.'

Mila and Carter sat in silence, side by side for a couple of moments while Mila assimilated this new information.

'What do we do now?' she asked quietly.

'We need to get the police involved. We need every resource there is out looking for them. We need to find them.'

Them.

Mila could not bring herself to ask him if he really believed that Briony was still alive.

'Call the police,' she said. 'Call them now.'

Carter picked up his phone, stood up, and wandered away, talking into the phone urgently, gesticulating with his free hand. Mila sat in the shade, watching birds come to sip water from the bowl of the fountain in the centre of the pond placed where two paths intersected. She felt numb. She couldn't hold a single thought in her mind.

Did this mean they were already too late to save Briony? What would she say to Mr and Mrs Moorcroft when she called them? How would she tell them what the witness in the supermarket had told Carter?

After a few moments, Carter returned.

'Sorted?' Mila asked. He nodded.

He stood in front of Mila in the shade of the tree, the sunlight falling through the leaves making lacy patterns on his skin.

'Where does this leave us, Carter? Do we keep on looking for her – *them*, or do we leave it to the police?'

'What do you want to do?'

'I want to keep looking.'

'Let's get back to the bike then,' said Carter. 'Let's keep looking.'

* * *

Mila and Carter spent the next couple of hours driving in the countryside around Lorient, pulling into lay-bys and exploring the old farm tracks and entrances to woodlands and fields, searching for the Moorcrofts' van. They might as well have been searching for a needle in a haystack. The area was full of tourist traffic and they hadn't even started going into the campsites, or the shopping complexes, or the resorts.

They drove through a great area of land that had been ravaged by fire. What should have been a pleasant drive along a green lane winding up the side of a hill was, instead, a safari through a jungle of charred tree trunks and fallen branches with ash beneath them. The leaves were gone, and so were the colours of late summer. Everything was monotone. Everything smelled of smoke.

Mila was on the back of Carter's bike. She could not wind up a window to mitigate the bitter odour. She could not escape the devastation.

What happens to the birds when there's a fire? Mila wondered. *What happens to the wildlife?*

By now, the afternoon was drawing in. Mila's concern for Briony Moorcroft's welfare was compounded by anxiety about Ani, who had been alone at the sea house all day. Mila felt even more guilty than usual about this, given the news she'd told Ani about the wreckage. Each time she'd messaged, Ani had replied cheerfully, but Mila knew she'd be thinking about her father; wondering if the boat on the rocks might hold some clue as to what had become of him.

There was an intercom system linking Mila's motorbike helmet with Carter's. She switched on her microphone and told him it was time for her to get back to Morannez.

'No worries,' said Carter. 'I'll take you back, get something to eat, then come back here on my own and carry on searching.'

'Would it be okay if we stopped at the harbour?'

'You want to speak to Monsieur Bolloré?'

'Yep. Ani is going to have a load of questions for me and I'd like to be able to answer them if I can.'

25

Morannez harbour was a small, man-made port inside the larger, natural Golfe du Morbihan – Ar Mor Bihan, or 'little sea' in Breton. Carter parked the bike on the concreted area behind the sheds where the fish were sorted and packed into boxes of ice. In the mornings, representatives from the local hotels and restaurants came to buy catches directly off the boats. By this time in the afternoon, the business was all done. A man in rubber overalls, tied at the waist, and heavy boots was hosing down the cobbles. Gulls were screeching overhead, darting down to grab a scrap of flesh or a discarded fish-head, then flapping up again, dodging other birds intent on stealing their prize.

Mila and Carter walked around the market and onto the harbour wall. The tide was out and the mud was exposed at the near end; pleasure boats, yachts and lobster boats tilted on their sides; barnacled buoys draped in seaweed; ropes drawing lines through the silt.

At the far end, where enough water remained, were the larger fishing craft, including Monsieur Bolloré's boat, *Ariane*, named after his wife, a formidable woman, who was sitting in a collapsible camping chair at the dock-edge knitting, a cigarette between her lips and a bottle of Lambig at her side, while her husband and their two daughters worked on the boat.

'*Bonjour!*' Mila called as they approached.

Madame peered over her needles. She was making a sweater, a string of blue wool emerging from the depths of her ancient handbag. It seemed incongruous given the heat.

The younger of the daughters, Solene, who had been one of the *Bande Sauvage*, stood up in the deck of the boat and waved a greeting. '*Salut*, Mila!' she called in a gruff voice. 'How's it going?'

'I'm good, thank you,' said Mila, because that was a lot quicker than telling the truth. 'I hope you don't mind me turning up like this.'

'Not at all. We'd have been surprised if you hadn't come.' Solene was a stocky woman with sun-bleached, short hair and a strong-featured face. She was holding a large wrench in one hand. Now she put it down and shielded her eyes with her hand. 'Who's that with you? It's not Carter Jackson, is it? It is! Oh my goodness, Carter Jackson! Is it really you?'

'It's really me,' said Carter.

'I heard you were back! I've kept looking out for you, but our paths never crossed! Oh my days, it's so good to see you!'

Solene climbed onto the side of the boat, grabbed onto the metal ladder that descended the harbour wall and was up in an instant. She was wearing heavy orange overalls, the skin on her face tanned a deep brown. Her older sister, Suzanne, was as quiet and withdrawn as Solene was extrovert. She remained in the boat concentrating on painting the old boards.

'Carter, you old bastard!' Solene threw her arms around him and gave him a hug that squeezed the breath from him, until her mother said: 'Put him down, girl!'

Then Solene stepped back, punching Carter in a playful way on the chest, then hopping from foot to foot and wiping the palms of her filthy hands on the side of her T-shirt. 'You remember Carter, Maman!' she said to the sphinx-like Ariane. Ariane glanced at Carter before continuing to knit. 'I used to have a huge crush on him, when we were kids.'

You too? Mila wondered.

'Aww,' said Carter, 'I had a bigger crush on *you*.'

Liar, whispered Sophie. *He only ever had eyes for me.*

'It's so good to see you, Carter!'

'It's really great to see you too, Solene, you haven't changed at all.'
Carter gave her one of his film-star smiles. Mila could imagine Sophie
making a two-fingers-down-the-throat gesture behind his back.

Solene was delighted. 'I hoped we'd bump into one another one day,'
she said. 'Trouble is, I'm always here, in the boat, and I heard you've got
a kid now, so you won't be down L'Alchimiste.'

That was a tiny bar in the heart of Morannez, owned by the Girard
family, with a reputation for staying open all night. It was a place, Mila
remembered, that Sophie used to frequent, although Charlie didn't like
it. He was always bemoaning the lack of British pubs and the fact that it
was impossible to buy 'a proper pint' in Brittany. He only did it to wind
up Sophie.

'So, what do you want to know, Mila?' Solene asked. She was rocking
her weight from foot to foot as if she were still on a boat at sea, adjusting
her balance.

By this time, Monsieur Bolloré had made his way up onto the
harbour wall. He was puffing and he had a limp. His huge wrists and
forearms were an unhealthy, purply-red colour and covered in scars. He
was entirely missing the left hand – an accident at sea, as Mila recalled.
He'd got his wrist caught in the net-winding mechanism. One of his
daughters had had to act quickly and cut off the hand with a fish cutlass
to save him being dragged into the sea – or that was the story Sophie
had told Mila when they were thirteen. It had given Mila nightmares:
she dreaded finding herself facing a similar dilemma with Patrick.

Was the story even true? Mila had no idea. She remembered Sophie
telling her horror stories about the disembodied hand, creeping along
the ocean bed, trying to find its way home.

The man took off his hat with his hook, and nodded a greeting to
Mila. 'You're Cecille Toussaint's stepdaughter,' he said gruffly, pushing in
front of Solene. 'I know why you're here. You want to know about the
wreckage we spotted.'

'That's right, Monsieur. If you have time to tell us.'

'I can only tell you what I told Cecille. We'd gone to a spot I've never
been to before, not in more than fifty years of fishing. No boat would

ever go there normally, too dangerous. But the sea was like a millpond that day and we followed the sardines around a deep channel. Got a good haul. Fine fish they were. You don't often see a shoal like that these days. It's the fault of the commercial trawlers coming into waters where they've no business being and...'

'The wreckage?' Mila prompted gently.

'Oh, yes. I could see what looked like the hull of a small sailing boat at the foot of the cliff. Right up amongst the rocks it was, wedged. It had been there some time. I couldn't get close enough on the *Ariane* to be certain, but I had a word with Arnaud Girard. He's going to try to get out there next time the weather and tides are right and, if it's possible, dive over to the rocks to take a closer look.'

The Girard family owned many boats. One of the family's pleasure cruisers, in her distinctively cheerful yellow and orange livery, was anchored nearby, bobbing gently. She and her sisters were used to take tourists on trips round Golfe du Morbihan and could be hired for parties. But the Girards also had a speedboat, a luxury yacht and a couple of smaller inflatables that would be ideal for this kind of expedition.

Mila had heard rumours that the craft were sometimes used for less salubrious purposes too; drug-running; people-smuggling even. She had never been sure how much of what was said about the Girard family's nefarious activities was true, and how much was myth – or legend.

'I'd like to go with Arnaud, when he goes out,' said Carter.

'Me too,' said Mila quickly. Carter wasn't even family. If anyone went on that boat, it should be her.

'What about the coastguard?' she asked. 'Has he been notified?'

Carter and Monsieur Bolloré exchanged a glance which made it clear they shared some kind of knowledge to which Mila wasn't privy. They'd talked about this already, she realised. They'd come to some agreement without consulting her. *Why?*

'Let's check it out ourselves first,' Carter said. 'If it turns out that it's just an old paddle-board or something, the coastguard won't appreciate being troubled.'

He looked uncomfortable.

What's going on? Mila wondered.

'If the weather stays as it is, we should be able to get out in the next day or two,' Carter continued. 'Another forty-eight hours won't make any difference.'

Carter wants to be the one who solves the mystery of what happened to Charlie and me, said Sophie. *He wants to be my knight in shining armour, still!*

Mila persisted: 'But if it is Charlie's boat, and different people keep going there, isn't there a risk of contaminating a crime scene?'

'Who said anything about a crime?' asked Solene.

Carter said: 'We'll talk about this later, Mila.' What he meant was that it wasn't a good idea to speculate in front of the Bollorés.

Monsieur Bolloré sniffed as if to signal that the matter was closed.

'While we're here,' said Carter, 'let me show you pictures of two young women we're looking for. Maybe you've seen them hanging round the harbour.'

He took out his phone and the Bolloré family passed it among them, each studying the photographs of Briony and Billie. Suzanne held the screen right up to her face and looked at the images for ages before shaking her head and passing it back to her father.

'Sorry,' said Monsieur. 'We can't help you.'

'It was worth a try,' said Carter.

Solene was standing close to Carter, her smile highlighting the missing incisor on her top gum and the apple-ness of her ruddy cheeks.

'We'll have to have a drink together, Carter,' she said, 'for old times' sake. Or get some wine and go out to one of the islands and camp, like we used to when we were kids.'

'Now that would be fun!' said Carter.

Camping expeditions had been regular occurrences for the *Bande Sauvage*. Mila had only joined them once. She had been seventeen years old and desperately in love with Carter. She tried not to think about that weekend, but now Solene had mentioned it, the memory assaulted her like a slap, every detail dancing through her mind.

At night, on the island camp, when most of the others were already sleeping, Mila had lain alone in the tent she was supposed to share with

Sophie, listening to Carter playing his guitar and singing. Sophie was with him, sitting by the embers of the fire.

After a while, the singing had stopped and she'd heard the two of them whispering. Mila, almost dying from loneliness, deduced that they were lying on their backs staring up at the sky, looking out for shooting stars.

Mila had wriggled into her sleeping bag, trying to block out the sounds of their voices, but there was no escape.

Eventually the whispering had stopped, and Mila only heard the sound of Sophie giggling, softly, and Carter telling her how lovely she was. A little later, she heard a soft cry of pleasure.

Despite all the intervening years, Mila had never managed to wipe that sound from her mind.

26

A little later, back at the office, Mila filled Ceci in on the events of the day.

Ceci, exhilarated after spending a couple of hours with Monique Girard, and buoyed by an excellent seafood lunch in the hotel owned by Monique's husband's family, listened attentively. The joy gradually faded from her expression, until Mila reached the part about Billie's most recent shopping expedition, when it disappeared altogether.

'Oh no,' she said.

'Carter's informed the police,' said Mila.

'It can only be a matter of time before we find them.'

'What if we're already too late?'

'Darling, we have to stay positive.'

'What should we say to Mr and Mrs Moorcroft?' asked Mila.

'I'll speak to them,' said Ceci. 'I'll tell them as much of the truth as I can without driving them to despair.'

'Don't you think they should be warned to expect the worst?'

'There's no point speculating. We must wait for the facts to reveal themselves.'

She took Mila's face between the palms of her two hands and kissed her forehead.

'You don't have to carry all this weight on your own, Mila. You look after yourself and Anaïs this evening. Concentrate on the two of you. Forget about everything else for now. This evening, the Moorcrofts are *my* responsibility and mine alone.'

* * *

Mila did as she was told. She bought some food in Morannez and cycled back to the sea house with the panniers full of supplies. A firefighting plane passed overhead, carrying a cargo of seawater. The smell of smoke was stronger in the air that evening – the direction of the wind must have changed.

Stop it, Sophie said, as Mila imagined a crude grave in the forest, flames crackling through the dry shrubs around it; trees burning and falling. *Why must you always imagine the worst?*

When Mila reached home, she found Ani in the garden, sprawled on the swing seat reading a book. She was lying sideways, pushing the seat with one slender, brown leg, resting her book against the bent knee of the other. Berthaud, the cat, was stretched out on a towel that lay on the grass beside her.

Mila's heart gave a little leap, when she saw her niece. She loved Ani. It made her happy to see her. The world could never be a terrible place with Ani in it; and Mila would never stop trying to make things better, for Ani's sake.

As Mila approached the gate, she glimpsed someone on the track that ran alongside the sea house's garden. Whoever it was had been standing beside the hedge, in the shadow cast by one of the big old trees. When they heard the squeak of the bike brakes, they moved on, walking quickly in the direction of the sea.

'Hey!' Mila called.

The man – she was almost certain it was a man, although he was too far away and in the shade for Mila to be absolutely sure – raised a hand in a conciliatory fashion, as if to signify that he meant no harm, and strode away.

Mila considered putting the bags down and cycling after him.

But then what would she say? The man hadn't done anything wrong. It was not a crime to walk along the sandy track that led to the sea. He hadn't been spying on Ani. Perhaps he'd stopped to check his messages or to admire the view or to take a breather, maybe even to relieve himself.

This was by no means the first time Mila had been spooked by someone walking along the track. Several times in the past, she'd raced after some hapless holidaymaker asking what they thought they were doing, only to have them apologise for doing absolutely nothing. Usually, they turned out to be a birdwatcher, or an amateur historian seeking out the menhirs dotted amongst the woodland that lay between the sea house and the sea. Once, embarrassingly, she'd challenged a man in the dusk who had turned out to be Arnaud Girard. She'd threatened him with a hand axe before she recognised him.

'I just came for a walk!' he had protested, turning both of his palms flat to show Mila that he wasn't holding a weapon, or a camera, or anything remotely sinister. 'It's such a lovely evening, and I was reliving the glory days of the *Bande Sauvage*, when we used to play manhunt in the woods here. I'm sorry if my presence alarmed you, but I meant no harm.'

'No, of course you didn't. I should be apologising to you. I overreacted,' Mila had said, feeling stupid; hysterical. She wanted to explain that sometimes she felt vulnerable in the sea house, it being so far from any other dwelling. Mostly, she felt perfectly safe, but it was so rare for anyone to use the track that when someone did, she automatically felt suspicious. But to admit this to Arnaud would be to reveal her weakness and her insecurity, so she said nothing.

'It's good that you're careful,' Arnaud had replied, glancing at the axe – it was the small wood-chopper that she'd grabbed on the way out of the garden, to show that she meant business. 'Good that you protect Sophie's daughter so fiercely, when the two of you are out here in the woods, alone.'

He wasn't being sarcastic, at least Mila didn't think he was. Arnaud was a sincere person. The opposite to his younger brother, who was a feckless playboy. Nobody would ever know Arnaud came from a family of millionaires, whereas Guillaume – well, you couldn't miss the fact that he liked to spend his money. You only had to look at his clothes, and his jewellery, his swanky car.

Mila accepted Arnaud's explanation that he had simply been out walking, at face value. But her subconscious must have noted some ambivalence in what he had said. A little while afterwards, she had dreamed of the encounter, and the dream had turned into a nightmare in which she was running through the woods chasing after Arnaud. He had Ani in a sack, and was making off with her like the wolf in Little Red Riding Hood. Mila had woken; paralysed for a moment, as she often was after nightmares, struggling even to breathe. She knew the inertia would pass but while it lasted, it was terrifying; like being buried alive. As it eased, she had tried to remember how the few words Arnaud had said to her had been spoken. Had there been an oh-so-subtle element of threat in his tone? Was he implying that Ani was vulnerable? Or had she misinterpreted the situation entirely?

Either way, Mila had been left feeling exposed and powerless. The encounter had continued to haunt her.

She'd seen Arnaud again, once or twice, on the track that went past the sea house, but they hadn't spoken. Mila had nothing to say to him and he, well, why would he want to speak to Mila, when the last time they met she'd threatened him with an axe?

27

Mila watched the man on the path until he had disappeared into the woods. Was it Arnaud Girard? She couldn't tell.

Unsettled, she came through the gate and called: 'Hello!' to Ani, who was wearing her earbuds and didn't hear Mila.

'Hello-o!' Mila called again, coming closer.

This time, Ani raised a languid hand in response. She'd been dyeing her hair again; electric blue streaks ran through it. Sophie and Mila had done exactly the same at her age.

Mila leaned down to kiss Ani. 'How are you, beautiful niece?'

'I'm good, averagely attractive aunt.'

'Cheeky bugger.' Mila pretend-slapped her and Ani pretended to have whiplash and grabbed her cheek and laughed. 'Have you been out today?' Mila asked.

'I've been to the beach with Pernille and the others.'

'What others?'

Ani closed her book and sat up. 'JP, Romeo. A few other people from school.'

JP, or Jean-Paul, was Pernille's older brother. Romeo was his best friend. Ani had a huge crush on Romeo that she denied but which was obvious to everyone, except Romeo, who had a thing for Pernille. The situation was so reminiscent of the triangle between Mila, Sophie and Carter that it was painful for Mila to observe. She knew she couldn't do anything to smooth Ani's path, but she would always be there to listen, to pick up the pieces, to shore up her niece's confidence and help her realise that she didn't need anybody else's approval or attention.

'Did you have fun?' Mila asked.

Ani shrugged. 'We played beachball.'

Ani wasn't sporty. Pernille was. Mila understood the subtext. 'Okay.'

'Romeo was in a funny mood,' said Ani.

'Oh? Why?'

'His father is in hospital.'

'What happened?'

'He's a firefighter,' Ani said. 'He got hurt rescuing some people.' She picked at a loose thread on the swing-seat cushion.

'Is he badly hurt?' Mila asked gently.

'Romeo said he's going to be okay. But his maman is crying all the time. She doesn't want him to do that job any more.'

'I can understand why she's worried. Those firefighters are heroes,' said Mila, 'all of them.'

She tailed off, well aware of the physical and mental damage caused by the kind of stress that Romeo's mother was enduring; unwilling to voice her thoughts aloud in case she triggered a painful reaction in Ani. But it was too late. Mila could tell from the faraway look in her niece's eyes that she was thinking of her own missing father; reminded of the constant pain of not knowing where he was.

Mila changed the subject. 'I've brought supper,' she said brightly. 'It's such a lovely evening: shall we eat out here?'

'Yeah. That'd be nice.'

Ani stood up and followed Mila into the house and she hovered in the kitchen while Mila unpacked the shopping. She gave Ani the job of washing the salad while she unwrapped the cheeses, put the olives into a bowl and cut the bread.

They helped themselves to food and then took their plates outside, together with a jug of Madame Abadie's homemade pink lemonade that Ceci had left in the fridge.

Ani ate a good third of a baguette stuffed with good things and drank a large glass of lemonade before she drew breath. Then she said: 'Is there any update on the wreckage?'

'As a matter of fact, there is. Carter and I called into the harbour to speak to the Bollorés this afternoon. When the weather and tides are right, they're going to go back and try to establish if the wreckage is *Moonfleet* and if it is, they'll call the coastguard.'

'Who's "they"?'

'Monsieur and Solene Bolloré, Arnaud Girard and Carter. I said I'd like to go too.'

'Could I come?'

'I don't think Arnaud would agree to that, Ani.'

Mila half-expected some pushback, but Anaïs didn't argue with this. Instead she asked: 'Mila, why do you think Maman and Papa went out sailing that day?'

Nobody knew the answer to that question. Nobody had the faintest idea why Sophie and Charlie had made that momentously bad decision and it was unlikely, now, that they ever would. Charlie was an experienced sailor; he would have checked the weather that morning and he would have known the conditions were dangerous. Sophie must have realised too. They had left behind no clues as to why they'd gone out to sea. They hadn't been drinking; as far as anyone knew, they hadn't had any kind of argument. Sophie hadn't messaged Mila to say that anything was wrong; she hadn't called her mother. She hadn't, as far as Mila knew, been in contact with anyone.

The only evidence that Charlie and Sophie had gone out had been a scribbled note, in Charlie's hand, left on the kitchen table for Anaïs to find if she got back from school before their return.

Gone sailing, it said. *Xxx.*

That was it.

That afternoon, the school bus had dropped Ani off at the end of the track. The storm had blown in by now, and she had walked back to the sea house, buffeted by gusts of wind, to find her parents were not there.

She'd picked up the note on the table, read it, laid it down again. The storm was roaring, bending the branches of the trees in the woods; lashing the leaves. Black and grey clouds were chasing one another across the sky, scattering rain as they travelled. Ani hadn't been worried at first. Rather, she had felt miffed at being abandoned, because she'd had an audition with the drama club at school that day. The play was *The Crucible* and Sophie had been coaching her, helping her learn her lines. Ani was keen to tell her mother that she'd been given the role of Abigail Williams, which was literally a dream come true. But Sophie wasn't there, and the only soul who Ani could tell about her achievement was Berthaud, who did not like bad weather, and who had stayed indoors, waiting for Ani to come home.

Mila and Ani had been over these details several times, trying to find a clue in Ani's memory that might help them unpick the mystery, but they'd found nothing.

'I don't know why they went out, Ani,' she answered her niece now. 'Perhaps it was simply that they felt like enjoying the sea. Perhaps they wanted to race the wind. It might have been no more complicated than that.'

'Do you think they capsized in the storm?'

'I don't know,' Mila said again.

'If they did, and the boat was blown onto the rocks afterwards, then Papa's body won't be in the wreckage.'

'No, darling, it won't.'

'He will still be lost.'

'Yes.'

'We won't know for sure that he's dead.'

'No,' said Mila. How many times had they had this conversation, or one like it? At least fifty times, she estimated. At least twice a month, and each time, Mila's heart broke a little more. She didn't care how many times she had to go through this speculation with her niece, she would always do so with patience and consideration. She just wished there was something she could say that would make things better.

'But,' said Ani, 'if they do find Papa in the wreckage...'

'Then we're all going to be terribly sad for a long time,' said Mila, thinking how cruel it was that Ani's grief was being eked out in this manner, 'but we'll look after one another, and eventually, after however long it takes, we will start to feel a little better, and in the end, although we'll never stop missing your maman and papa, we will be okay.'

'Will we?'

'I promise you, we will.'

28

Some time later, after Ani had gone up to bed, Mila checked her phone to see if there were any updates from Carter. There weren't – but there was a message from Ceci to say she'd spoken to Mrs Moorcroft, and six missed calls from Luke – oh God! Before she left Portsmouth, she'd promised she'd call him this morning to let him know she was back safely and she'd completely forgotten to do so. There was also a missed call from her father and a message asking her to call him back.

She couldn't muster the right kind of energy to speak to Luke, so she contacted Patrick first. He answered the phone almost at once.

'Hello, number one and best beloved daughter, how are you?'

'I'm okay. Where are you?'

'In Glasgow. I've just finished filming a new police drama.'

'Are you playing a gritty detective?'

'The grittiest. One minute, honey.'

She heard her father murmur a few words to a companion. Less distinctly, she heard laughter, and the glug of something being poured from a bottle.

'Is it a bad time for me to call you?' she asked.

'It's never a bad time for you to call me, Mila, you know that.' A pause. 'You sound a little deflated, darling.'

'I'm tired, that's all. I only got back from England in the early hours and it's been a long day.' She wondered whether to tell him about her fears for the missing Briony, and decided against it. She didn't want to bring down his evening. 'Have you spoken to Ceci lately?'

'She called to tell me about the wreckage. That's why I called you. I wanted to make sure you were okay.'

'I'm fine.'

'And Ani?'

'She's being very grown-up about it.' Mila heard a woman's voice; shrill, laughing. 'Are you in a restaurant?'

'Yes, but we're not at our table yet, we're in the bar.'

'We?'

'I'm out with my second family.'

He meant the production crew and his fellow actors. Patrick never missed an opportunity to enjoy himself.

'So apart from the wreckage, is everything else all right?' Patrick asked.

Mila took the bull by the horns. 'I need to talk to you about Mum. Not now, while you're with your friends, but sometime soon. She's not looking after herself or the house and I'm worried about her.'

There was the slightest beat of hesitation. Mila imagined her father holding his forehead between his thumb and forefinger and squeezing, a shadow darting across his face as it always did when the topic of Lydia was raised. She wondered, briefly, if it was unfair of her to ask for her father's help. He and Lydia had been divorced for more than two decades. It was, perhaps, unreasonable to expect him to take responsibility.

'Of course, we will talk about your mother,' Patrick said. 'It's her seventieth this year, isn't it?'

'Next month, yes.'

'Perhaps I should take you both out to lunch. What do you think? Would Lydia like that?'

'I don't know, Dad.'

'Think about it. There's still plenty of time to make plans. I'll call you when I'm back in London, okay?'

'That'd be good,' said Mila.

'But if you need me in the meantime... If anything transpires with the wreckage, get in touch, won't you? Promise?'

'I promise.'

'Okay. I love you, Mila.'

'I love you too. Enjoy your meal.'

Mila disconnected the call and stared at the phone in her hand. Patrick had sounded relaxed, but then he always did after a shoot had finished.

She searched the internet on her phone for *Patrick Shepherd, Glasgow, police drama* and was rewarded with a host of pictures from the Glasgow Live news website of filming in progress. Playing a female crime boss opposite Patrick was a glamorous actor in her sixties with whom Patrick had been romantically linked at about the same time as his marriage to Ceci ended. An interview with the show's director mentioned 'special chemistry' between the two characters. Perhaps they had picked up their relationship in real life and hers was the voice Mila had heard in the background of the call. Perhaps Patrick was about to make his co-star Mrs Shepherd number three. Oh dear God, imagine what Lydia would have to say about that!

Mila went into the kitchen, opened the bottle of red wine that she'd filled from the self-service keg in the grocery shop earlier and poured herself a glass. She went out into the garden and sat on the swing seat, with her back against the pillows that Ani had stacked to one side and her legs stretched out on the cushions, covered in a fabric printed with cocktail glasses and cocktail umbrellas that used to be colourful before the sun had bleached everything to pale pastels. She closed her eyes and felt the peace of the cooling air on her skin. Ani had left a cotton throw on the swing, and as the last wisps of sunlit cloud faded into the night, Mila pulled the throw around her like a cloak.

Her mind was busy, veering between thoughts of her father, her mother, Ani, the wreckage, and Briony Moorcroft. Everything was uncertain; nothing resolved. She prayed that Briony still be alive, but then she thought of Billie Dexter walking out of the supermarket with her bag-for-life full of bleach, and her new spade tucked under her arm, and it became difficult to be optimistic about a positive outcome for Briony.

At some point, she must have fallen asleep because when she woke, the constellation of stars that had been directly above her had slid down towards the horizon and the moon had risen above the trees. She looked to the sea house and saw that the light in Ani's bedroom had been extinguished.

Mila pulled the throw around her, slid off the seat and went back into the house. She hadn't taken her phone outside; there it was on the side, in the kitchen, its battery completely flat. She had no idea where the charger was. It was almost midnight and she still hadn't called Luke.

'Sorry, Luke,' she whispered into the night air, knowing he couldn't hear her.

29

Mila was woken the next morning by the sound of the shower. She went downstairs to make coffee for herself and hot chocolate for Ani, and when she came up, Ani was in her bedroom, wrapped in a towel, blow-drying her hair in front of the mirror.

'Are you going out?' Mila asked.

'I'm meeting Pernille and her maman in Morannez,' said Ani. 'Madame Sohar is taking us shopping in Rennes and then we're having lunch somewhere smart. I thought I could cycle in with you and wait for them at Jenny's café.'

'Good plan,' said Mila. She put the bowl of chocolate on the chest that served Ani as a dressing table, steam wisping from its surface. 'We'll need to leave by seven thirty.'

'I'll be ready.'

Downstairs, moving between the oven where a tray of pains au chocolat were warming and the fridge, and trying not to trip over Berthaud who was doing what Ani called her 'magic cat-weave' dance between her legs, Mila messaged Luke on the now fully charged phone. Or she tried to devise a message.

Sorry I didn't call last night

she typed.

No! said Sophie, *absolutely do not apologise. Be assertive.*

Mila deleted the text and tried again:

Hi, good morning, was tied up yesterday, can I call you at lunchtime?

Sophie had issues with that draft too. *What if you can't call him at lunchtime because you're busy?*

Again, Mila deleted the text.

Hi,

she wrote. Then she was stuck.

It was ridiculous! She and Luke had been a couple for more than twelve years; they were engaged, they knew every intimate thing about one another and she couldn't compose a straightforward message.

And now, perversely, she was feeling cross with Luke because of a call that she'd forgotten to make.

Ani breezed into the kitchen and Mila dropped the phone as if she'd been caught doing something she shouldn't have. She turned her attention to her niece, who was wearing a pair of cargo trousers that sat low on her hips and a crop top; bangles on her wrists, rings on her fingers and strings of the kind of silver-plated jewellery that the Sohars sold in their chain of holiday-wear boutiques strung around her neck. She had painted her nails and her face was made-up; she was wearing enormous hooped earrings and her hair, normally loose and wavy, was pulled severely back from her face.

Mila tried not to comment on Ani's appearance unless her opinion was requested. As a teenager, she had hated how Lydia had made her feel about her looks; a barrage of criticism that had battered Mila's self-confidence. Mila was determined not to make her niece feel as she used to feel under Lydia's gaze, either ashamed or patronised. And, in any case, she was trying to raise Ani by the mantra that what was inside a person was far more important than how they looked on the outside.

But this morning Ani appeared so grown-up and stunning, and so unlike the girl that Mila knew and loved, that it was hard for her to hold back a gasp of astonishment. She suspected that Ani was trying to keep up with Pernille who, thanks to her parents' business, had access to all the latest fashions. Ani scooped Berthaud up into her arms and pressed her face into the cat's fur, subtly hiding how much bare skin she was showing, which confirmed, to Mila, that Ani, herself, felt that the outfit was too revealing.

But what should the responsible adult *do* in such a situation? What should they say that would neither hurt nor offend?

Mila had spent ages browsing the internet for a book that would teach her how to deal with teenagers in a sensitive and appropriate manner, and she'd found nothing that addressed the issues she faced almost daily.

If Mila had come downstairs in the Maidenhead house in clothes as skimpy as Ani's, Lydia would have forbidden her from going out but all Lydia's extensive rules and excessive strictness had done was make Mila an expert in petty deceit and circumvention. Young people, she knew, needed a degree of freedom to experiment: to make their own mistakes and also achieve their own successes. Briony Moorcroft was a good example of how too much parental care could be detrimental. Wrapping Briony in cotton wool and separating her from the big wide world hadn't protected her. It was arguable that her naivety and lack of experience were what had made her so susceptible to Billie Dexter's predation.

When it came to bringing up Ani, Mila found herself relying on instinct; asking Ceci's advice if ever she and Ani came to loggerheads over something; but this was rare. Mila had no idea what Ceci would think of Ani's current outfit, but was certain that she would not make a big deal of it.

Mila recalled a promise she'd made to Sophie, that she would always support her niece, in whatever way she could. She put a hand gently on Ani's bare shoulder. 'You are wonderful,' she said. Ani smiled, shyly. 'I'm so proud of you,' said Mila. She placed a pain au chocolat wrapped in kitchen paper onto the table beside Ani's bag. 'You're going to have to eat it en route. We need to go now.'

* * *

It was a pleasant bicycle ride from the sea house into Morranez town, the narrow roads winding between fields of maize and sunflowers, but already the air was thick and warm and there was a pervasive hint of smoke. The heatwave had lasted so long that Mila craved a fresh breeze; the kind of clouds that presaged a rainstorm; anything that would bring respite from the relentless warmth.

Between the trees and hedgerows, she caught glimpses of the sea, blindingly bright where the sun was catching on the water. Even the temperature of the Atlantic was rising; Mila had heard an expert on the radio talking about an encroaching marine crisis; about the stress that unseasonably warm water would place on fragile ecosystems.

Yet along their route, everything was reassuringly the same; as it always had been. Mila and Ani cycled past rustic old cottages and farm-houses; the occasional dolman standing in someone's garden with a washing line passing right beside it, underwear shadowing the ancient stones, and menhirs in fields with sheep grazing all around.

When they arrived in Morannez, they wove through the streets, stopping outside the Toussaints offices and securing their bikes. Ani said she'd wait for the pâtissière, Mademoiselle la Caze, to open up her shop. Mila gave her money to buy some treats to give to Pernille's mother as a 'thank you' for her many kindnesses.

Carter was preparing to leave the office when Mila arrived, shrugging on the fringed leather jacket that was so worn it had taken on the shape of him.

'I'm going to look for the Moorcrofts' van,' he said. 'If I go early, there's more chance of spotting it while Billie's still sleeping.'

'No word from the police?' Mila asked.

'Sandrine, my buddy in the traffic office, says the van hasn't pinged any automatic number plate recognition cameras in the last twelve hours.'

'So the van hasn't moved?'

'Or it's kept to the lanes and back roads.'

'Right.'

'Sandrine's going to search back through the records to see if she can spot any patterns. That might help us work out where Billie and Briony are – or where they *were*.'

What was it about Carter, Mila wondered, that made everyone so willing to help him? Was there some kind of honour-amongst-thieves network within the police internationally or was Carter simply so adept at charming people that they fell over themselves to cooperate – especially women?

'Have you heard from Arnaud?' she asked.

'I spoke to him first thing. He said the tides are wrong to attempt to get a boat close to the wreckage today.'

'Okay. But you'll keep me in the loop?'

'Of course,' Carter said. He gave Mila a mock salute and clambered down the narrow staircase, going sideways so that the steps could accommodate his enormous biker boots.

30

Ani came up the stairs with a box from the pâtisserie and, soon after, Ceci breezed into the office in a waft of Dior. Mila saw her do the briefest of double-takes when she saw Ani's outfit, but she didn't miss a beat before kissing her granddaughter, and embracing her with her usual affection.

'How are you, my darling?' Ceci asked Mila.

'Worried about Briony. Did you speak to the Moorcrofts last night?'

'I did. I told them we are getting closer to identifying where Billie and Briony have been staying.'

Mila glanced at Ani who was staring at her phone.

'You didn't mention the spade?' she asked quietly.

'No.' Ceci paused. 'I had to persuade them to stay put, for the time being. Mrs Moorcroft was all for coming out here and helping join the search herself.'

'You don't think they might turn up, do you?'

Ceci shook her head. 'I talked her out of it for now. I promised I'd stay in close touch.' She paused, and Mila knew that she was thinking about the next phone call she might have to make to Mr and Mrs Moorcroft, and how difficult that call might be.

When the computer was booted, Mila found an email from Carter's colleague in the traffic police.

Attached to the message was a computer-generated map of all the locations where the Moorcrofts' Maid Services van had been pinged by ANPR cameras over the past ten days. It had made several journeys into Lorient town, twice being parked close to an internet café on the Rue de Carnel.

The officer had also outlined the area where she thought the runaways must have been hiding out. It was a rural part of Brittany, comprising mainly of farms and rough woodland. Mila and Ceci pored over the map.

'We'd need a helicopter to search that area thoroughly,' said Mila.

'But not all of it is accessible to a vehicle,' said Ceci. 'Call Carter and get him to check out the internet café and, meanwhile, I'll study the map and see if I can narrow it down.'

* * *

A little later, Mila walked with her niece to Jenny's café, where Ani had arranged to meet Pernille and Melodie Sohar. They weren't there yet, but Jenny was rushed off her feet. Her old waitress, Betty, had recently returned to Germany and the new hand, an Albanian woman called Marsela, was struggling to cope on her own.

'I'll help! What can I do?' Ani asked.

'You're an angel!' said Jenny. She tossed a clean apron to Ani. 'Marsela's in charge, just do whatever she tells you, okay?'

* * *

Mila was almost back at the office when Carter called.

'I've just left the internet café,' he said. 'Sandrine was right. Billie was there a couple of times.'

'Do you know what she was doing?'

'Looking at medical websites, researching rare cancers, their symptoms and their treatments. Autoimmune diseases too.'

'Briony's illnesses?'

'Yep. And specifically, she searched for: *How to recognise when someone is close to death.*'

Mila stepped into the shade. 'Oh no,' she whispered.

'Yeah,' said Carter. 'Hold on, there's another call coming in. I'll be back with you in a second.'

He disappeared off the line and Mila waited, stepping back against the wall so that she wasn't blocking the pavement, which was busy now.

After a few moments, Carter came back. 'Mila, are you still there?'

'Yes.'

'That was Solene Bolloré. There's a woman, she's pretty sure it's Billie Dexter, walking round the market at Morranez harbour right now. It'll take me an hour to get back...'

'It's okay,' said Mila, 'I'm on my way.'

'Mila, if it is her, don't say or do anything. Follow her but at a distance.'

'Yep.'

'And stay in touch.'

31

Mila jogged the small distance back to the office and grabbed her bike. Cycling was the quickest way to navigate Morannez's narrow streets at any time of the day, but particularly in the morning, when the town centre was busy with shoppers and holidaymakers. She cut through the old service alleyways at the backs of the shops, bumping down the stepped cut-throughs used by fisher-people and townsfolk for centuries, past the lovely old buildings with their slate roofs and sun-bleached shutters and all the colourful hanging baskets and window boxes.

She slowed as she approached the harbour, letting the bike coast to a halt before securing it in one of the racks at the water's edge.

The tide was in, green water lapping at the huge stones in the harbour wall and reaching up to the concrete ramp from which small boats could be launched directly from the dock. Small shoals of fish were weaving through the shallows, the sun, every now and then, catching their scales, refracting silver like tiny mirror balls.

Mila dodged the fishermen carrying trays of sardines packed in ice and wended her way through the vans and trucks in the car park. The market stalls, with their striped awnings, were arranged in lines and already the crowds had gathered. Gulls perched around the perimeter, extending their throats and calling. Music was playing within the market and many voices were competing with each other, all at once.

Mila walked along the edge of the harbour wall until she reached the line of fishing boats tethered to their bollards. She spotted Solene a little way ahead, passing lobster pots down to her sister on the deck of the *Ariane*. Solene waved and gestured towards the market, indicating where she believed Billie to be. Mila gave her the thumbs up, stepped off the wall and merged into the crowd thronging around the stalls.

In the shaded walkways between the tables, shoppers were perusing everything from pairs of flip-flops held together with pieces of string to pots of olives. Old men and women were holding shouted conversations. A wizened man with skin like leather and only one single tooth in his mouth was standing on the tailgate of a lorry auctioning unopened boxes to a rapturous group gathered around him – undelivered internet shopping parcels.

Mila walked through the people, her eyes scanning the heads, looking for a tall, statuesque young woman with short hair. She squeezed past a stall where a jolly soul with her sleeves rolled up and wearing dangly gold earrings was selling bits of dried animals – pigs' feet, rabbits' ears, bulls' pizzles – as treats for dogs, scooping them out of plastic buckets and wrapping them in newspaper. Beside it was a stall that sold rose-coloured drinking glasses, cutlery, crockery and knick-knacks that looked as if they'd been collected from house clearances. This would be the ideal place to offload some of the junk in the sea house, Mila thought.

'*Excusez-moi*,' she murmured, slipping through the shoppers. '*Pardonnez-moi*.' Her eyes began to ache from concentrating so hard but finally, standing in front of the car breaker's stall at the far end of the market, she spotted a tall, broad-shouldered woman with her back to her, a cigarette held between her fingers and a baseball cap, back-to-front, on her head.

Mila moved a little closer. Her phone buzzed. Luke was calling. She cut him off.

Careful, Sophie whispered. *Go carefully.*

Mila walked through the sunlight up to the stall and stood beside the woman. She had short hair, strong, tanned arms; she was at least four inches taller than Mila. She was talking to the stallholder in fluent French. Mila looked up into the woman's face, but she knew already.

She wasn't Billie.

* * *

Mila texted Carter to let him know. While she was at the market, she showed the stallholders pictures of Billie and Briony, asking if anyone had seen them. They hadn't. She also spent a few minutes talking with the market's security team – two muscled young men who were keen to help, especially when they found she was a colleague of Carter Jackson's.

'Give him our regards!' they said, beaming. 'Tell him we'll catch up soon.'

32

Mila and Carter spent the afternoon as they had spent the previous one: searching the countryside between Lorient and Morannez for the Moorcrofts' van. With every moment that passed, it seemed less likely, to Mila, that the endeavour would have a happy ending. She doubted that Briony Moorcroft was still alive. And while she wanted to find the van so that this nightmare task would be over, she dreaded it also, with every atom of her being.

Briony's parents, unaware of the sinister turn the case had taken, were still hoping for a positive outcome. Although there had been no further developments, Ceci spoke to them again that evening, assuring them that the agency team was committed to doing all it could to find their missing daughter. She asked if they'd heard from Billie: if there'd been any threats made, or demands for money. There had not.

The apprehension that Mila was carrying weighed ever heavier on her shoulders. She barely slept that night for worrying about Briony; imagining her dying alone while Billie Dexter pored over a computer screen in a public internet café.

When she woke, there were a few seconds of respite before the anxiety piled in again. The feelings of panic and helplessness triggered the memory of other dreadful times; specifically, the days between

Sophie and Charlie going out in the boat, and Sophie's body being found. Sophie being missing hadn't ended well and there was no reason now to believe that this investigation would fare any better.

Mila and Carter resumed their search for Briony Moorcroft the following morning soon after dawn, when the roads were quiet and the air was a fraction cooler.

Mila ignored the stress headache drumming at her temples and worked methodically, zigzagging back and forth through ancient bridle-ways and droves on her bicycle. She marked them off on her map when they'd been covered. There were numerous little hamlets at the ends of stony tracks, farmsteads that she hadn't known existed; tiny villages with war memorials and bakeries and working wells. If her quest hadn't been so urgent, she'd have enjoyed seeing the sights. But, all the time, at the back of her mind, was the gnawing anxiety about the fate of Briony Moorcroft and the prospect of Ceci having to break the news to her parents that she was dead and that she, perhaps, had been dead for some days.

Carter, meanwhile, was tracking the roads on his motorbike. He could cover greater distances more quickly, although he stopped often and chatted to people, gathering information. Yet nobody he spoke to recalled seeing the Moorcroft's Maid Services van or the distinctive pairing of Billie Dexter and Briony Moorcroft.

He and Mila stayed in touch. Each time her phone pinged, Mila hoped it would be good news – but it never was. It was more of the same:

No luck so far. How about you?

Nothing.

When Mila was hungry, she went back to the café and took a seat outside, waiting for the queue at the counter to die down. She texted Carter to let him know where she was, and called Luke, who didn't answer. It seemed a long time now since she'd last spoken to him in Portsmouth, but it had only been a couple of days.

Eventually, Jenny came out with two cups of double espresso and two peaches on plates, together with slices of dry, dusty cheese. On the edge of each plate was a drizzle of honey. She sat down next to Mila and proceeded to expertly slice the fruit into segments. Mila lay the phone on the table.

'Eat a piece of peach with a little of this,' said Jenny, cutting a triangle of the dry cheese and dipping it into the honey.

Mila did as she'd advised. The combination of honey sweetness and the saltiness of the cheese, with the cool texture of the fruit, was wonderous. 'Oh,' said Mila, 'that is heavenly!'

'Sometimes the simplest things are the best,' said Jenny.

They sat quietly and ate. Mila kept an eye on her phone, but nobody called.

Around them, Marsela cleared the tables.

When the meal was finished, Jenny asked Mila what was troubling her, and Mila, trusting Jenny not to gossip, explained about Billie and Briony.

'We know roughly where they've been staying, and it's not a huge area, but trying to pinpoint the location has proved impossible,' said Mila.

'I could ask Marsela,' Jenny said.

'What makes you think she could help?'

'She's friends with the seasonal workers of all nationalities. I swear we've been busier since she started working here because so many people come in to see her. She's like a sister to them.'

Jenny called Marsela over. The two of them had a lively discussion for a few minutes, speaking, as far as Mila could gather, a combination of French, Albanian and some third, unidentifiable language before Marsela took her phone out of her pocket.

'I'll call a friend,' she said, with a nod to Mila.

Mila watched as Marsela paced up and down the road outside the café, speaking to whoever was at the other end of the line. She finished that call, and then spoke to somebody else. After that, she stared fiercely at the screen of her phone until it pinged to signal an incoming message. She returned to the table, said something to Jenny, and passed her phone to Mila.

On the screen was a map of more or less the same area that had been delineated on the police map, to show where Billie and Briony might be holed up. Jenny tapped a digital pin with her fingernail: 'A couple of young women matching your description have been staying in a shed in the grounds of the commune close to the water park.'

'Definitely two young women?'

'Yes.'

'And they've been living in a shed?'

Marsela and Jenny spoke for a moment.

'It's more of a barn,' Jenny explained, 'that's used for birthing lambs in the springtime. A sheep shed.' She leaned forward. 'They have to be the same women you're looking for, don't they?'

'I don't see how Billie and Briony could have known about this place. It's so remote.'

Marsela said something to Jenny, who translated.

'One of the girls was in the same British prison as a regular at the commune. They stayed in touch. The communard told her the shed would be a good place to hang out if you didn't want to draw attention to yourself.'

Mila's heart rate quickened.

'That makes sense,' she said.

She passed the phone back to Marsela, pushed back her chair and stood up. 'Thank you, Marsela. Thank you so much. I'll let you know how we get on!'

33

Mila reached the gates at the entrance to the commune on her pushbike before Carter arrived on his Harley-Davidson. She left the bike propped behind a hydrangea bush whose floral clusters had browned in the heat and were hanging, face down, like withered baubles on a dead Christmas tree and walked up to the enormous, cast-iron gates. Each was attached to massive hinges set into a solid stone wall. It surrounded the grounds of a building that had once been a convent, but which was now home to a community of people who kept themselves very much to themselves. Mila knew little about them, beyond the fact that they eschewed the modern ways of living; they had no phones, no laptops, no internet; they weren't even connected to the power supply. She had heard rumours of cultism swirling about Morannez, but it was, as far as she could tell, conjecture.

The communards were of various nationalities, ages and back-grounds and almost completely self-sufficient, only coming into Morannez when they needed to purchase something they could not grow, make or farm themselves, or, if they could, make a trade. They were easy to identify. They wore old-fashioned clothes, no jewellery or adornment of any kind. The men were bearded and the women had long hair. They rarely brought their children out from behind the boundary walls.

That day, the gates were open. Mila had promised Carter she'd wait for him outside. Yet the temptation to look, combined with a desperate desire to find Briony Moorcroft, was irresistible. She wandered a little way into the grounds. Huge trees with great, thick branches grew out of extensive meadows. Beneath them, grass and what would once have been a carpet of wildflowers running riot had been scorched by the sun and was now a mat of dry, yellow-brown stalks, gone to seed. If the wild-fires reached here, Mila thought, they'd be impossible to stop.

The trees, however, were big enough and their canopies so broad that, inside the walls, it felt as if the air itself was a few degrees cooler; everywhere dark and green and shady; birdsong trilling; and the insects, that Mila hadn't noticed until that moment were strangely silent else-where that summer, were noisy here. Somewhere beyond the trees, sheep were baaing.

Mila walked a little way down the drive until she could see the great Gothic buildings of the old nunnery. Washing was strung over bushes, children were running around playing, and women were sitting on the terrace at the front of the building, leaning back on their hands in the shade. It looked, from this distance, idyllic.

Something hung from the branch of the nearest tree, spinning in the light breeze at head height. Mila walked forward to investigate. It was a crude puppet, with a coconut-shell head and a body made of sticks, tied together. The face was grotesque. It was a holding a sign.

Private, the sign read. *Keep out.*

Mila looked around. There were dozens of similar voodoo-esque puppets hanging from branches of the shrubs and trees around the entrance. Tacked to one tree was a laminated poster. In the style of the famous Lord Kitchener *Your Country Needs You* image was a picture of a human skull, a skeleton finger back at Mila. *You're Being Watched!*

Instinctively, Mila looked around for a camera. But then she remem-bered that the commune didn't have electricity, or Wi-Fi, or indeed, any of the technology necessary for the successful implementation of closed-circuit television.

She wasn't being watched. The poster was a warning, designed to deter intruders like her.

The entrance to the old convent was off the beaten track. But only fifty or so metres away was a different road, the road that led to the AquaSplash water park on the way to Bloemel-sur-Mer. From where she stood, Mila could hear snatches of blaring pop music and the screams of teenagers going down the waterslides. They were geographically close, but this place was like a different world. How must the children of the commune feel listening to the sounds of their contemporaries, having so much fun on the other side of the wall? Were they envious, or were they content with their own lives?

Mila walked a little further, until she began to feel uneasy. If she were to encounter Billie and Billie was armed, there would be no witnesses. Nobody would come running to help Mila. There would be no video evidence to show what had happened.

It was foolish to make herself vulnerable.

Mila moved back out of the gates, found a shady patch and leaned against the wall. It wasn't long until she heard the familiar rumble of Carter's motorbike.

He turned off the Harley's engine and coasted to a halt. He bumped the machine onto the verge and put it on its stand, close to Mila's pushbike.

Mila raised a hand in greeting as he took off his helmet and his jacket and lay them on the grass, in the shadow of the bike. A sheen of sweat covered his skin and there were dark stains on his shirt too. His expression was less relaxed than usual and he had the focus of a hunter in his eyes.

'Okay?' he asked.

Mila nodded.

'Come on then,' he said. 'Let's go find the sheep shed.'

34

They walked around the outskirts of the grounds, keeping close to the perimeter wall. Mila was holding her phone in her hands, watching their digital progress as they moved towards the shed. With each step, they came closer to the pin, and with each step, Mila became more aware of the tension in her body; the adrenaline kicking in, preparing her for whatever trouble they might encounter. Her mouth was dry. She felt alert and alive; she could think of nothing but the next moment, the next footstep, the next breath.

Soon enough, they reached a series of tumbledown barns and sheds: the convent's old agricultural buildings. They were situated on waste-land; weeds recolonising an area that had been covered in concrete which was now crumbling. A couple of ancient vehicles were rusting quietly; rotten tyres were heaped in a pile, the black rubber shining in the heat. An ancient bale of hay had burst out of its plastic wrapping. A feral cat was stretched out in the sunshine. It rolled over, extending its claws. Apart from birdsong and the occasional burst of noise from the AquaSplash, the place was creepily quiet.

'It looks like Billie parked the van here,' said Carter, pointing to tyre tracks in the dust. 'This must've been as far as she could bring it.'

It was far enough. In this spot, the van would have been completely hidden. Nobody passing by on the other side of the wall would have had any idea it was there. Next to the tracks, an empty two-litre paint can lay on its side, the lid a little distant.

'The van's not here now,' said Mila.

'Doesn't necessarily mean Billie's not around. I'll message Sandrine and ask if the van's been pinged anywhere. Either way, we need to take it slow, okay? And if we see Billie, you leave the talking to me.'

Carter was skilled in negotiating with terrorists in hostage situations. He also knew how to talk to someone off their head on crack. Mila didn't usually like being told what to do, but on this occasion was content to play deputy.

'Which building is the sheep shed?' Carter asked.

'None of these. It's over there, behind the barn.'

They walked across the disintegrating concrete, around the side of a dilapidated barn, and there, beyond, was a long, low shed with a corrugated metal roof.

Carter glanced back at Mila.

She nodded. 'That's it.'

It was obvious from the dead, flattened grass and the paths tramped through the dirt that the shed had been in recent use. A thin, heavily stained, single-size mattress was propped against the outer wall, sagging in the middle. Someone had attempted to clean it – there were bleach stains in the middle and spatters where buckets of water had been thrown at it, but it had been given up as a bad job and the mattress left outside to dry in the sunshine.

Mila's body prickled with tension. She was on the highest alert, jumping at a scuffling sound, but it was only a ragged hen scratching in the undergrowth.

Carter walked carefully forward. Mila followed in his footsteps. She tried to imagine how Briony must have felt when Billie brought her to this place, the young girl who spent all day, every day in that modern, spotlessly clean house at the top of the hill in Carnarth. She had never been anywhere isolated or lonely or filthy in her life.

How did Briony react when she realised the old sheep shed was to be their accommodation? Or was she too sick to understand what was going on? Did she think, in her naivety, that it might actually be fun to stay here? Like camping?

Carter kicked the base of a rusty metal door with the toe of his boot. When it swung open, he stepped inside. Reluctantly, Mila followed him.

The interior of the shed was dark and hot. The sun was beating down on the metal roof and the air inside had no means of escape. It took Mila's eyes a few moments to adjust. The only light came through a small, four-paned window in the craggy old wall. Ancient cobwebs were draped across the rafters, their silks blackened and dusty.

The heat was one thing; the smell was something else. The shed stank of unwashed bodies, of vomit, of faeces; organic, musty, sick-making smells masked by a miasma of bleach. Flies were buzzing around an open drain in one corner of the space. Mila pulled the front of her dress up over her mouth and nose and breathed through her lips. Beside her, Carter did the same with his shirt.

The building's original purpose, as a lambing shed, was evident in the tiled floor; the racks of partitions piled high against one wall; several old crooks, a pair of rusty shears, abandoned clippers; ropes, a bundle of barbed wire.

But part of the interior had been cleared of agricultural detritus and the floor had been swept. Up against the wall was a metal bed frame, a single bed, with wire stretched across the base – no mattress, that was outside – but beneath it was a washing-up bowl that had been used as a chamber pot and was a magnet for flies. There was a table in the corner with a camping stove on top of it and also a bottle of bleach, and a couple of folded bin bags. There was a second bowl containing a few filthy items of crockery and cutlery and a single wooden chair and a half-used roll of toilet paper on the floor. Empty water bottles, presumably the same ones that Billie and Briony had purchased at the Intermarché Super in Lorient, were jumbled in the corner.

Carter stood by the bed.

Mila took a few steps towards him and then he held out a hand to indicate that she shouldn't come any closer.

Stuffed between the bed frame and the wall was a handful of blood-stained tissues. Attached to one side of the metal frame was a pair of handcuffs. Hanging loose, on the other side, was a length of washing line.

'Billie tied her to the bed,' Carter said.

'Why would she do that?' Mila asked, and mentally answered her own question. To restrain Briony, of course. To keep her captive while Billie did what?

Tortured her?

Mila couldn't stand being in that awful place for another second. She turned and walked out of the shed. Outside, the bright sunlight blistered her eyes. Beyond, a thin, wide curtain of smoke was masking the sky, turning blue to grey, dirtying the day.

What's wrong with people? Mila wondered. *Why do they have to hurt one another? Why do they start fires in areas of drought? Why must they spoil everything, destroy everything?*

She walked away from the building, into the wooded area beyond. She leaned against a tree, and looked up to the sky and took deep breaths of fresh air. The fallen leaves beneath her feet crackled. Briony Moorcroft's collapsible wheelchair had been dumped on its side nearby. The metal frame was bent and twisted; the seat and backrest padding ripped and torn as if someone had attacked it with a hammer.

Mila covered her face with her hands, trying to press away the thought of the frail girl, tied to the bed; her thin legs pulled up to her body as she lay on that disgusting mattress with Billie towering above her. Billie, who had researched Briony's condition, and the signs that would show that she was dying; Billie who had known nothing but how to inflict cruelty and neglect.

God, it hurt to imagine what poor Briony must have endured here!

'Mila!'

Carter was calling. Mila pushed herself up to a standing position. Her head was heavy; her body weighed down by the horrors she was imagining.

'*Mila!*'

'I'm coming.'

It was like being hungover; in a nightmare. She felt as if she was moving in slow motion.

'Where are you?' she called.

'Round here, on the other side of the shed!'

He was standing beside a patch of land that had been fenced off. It looked as if it had once been used to grow vegetables and fruit, but now brambles were pushing their way through the broken panes of a derelict greenhouse and the area where Carter was standing was covered in rusty chicken wire. The shredded remains of polytunnels were evident. The land had been dug before, which made it the logical place to dig if you had something you needed to bury.

The spade, with its Intermarché price sticker intact on the handle, was propped against the fencing; clumps of red clay stuck to its blade.

Nearby was an area of disturbed dirt. It wasn't a huge area, and it wasn't shaped like a grave, but Briony was a very small person, one who didn't take up much room when she was alive, and certainly wouldn't when she was dead.

Mila took in the scene. She took it all in and then she turned and walked away.

35

Mila waited for Carter on the outside of the boundary wall of the former convent, sitting on the ground with her back pressed against the warm old stones; her arms wrapped around her legs. She was in the shade of a giant ash tree that reached its branches over the fence like enormous arms. Distantly, she could see great plumes of smoke billowing into the sky. A whisper of breeze lifted her hair. The fires were still a long way away, but they were coming closer.

Eventually, Carter appeared. He wandered over to where Mila was sitting and put a hand on her shoulder, squeezed in a brotherly fashion. 'You okay?' he asked.

'Yep,' she said.

'The police are on the way.'

'Did you contact Sandrine? Did you find out if there's been any sign of the van?'

'It hasn't gone past any cameras in the last few days.'

'So it's still around here somewhere – hidden maybe?'

'Or else Billie's changed the number plates.'

'Of course,' said Mila. 'That's what she'll have done. Changed the plates and painted over the logo. Why didn't we think of that before?'

'I did,' said Carter. 'The cameras were always a long shot. Anyway, it doesn't matter. Billie won't come back here now.'

'No.'

Mila didn't care about Billie Dexter. Sooner or later, she would be found, and arrested and she would face justice. The police and the courts and public opinion would not be sympathetic when they found out what she had done to Briony Moorcroft. Probably she had meant to demand a ransom from Mr and Mrs Moorcroft. It was even possible that the two young women had concocted the plan between them. But Briony's condition had deteriorated before they had chance to see the plan through. Instead of asking for help, Billie had panicked. She'd tied Briony to the bed and left her to die.

And now Billie Dexter was gone.

But, so what? It was too late to change anything. The damage had been done. And Mila knew she'd never be able to get the loneliness of that patch of derelict land behind the sheep shed, nor its dreary desolation, out of her mind.

'You don't need to hang around here, Mila,' Carter said. 'Go home if you want. I'll wait for the police.'

'What should we tell Mr and Mrs Moorcroft?'

'Leave it to Ceci to decide. But this isn't the kind of news that should be delivered over the phone. We should let the police handle it going forward. If this is a murder investigation, they won't want us muddying the water.'

He looked about, squinting against the bright sun in his eyes. Then he looked again at Mila.

'You don't look great. Shall I call Ceci and get her to come and pick you up?'

'No, it's okay. I'll call her.'

Carter reached his hand down to her. She took it and he pulled her to her feet. He brushed a cobweb from her shoulder.

'Mila,' he said, 'what happened here wasn't our fault.'

'I know.'

'We're not responsible for other people's actions.'

'No.'

Carter looked at Mila intently. His gaze made her uncomfortable.

'I'm alright,' she said.

She dusted down the back of her dress. 'I don't suppose you have a cigarette on you, Carter?'

'You don't smoke.'

'I feel like a cigarette.'

'I don't have one. Sorry.'

'Okay.'

Mila picked up her bike and kicked up the brake. Carter watched her.

'Mila?'

'Yes?'

'You really okay? You seem a bit weird.'

Mila shrugged. She pushed the bike off the verge and onto the lane. Already, faintly, she could hear sirens approaching, although their sound was muffled by the happy screams and shouts of laughter coming from the direction of the AquaSplash.

Life goes on, Sophie whispered. *Always, life goes on.*

36

Mila cycled to the end of the lane and turned onto the busier road at the T-junction. At the last minute, she decided not to go back to Morannez, but to head the other way, taking a different route and cycling uphill, standing on the pedals, each rotation a huge effort as she struggled to keep the bike upright and not crash into the hedge. She didn't stop until she reached the cemetery at the very top of the hill, spread over the summit like a blanket.

Mila went through the gates and into the graveyard, with its neat paths and its well-maintained monuments to the dead. She parked the bike and she walked a little way and stood for a moment, gazing at the sea beyond the far boundary wall. She could still smell the interior of the sheep shed. She feared it would haunt her for the rest of her life.

She turned to look the other way. Hanging above the land horizon was a long, thin strip of grey, the accumulated smoke from the wildfires, hanging over Finistère; a pall for all the animals and trees that had been destroyed in the fire's wake.

Mila found a bench and sat on it. She watched an old woman with a tiny dog wearing a diamanté collar as the two of them stood beside a headstone. The woman was talking to the dog; a constant stream of words that Mila could not hear. Every now and then, the woman opened her handbag, took out a cocktail sausage, broke it in half and fed the two halves to the dog, which wagged its little tail furiously.

See, said Sophie quietly, *not everything in the world is bad.*

But Mila felt devastated.

When she was a little calmer, she called Ceci and told her what she and Carter had discovered. Ceci complained that she couldn't hear what Mila was saying.

'It looks like she's buried the body in the old vegetable patch behind the sheep shed,' Mila yelled.

The old woman and the dog turned and stared.

Sorry! she mouthed and turned away.

'Where are you?' Ceci asked.

'At the cemetery.'

'Right. Go to Le Liège and order a glass of brandy. I'll meet you there in twenty minutes.'

Le Liège was Ceci's favourite restaurant. It was situated almost next to the cemetery, a little way distant from Morannez town.

Mila didn't want brandy. She didn't want Ceci's kindness. She wanted things to be different. She wanted Briony Moorcroft to be alive and well; she wanted to be able to call Mrs Moorcroft and tell her that Briony was safe. She wanted to take Briony back to the sea house and let her bathe and sleep and then hand her back into the care of her parents. She wanted a happy ending to Briony's story, not this nightmare that was playing out in front of her eyes.

She wandered along the paths heading to her stepsister's grave; the very act of following a route so familiar was soothing in a perverse way. Missing Sophie was an old hurt. Mila was used to it.

Sophie's grave was in a quiet spot, separate from the pathways lined with the final resting places of dignitaries and wealthy residents; an unobtrusive plot with its head against the wall. The grass had grown long and silver, waving its seedheads, the stone behind it was grey, patched with white and orange lichen, tough little flowers rooted between its cracks, and beyond everything was blue and white: the blue sea, the blue sky; white horses galloping on the breaking waves.

Mila sat on the mown path at the foot of Sophie's grave and she said: 'Hi. It's me.'

Sophie didn't answer.

Mila ran the palm of her hand along the edges of the grass. They felt rough. Mila craved softness. She moved closer to the grave, half-tempted to lie on it.

Even now, after two years, she struggled to believe that Sophie was really gone; that her body was here, under the ground; that she was never coming back, that she would never see her again. Never. It seemed ridiculous, like a joke. It didn't seem real.

'Why did you leave me, Sophie?' she asked. '*Why?*'

Sophie didn't answer, but Mila imagined she heard her laughing.

'Why did you go out on that stupid boat in that stupid storm? What was the point? It was such a stupid, fucking selfish thing to do! You lost everything and we lost you! And for what? For what?'

Mila rocked back onto her heels, holding herself, skewered by anger and grief and frustration. She tried to cry, to let out some of the tension, but she hadn't been able to cry in all this time and still the tears wouldn't come. What was wrong with her? Why was she condemned to hold her emotion inside; a compact, hard thing that seemed to become heavier with each passing day.

Where was the end to her grief? How could it end?

She felt nauseous. She knew, at a rational level, that much of the problem was the adrenaline that had flooded her bloodstream when she and Carter had entered the sheep shed. The fight-or-flight hormone had nowhere to go. She needed to run or swim or burn energy in some other way.

Mila stood and walked around the cemetery's perimeter path, trying to make herself feel better. Trying to let go.

After a while, she came back to Sophie's grave and noticed what she hadn't seen before; that someone had left a small bunch of heather on the grass. The sprigs were weighed down with a pebble carved with the Gallic triskele – the symbol of the *Bande Sauvage*.

So, one of the old gang had been here: Solene, Carter, Arnaud,

Melodie, Denis, Guillaume or Emmanuelle. Though the most likely candidate was Carter.

Mila knew how deep his passion for Sophie had run and perhaps still did. And there was something else; something she'd almost forgotten. Not long before her death, Sophie had mentioned a secret to Mila, about 'someone we used to know.'

They'd been speaking on WhatsApp video. Mila had been annoyed with Sophie at the time; she couldn't remember what the problem had been now, but back then she hadn't wanted to gratify Sophie by appearing curious about the secret. As a result, she hadn't pushed Sophie to tell her, which was what Sophie wanted, so she'd never found out. And, a few days later, Sophie had been lost at sea, and now whatever it was she had been hinting at would always be a secret.

Mila was pretty certain, though, that the 'someone' had been Carter. At the time, his marriage had been disintegrating and he and his wife (now ex-wife), Emmanuelle, were planning on moving back to Brittany from Canada. It was logical that he would have made contact with Sophie. Perhaps he had harboured hopes of rekindling their romance. Only Sophie would have told him that she was married to Charlie now, and that they had a teenage daughter, and that any kind of relationship beyond a purely platonic friendship was out of the question.

She would have told him that, wouldn't she?

Out at sea, the waves rose and fell, stretching back to the horizon. The wind slid over the surface of the ocean, and it crept up the cliff face and over the wall and, gentler now, it smoothed the grass growing in the cemetery, whispered over the graves before it continued across the country to where the fires were burning, fanning the flames.

The sun shone through the clouds and the gulls wheeled in the sky, and Mila Shepherd gazed down at her stepsister's last resting place. A butterfly fluttered above the grave and disappeared.

'Tell me, Sophie,' Mila begged. 'Was Carter the secret? Had he been in touch with you? Was that what you were going to tell me?'

But Sophie was silent, keeping all her secrets to herself.

37

Ceci was already seated at her favourite table in the garden of Le Liège when Mila arrived. She stood when she saw her stepdaughter. 'Oh Mila,' she said, 'I'm so sorry. What a dreadful morning you've had.'

They embraced and then Mila took a seat and drank from the glass of mineral water that had already been poured. It was chilled and lemony and cut through the after-taste of the air inside the old sheep shed; that and the smell of the goats that the Pinet family, who ran the restaurant, kept for their milk.

Ceci was looking at Mila in a way that made her realise Carter had also called Ceci and told her he was worried about Mila.

'I'm all right,' Mila told her.

'Evidently you're not. You've had a shock.'

'You didn't see the shed,' Mila said, 'or the mattress. You don't know how dirty it was, Ceci. How degrading.' She dropped her head into her hands. 'If only we'd got there sooner.'

Ceci rubbed Mila's back between the shoulder blades. 'You've been searching for Briony almost every waking moment since you came back from England,' she said. 'You and Carter, both of you, you haven't stopped. Nobody could have tried harder to find her. There was nothing, not one single thing, more that either of you could have done.'

Mila nodded miserably.

'The people who should be feeling ashamed are those who knew Billie was keeping Briony prisoner in the sheep shed, and didn't intervene.'

'You think the communards knew?'

'Some of them must have. Thankfully, their consciences aren't our business.'

'What about Mr and Mrs Moorcroft?' Mila asked quietly.

'The police will look after them. Still, I intend to fly to Cardiff in a day or two to offer my support.'

Ceci sipped her water. The sunlight caught in the glass and reflected from its bowl.

'Today is a bad day,' said Ceci, 'a terrible day. But we will get through it and tomorrow will be a little easier. We'll help one another. We'll be all right.'

She was using more or less the same language that Mila had used when she'd told Ani about the discovery of the wreckage. Mila must have learned the strategy for managing emotionally traumatic situations from Ceci – these weren't the kind of words Lydia would ever use. Lydia was all for 'least said, soonest mended'. Mila felt momentarily disorientated, as if she and Sophie had become interchangeable; daughters, sisters, soulmates.

A dusty figure came into the garden area of the restaurant: Carter. He was walking with the cowboy stance of someone who spent a lot of time riding a classic American motorbike over potholes and along bumpy, awkward-to-navigate lanes. His brow was furrowed, his eyes dark. He shrugged off his jacket and hooked it over the low wall that held back the garden, leaned to kiss Ceci, touched Mila's shoulder in a brotherly fashion and took his seat.

'Are you okay?' Ceci asked.

'Yep.'

'Have the police arrived at the commune?'

'Yes. And reinforcements are on their way with cadaver dogs.'

'Oh God,' whispered Mila, imagining the dogs alerting, a small, dead hand emerging from the dusty soil, the fingers curled towards the palm.

At that moment, Madame Pinet, mother of the chef and chief wait-ress at Le Liège, came out of the kitchen, carrying a tray on which was a single large plate. She paused by a different table of four diners, who, with their napkins tucked into their collars and their cutlery laid out in front of them, were looking hungry and expectant. Madame Pinet was on the very point of putting the contents of the tray down on that table when she noticed that Carter had joined Ceci and Mila. She hesitated, then came over to Ceci's table and put the plate down in front of Carter. On it were four freshly cooked galettes. Ham and cheese, with a fried egg nestled in the middle of each, sprinkled with parsley.

'For me?' asked Carter.

'For you,' said Madame, nodding and smiling with pride.

The waiting diners were making what-just-happened? faces at one another.

'Wow!' said Carter.

Fucking four! said Sophie.

Madame flushed with pleasure, clasped her hands together. 'I'll fetch you some bread,' she said. She wagged a finger playfully in Carter's direction. 'I know how you Canadians like bread with your meal!'

'Well, that would be just wonderful,' said Carter. 'And some butter, please, Madame, if you don't mind.'

Madame Pinet scuttled off back to the kitchen, pausing only to scold the waiting diners at the other table for their impatience.

Mila leaned across to Carter.

'How could you accept that food?' she asked, appalled. 'How can you eat at a time like this?'

Carter cut a large piece of galette, folded it and put it into his mouth. 'I just can!' he said, wiping a dribble of yolk from his chin.

Ceci was trying to avoid eye contact with the other diners.

'Oh, mon Dieu,' she murmured, the fingers of one hand pressed to her forehead to shield her face.

Madame Pinet returned with a wicker basket containing freshly made bread rolls. She placed it beside Carter, tilted her head to one side and beamed down at him. She had refreshed her lipstick since the last time she was at the table.

'Could you please ask Etienne to make a vegan galette for Mila, Madame?' Ceci asked.

Madame sniffed.

'Excuse me, Madame!' called one of the waiting diners.

'What's wrong with you? Your food is coming! You're not going to starve!' Madame Pinet called back. 'Mushrooms suit you?' she asked Mila, in a tone that implied mushrooms would be a great deal of trouble.

'Perfect,' said Mila.

Madame scuttled away.

Mila felt her phone vibrating in the bag at her side.

'Excuse me,' she said.

The incoming call was from a number she didn't recognise. She hesitated. It was the height of bad manners to prioritise one's telephone over lunch but these were exceptional times.

'You'd better pick up,' said Carter. Ceci gave a slight nod, to show that she concurred.

Mila answered the phone. 'Hello?'

'Is that Miss Shepherd?'

'Yes, this is Mila.'

'It's Désespéré here. Didier Désespéré. I met you by the seafront in Lorient. We spoke about my work as an oceanographer.'

'Of course. Monsieur, I remember. How are you?'

'I'm good.' He spoke carefully and slowly, as if he was struggling to make the shape of each word in his mouth. 'I promised I would let you know,' he continued, 'if I saw either of the women for whom you were looking.'

'Yes.'

'Well, good to my word, I'm calling to inform you that the tall woman is here, now.'

'The woman whose picture I showed you on my phone?'

'Yes.'

Carter stopped eating, fork midway to his mouth, and stared at Mila.

'Monsieur, forgive me,' she said, 'but are you absolutely sure it's the same woman?'

'I'm an alcoholic, Ms Shepherd. I'm not blind.'

'Of course not. I'm sorry,' said Mila.

'She's gone into the museum.'

'Thank you. We'll get on our way. We'll be with you shortly.' She paused. 'Monsieur, in the meantime, could you watch the museum in case she leaves?'

'It will be my pleasure... One more thing, Miss Shepherd. She's not alone.'

38

Carter took the straighter, newer roads to Lorient and opened up the bike's throttle. Mila, behind him, sat forward so that his body protected hers from the wind. She held onto him, trying to relax; leaning into the corners, gripping the sides of Carter's jacket when he accelerated to pass a car towing a caravan, or a lorry. She was used to riding pillion on the Harley; she wasn't used to the speed at which Carter was driving, nor the strength of the air that buffeted her as it was displaced by the bike. Carter was concentrating on the road, and not chatting to her, as he normally did, via the communication system in the helmets.

Insects and dust smashed into the visor of her helmet. When they turned a corner, the road seemed to come up close to meet her. She tried not to think about how it would feel to fall, her body tossed along by the forward momentum like a rag doll.

As they zoomed past fields and patches of woodland, through small towns, past beautiful old farmhouses with their shutters and their gables, to distract herself from the speed at which they were travelling, she tried to imagine how the scenario ahead of them might play out. At least, she thought, if she and Carter positively identified Billie to the police, it would be a cathartic experience. Mila would be able to say to Mr and Mrs Moorcroft at some point in the future: 'I was there when

Billie Dexter was arrested. She'll never be at liberty to harm anybody else again.'

It would be a form of closure.

They went over the river, reached the outskirts of Lorient and ran into the inevitable queues. Carter wove the bike through the traffic, making his way to the front of the lines for traffic lights, and, when he could, taking the back roads. He had an instinct for finding shortcuts, which was a blessing in a busy town like this, although it became increasingly difficult for Mila to orient herself, given all the twists and turns.

Soon enough, they turned into the car park at the back of the Cité de la Voile Museum. Carter parked the bike and Mila climbed off and removed her helmet. She shook out her hair and looked towards the great concrete and glass structure.

Carter nodded towards a small, scruffy van parked a few spaces away.

'Is that Billie's?' Mila asked.

'Yep,' said Carter.

The sides of the vehicle had been crudely painted to obliterate the Moorcrofts' Maid Services branding. Billie had also replaced the original number plates with French ones. As disguises went, it wasn't sophisticated, good enough to fool the ANPR cameras but any police officer who spotted it would recognise it for what it was.

If Billie Dexter's plan was to flee in that van, it was destined to fail.

'Billie can't have gone far,' said Carter.

'Monsieur Désespéré said she was in the museum. Should one of us stay here and watch the van?'

'No need.' Carter took a bottle of water from his jacket pocket, had a drink and then passed it to Mila. While she drank, he went over to the van, crouched down and did something to one of the tyres. That corner of the van sank as the tyre deflated. 'Nobody will be going anywhere in that now,' Carter said.

He and Mila fastened their helmets to the bike and walked towards the quay. They found Didier Désespéré in the same spot as before, sitting hunched, an old blue raincoat hooked over his shoulders, a paper bag containing a bottle clasped between the palms of his hands. He looked up as they approached.

Mila smiled and walked over to him. The light reflecting from the concourse tiles was blinding.

'Good afternoon, Monsieur,' said Mila.

'You took your time.'

'We came as quickly as we could. The traffic was awful.' She passed him a napkin from Le Liège. It was wrapped around the galettes that Carter hadn't managed to eat, and slices of the restaurant's delicious bread. 'We brought you some lunch.'

'You're too kind.' He opened one corner of the napkin. 'Wonderful!' he exclaimed, his eyes lighting up. 'Real food!'

'Has she – the woman you spotted – come out yet?'

'No, she's still inside. She and her companion. Do you mind if I...?'

'Tuck in,' said Carter.

Monsieur Désespéré took a big bite. His breath reeked of alcohol. He looked in a worse state than he had done the last time Mila saw him; thinner and frailer. His face and the top of his head were horribly sunburned and his lips were bloody and raw.

From the speed with which he wolfed down the galette, it seemed likely he hadn't eaten in days.

'Could you describe the person she's with?' Mila asked, 'so we know who to look out for.'

'Woman,' said the homeless man, wiping a smear of olive oil from his lips. 'Red-head. I didn't get a good look, but old, I think.' He hunched his shoulders to demonstrate the demeanour of Billie's companion.

Mila and Carter exchanged glances.

'Maybe the ex-prisoner she knew from the commune?' Mila suggested.

'Maybe. Thanks, buddy, for being so observant and calling us,' said Carter. 'We owe you, big time.'

The man, still eating, raised a hand to his forehead in a mock salute. 'I am happy to help the forces of law and order. Especially those that come bearing gifts of food.' He was trying to keep a normal voice, but he was struggling, slurring badly, and his eyelids seemed swollen and heavy. There was a cut on his nose and flakes of saliva were crusted onto his chin.

Carter passed him what was left of the water.

'Let us buy you another meal,' he said, taking a couple of notes from the wallet he kept in his back pocket and passing them to Monsieur Désespéré, who took the money and tucked it inside his shirt.

'Very kind of you,' he said. 'Very kind indeed.'

He'll only go and spend it on vodka, Sophie said.

She was right, but Mila thought: *If it makes him happy, so what?*

39

Mila and Carter went into the museum building.

It was large and airy; echoing with children's voices and busier than Mila had been expecting; full of families seeking respite from the sun. There were also tourists of many different nationalities, and groups of young people wearing holiday club baseball caps and T-shirts.

Mila and Carter decided to split up: Mila heading to the top of the museum, Carter starting at the bottom, and they stayed in touch via their phones as they searched, gradually working their way back towards one another. Mila held her phone tightly in her hand as she wandered around the exhibits, her heart beating with a mixture of anticipation and apprehension.

She and Carter had agreed not to approach Billie themselves. It was too risky. If she felt threatened, the worst-case scenario was that she might grab a child and use him or her as a shield; bystanders could be hurt in any scuffle that might ensue. And, of course, Billie might be armed. She could be carrying a knife, and if she was, and she was cornered, she would use it. They believed she was already responsible for Briony's death; adding actual bodily harm – or worse – to the list of her crimes wouldn't be such a big deal. Luke had told Mila countless times that the more desperate a person, the more dangerous they were.

And there was the red-headed woman to consider. She might be an innocent, drawn into Billie's sphere as Briony had been but it was more likely she was an accomplice. She might also be violent.

Instead, the plan was for Mila and Carter to find Billie, hone in on her, one on either side, so she could not give them the slip, and then alert the police to their exact location. Billie didn't know that Mila and Carter were looking for her. She didn't know them from Adam, which meant they had a massive advantage over her. As long as they were careful, they should be able to get as close to her as necessary, without Billie suspecting anything.

Mila went into the cool gloom of the museum's cinema, where a film of Éric Tabarly skimming the seas aboard *Pen Duick* was playing. She waited a few seconds for her eyes to adjust to the low light and then studied the backs of people's heads, until she was certain that Billie and the red-haired woman weren't there.

She walked out, wandering amongst the displays. Two brothers were excitedly talking to their parents about a submarine simulator. Mila was searching for the entrance to that exhibit, when she received a message from Carter.

Indoor boating lake. Now.

Mila found it easily enough. Model yachts were skimming across the water; people were gathered around watching. Mila spotted Carter almost at once. He was leaning on the Perspex barrier, watching the boats and chatting with a couple of young boys at his side. He barely acknowledged Mila, but when she came into his eyeline, he nodded subtly in the direction of the raised podium on one side of the lake from where the yachts were controlled.

Standing in the middle, behind one of the controls, was a tall, athletically built woman with short hair, her arm muscles bulging from the sleeves of a navy-blue polo shirt. She had broad shoulders, a thick neck, a large nose that had, at some time, been badly broken. Mila recognised her at once. Billie was as bullish in real life as in photographs and videos. Mila's instinctive reaction was one of revulsion; to be so close to someone who had caused so much pain and done so much damage to the Moorcroft family.

In front of Billie was a tiny woman with a shock of bright red hair who was struggling to control the boat. As Mila watched, the red-head gave a peal of childlike laughter and Billie slapped her, hard enough to jolt her forwards, on the back. The red-head laughed again. The laughter sounded artificial; forced.

Mila drew closer. It was the redhead who held her eyes. Slowly, she took her phone out of her pocket and, holding it in front of her, she scrolled back through the photographs. She looked at the picture of Briony, and then at the girl standing in front of Billie Dexter. There were distinct similarities. Did Billie have a thing for small, frail, young women?

She texted Carter.

The red-haired girl looks like Briony.

Carter texted back.

She is Briony.

What?
No, she couldn't be. Could she?

Mila held onto the rim of the barrier. Carter must be mistaken, she thought. She looked again. The young woman did look like Briony Moorcroft, although Briony didn't have red hair, and surely Briony was dead.

Wasn't she?

Mila looked again, and no, there was no mistake. The redhead was Briony Moorcroft. She was not dead and buried in the grounds of the commune, but alive and looking pretty well, all things considered.

As the shock faded, it was replaced with relief.

How can this be? Milla wondered. How could Briony Moorcroft be here, standing, breathing, laughing when such a short time earlier, Mila had been convinced she had been crudely buried outside the sheep shed at the commune?

But then she realised it didn't matter how, all that mattered was that it was true.

Thank God, Mila thought, there will be good news for Briony's parents.

Thank God they won't have to hear that their daughter is dead.

40

Briony was alive. She was pale and very thin, but a pale, thin Briony was a massive improvement on a dead-and-buried Briony.

I can't believe it, Mila thought, still struggling to come to terms with this new reality.

Surreptitiously, she took a photograph of the two young women. She enlarged the image with her fingers until she was looking into Briony's eyes. They were not the heavy-lidded eyes of the sick girl she'd seen in the other photographs. This young woman was undoubtedly Briony Moorcroft, but something about her, besides the dyed hair, was different. She looked at Carter again. He made a small gesture with his hand, indicating she should stay put. Then she received another text.

Stick to the plan. I'll notify the police.

That was the sensible option. The whole objective of everything Mila and Carter had done so far had been to remove Briony from Billie and return her safely to her parents, and that was still their aim.

Briony did not appear to be being coerced, but appearances could be deceptive. The happy tableau that she and Billie were presenting didn't mean that everything was really okay. Billie Dexter was a dangerous woman with a violent and destructive track record. Briony had been manipulated into running away with her, and no doubt was still being controlled by the older, stronger girl. Whatever had transpired between Billie and Briony over the past days, it didn't mean that Briony was safe. It didn't change anything.

Mila remained in position, ostensibly looking at her phone, but really keeping an eye on Billie and Briony. Eventually, they moved, walking past Mila, so close that she heard Briony say she was hungry. Her voice was high-pitched and tinny, like a child's.

'We'll go get something to eat then,' Billie replied gruffly.

Mila messaged Carter.

They're going for food.

Police coming.

he replied.

Briony and Billie walked through the museum, heading for the exit. Mila followed. As she watched, Billie leaned down and picked up a bag that someone had placed at their feet. She whisked out a purse, pocketed it, and dropped the bag. It was a seamless manoeuvre.

Impressive, Sophie murmured.

Mila was sorry for the woman who was shortly to find out she'd been robbed, but to intervene now would alert Billie to the fact she was being followed, and could mean losing her, and Briony forever.

Carter had witnessed the theft too. He was there, to the other side of them, exactly as per the plan. He and Mila accompanied the couple, at a distance, as they left the museum and went out into the heat of the day.

They weren't in any rush. They walked a little way from the building and stood in the sunshine, Briony keeping watch while Billie opened the stolen purse, removed the cash and a couple of bank cards and dropped the purse into a waste bin.

Then they set off, not heading back to the van, but in the opposite direction, along the quay. On the way out, Billie grabbed a phone that a man had put down while he attended to his toddler's sunhat, and slipped it into her pocket. She didn't look back, to see if she'd been observed, but carried on walking with a hint of a swagger. Briony, however, glanced furtively about, clearly uncomfortable with Billie's blatant lawbreaking.

But Billie was good; a consummate thief and a slick opportunist. She would stand out a mile in any line-up, but she was so skilled a pick-pocket that probably she got away with it most of the time.

The two young women, unaware they were being accompanied by Mila and Carter, walked on, through the sunshine, weaving in and out of the holidaymakers milling about on the quayside. Mila wondered how long it would take for the police to arrive.

She tried to relax. Tried to stay calm; keep her focus on Briony. Having found her, being so close to her, they must do nothing to risk losing her again. The tension was making her light-headed.

Hurry up, she willed the police. *Where are you?*

Eventually Billie and Briony reached a Lebanese café housed inside an old shipping container. The outside tables were busy, and the aroma of cooking spices, chilli and garlic filled the air. They stopped to look at the laminated menu pinned to the side of a sapling outside. They must have agreed they would eat there because Billie took off her cap, took the stolen phone out of her pocket and gave both items to Briony. Briony took a seat at the only vacant table, in the dappled shade of the small trees, and Billie went inside.

Carter followed Billie, but before he disappeared through the plastic ribbons at the entrance to the container, he looked across to Mila.

Stick with Briony, he mouthed.

Mila gave a small nod. She walked over to the table where Briony was sitting, took hold of the back of a chair and smiled her most reas-suring smile at Briony Moorcroft. It was thrilling to finally be so close to the young woman for whom she'd been searching.

'Hi, I'm Mila. Do you mind if I sit here with you?'

Briony frowned. She looked about and observed that all the other tables were full. She shrugged to show that she did mind, but didn't feel as if she had any option but to share the table with Mila.

Mila sat. She kept her movements slow, her body language

respectful and unthreatening, even though her heart was racing. Briony moved the stolen phone closer. Her hands were tiny, the skin flaky and red, the cuticles raw, the nails bitten down. Both wrists were bruised. She looked towards the café entrance, scanning for Billie.

'Isn't it a lovely day?' said Mila, eager to win Briony's attention.

The younger woman ignored Mila. She was concentrating on the coloured ribbons that kept the flies out of the establishment, waiting for Billie to return, like an anxious dog left outside a shop.

Her behaviour wasn't normal. She was afraid of something.

She must be afraid of Billie Dexter.

Mila knew about Stockholm Syndrome, in which hostages develop a psychological bond with their captors. She wondered if this was at play here, or if Briony had simply become dependent on Billie and was being controlled by her. Briony, unused to making any decisions for herself, would slip seamlessly into the role of victim, without even realising she was being manipulated, exactly as her mother had predicted.

Close up, her skin was pallid. She was small as a bird, and her veins seemed too close to the surface. Her eyes protruded and the whites were bluish. Her breathing was shallow and laboured and she smelled sour.

'Are you enjoying your stay in Brittany?' Mila asked.

Briony did not answer, but blinked several times as if her eyes were dry. She was clutching tightly to Billie's cap. The bright scarlet colour of her hair was glaring in the sunlight. Maybe it wasn't intended to be a disguise. Perhaps it had been a choice, a colour that Briony had wanted to try. Billie must have helped her with the dye. Mila pictured them together, outside the sheep shed, Billie's big fingers massaging the colour through Briony's sparse hair; Briony's small head tilted forwards, her shoulders white and bony, and the nobbles in her spine making a track down her back. She imagined spots of dye, like blood, dotting Briony's milky skin.

'Is your friend ordering food?' Mila asked, mentally calculating how long that might take.

'How do you know I speak English?' Briony replied. 'Who are you? You were in the museum.'

'I'm Mila Shepherd. Yes, I was in the museum.'

'Are you following me?'

Mila hesitated. A reassuring lie would be easiest, but she wanted to gain the young woman's trust and the only way to do that was to be honest.

'I'm here to help you,' she said gently.

'I don't need help,' said Briony.

Her voice was babyish but her eyes were shrewd, and it was obvious that her mind was ticking over; trying to work out what was going on, and calculate if Mila represented a threat.

'Are you here because of my parents?' Briony asked, a note of panic now in her tone. 'Did they send you?'

'How did you get these marks?' Mila asked, gently touching the weals that circled Briony's wrists like bracelets.

Briony put her hands under the table.

'None of your business. Are you here because of my parents?' she asked again.

'Your parents want you to come home, yes.'

'I knew it!' said Briony. 'I knew they'd sent you!'

'Briony, they're desperately worried about you. They're your family. They want to look after you.'

'You don't understand.' Briony picked up the stolen phone and pushed back her chair. She stood up: standing she was barely taller than the sitting Mila. 'Billie's my family,' she said. 'She looks after me now.'

'Briony...'

Briony leaned forward. She narrowed her eyes and hissed: 'Get away from me, don't touch me! If you come anywhere near me again, I'm going to scream. I *mean it!*'

She had a look of such determination in her eyes, like a cornered wildcat, that Mila believed her.

41

Briony Moorcroft held an arm out in front of her to stop Mila coming any closer.

Any second now, thought Mila, Billie would come through the doorway of the shipping container restaurant and see Briony standing in that dramatically defensive posture and realise that something was going on. Carter would be tailing her, but Billie might panic and the situation could easily escalate out of control. The area outside the restaurant was packed with tourists and holidaymakers, there were dozens of children milling about, including babies in pushchairs. Someone could be hurt.

Where were the police?

Mila glanced towards the doorway. A young waitress in an apron was blocking it. She was holding a tray of used crockery, resting one side of her body against the doorframe, chatting with a friend.

Mila turned back to Briony Moorcroft.

'Briony, please, sit down. Your mother... actually *both* your parents are desperately worried about your health.'

'Listen,' said Briony, leaning forward so her face was close to Mila's. 'I can guess what my mother told you about me and all my various illnesses, blah blah blah, but I'm not ill, I never have been. *She* was the problem, not me. She's been poisoning me!'

'No, Briony, that's not right.'

'It *is*! Billie explained everything. I was addicted to the meds Mummy was giving me like Billie used to be addicted to heroin. And Billie helped me get clean and now I'm fine. So please will you just go away and leave us alone. I want to be with Billie and you can't stop me. It's my life and my choice and it's nothing to do with you!'

Experience had taught Mila that arguing with people who were convinced something was true, even if it was some crackpot theory they'd read about on the internet, was a waste of time. It was almost impossible to change somebody's mind when it was made up. Briony would argue her case until her body caved in and she was taken to hospital as an emergency.

'I can tell you don't believe me,' Briony said, as if she could read Mila's mind, 'but everything I've told you is *true!*'

'Okay, Briony,' said Mila. 'I am listening to you. I understand what you're saying. All I'm asking is that you let me take you to see a doctor...'

'I don't need a doctor! I just told you, I'm fine. For fuck's sake!'

It was a shock to hear Briony Moorcroft swear in that fashion.

Throughout this exchange, Mila had been keeping an eye on the waitress at the doorway. Now, she stood up straight, said goodbye to her friend and disappeared through the plastic ribbons with her tray. She must have walked right past a man who, a few seconds later, exited the container, folding a receipt into his wallet.

A child was blowing bubbles that drifted in the air. Sparrows fluttered into the trees, their wings making little dark shadows.

Where were the police? What was Billie doing inside the container? Was Carter still with her?

'Are you the police?' Briony asked in her little-girl voice, suddenly meek again.

'No. I work for an agency that specialises in tracking down missing people, like you.'

'But I'm not missing. I left of my own accord to save myself from my mother.'

'Was it really your decision, Briony? Or did Billie convince you that it would be a good thing to do.'

'I'm not an idiot,' said Briony. 'I have a mind of my own.'

Before Mila could reply, Briony turned back towards the old shipping container, as if she'd intuited that this would be the exact moment when Billie would come lumbering out from between the plastic ribbons hung at the door.

And she was right. It was.

42

Billie Dexter was holding a tray, laden with a board of snacks and some plates. Carter Jackson was a few steps behind her.

She stopped and looked around: her eyes scanning the shaded area beneath the trees. Briony raised the hand holding the stolen phone.

'Billie! Over here!' she called.

Billie spotted her. Her eyes flicked to Mila, and back to Briony again, as she tried to work out what was going on.

Frowning, she stepped forward.

'Briony...' Mila began again, but all Briony's attention was focused on Billie, walking towards them through the dappled sunshine, holding the tray. Carter followed.

Behind the container, and still some way distant, Mila spotted four people – three men and one woman – approaching. They moved more quickly than the tourists; and their body language was purposeful. They were not in uniform, but all were wearing trousers, close-fitting T-shirts and heavy-duty trainers. Mila recognised them at once as police officers. Carter could not have seen them, but Mila was certain he knew they were there. She felt sweat prickle in the small of her back. What if Briony noticed them? What if she realised they were police and alerted Billie?

She glanced at the younger woman, but Briony only had eyes for Billie.

As they drew nearer, the police broke into two sets of two – they were going to approach Billie from both sides. They were confident and resolute; like a pride of lions stalking their prey. Briony and Billie were oblivious to what was about to happen but Mila's mouth was dry.

Billie reached the table, and set down the tray. Mila resisted the instinct to back away. Carter was nearby. The police were almost upon them.

Even so, the situation felt dangerous.

Billie was several inches taller than Mila: physically imposing. There were sweat stains beneath the arms of her shirt, and she had a strong, musky smell. The sun caught in the fuzz of the shaved hair at the base of her neck. Beneath her left ear was a tattoo: a heart with a banner above it bearing the word *Tadcu*. What was that? Mila wondered. The name of a boyfriend?

'Alright?' Billie asked Briony.

'I would be if she wasn't here!' said Briony, indicating Mila.

Billie glared at Mila. Mila tried to stay calm. From the corner of her eye, she could see the police officers, only a few metres away. For the first time, she noticed the ceramic pot in the middle of the table containing cutlery. Knives. Not sharp knives, but capable of inflicting damage.

'What's going on, *bychan*?' Billie asked Briony.

'My parents sent this woman.'

Billie turned to Mila. Her eyes were dark and strong, heavy-browed. She moved her face closer to Mila's, so close that Mila could feel the warmth of her exhaled breath.

'Is that right?'

Mila straightened her back so that she stood a little taller. 'All Mr and Mrs Moorcroft want is for their daughter to take her medication and come home.'

'Abso-fucking-lutely that's all they want,' said Billie aggressively. 'They want to drug her up again so she can't go telling anyone the truth about what they've been doing to her.'

'Don't talk to her, Billie,' Briony said. 'Let's just get out of here.'

The police to the right of them were weaving through the restaurant tables like panthers. They were almost within touching distance.

'We need to get Briony to a hospital,' Mila said to Billie.

'*We*? There's more than one of you?'

'Billie!' Briony cried. 'Look out!'

Billie turned, but not quickly enough. The officers, assisted by Carter, were professional: swift and brutal. Billie was snatched from the table and pulled backwards. One of the police twisted Billie's arm behind her back and she, unfooted, half-fell and was half-helped to lie face down on the ground, her cheek pressed into the paving slab. From that position, she swore at the police.

'Don't hurt her!' Briony screamed, hopping from foot to foot like a toddler. 'Don't you dare hurt my Billie!'

'Get your fucking filthy hands off me!' Billie yelled.

'It's okay,' Carter told her. 'Try to stay calm. The more you fight, the worse it'll be for you.'

'Go fuck yourself!' Billie yelled.

'Ta gueule!' said the officer whose knee was restraining Billie's legs.

Briony tried to help Billie. Mila, fearing she'd be hurt in the fracas, held her back.

Billie was handcuffed and then pulled to her feet, still struggling. One of the officers had a bloody nose, another doubled over in pain when Billie lashed out, kicking him in the stomach. A third was talking into a microphone clipped to his collar, giving instructions in French. Carter assisted the bleeding officer. Billie yelled abuse indiscriminately. The fourth officer was attending to Briony, alternately restraining and comforting her.

'Bastards!' Billie shouted. 'Fucking bastards! I'm the good guy here! I'm the hero!'

'Tais-toi!' said the female officer. *Be quiet.*

The diners outside the restaurant, watched in alarm: holidaymakers grabbed their children's hands and led them away. Teenagers were videoing the arrest on their phones to garner social media 'likes' later. Mila, her own heart pounding fiercely, attempted to placate Briony who was close to hysteria and flailing at the officer who was attempting to calm her. It wouldn't help matters if Briony got herself into trouble too.

It felt like forever, but, in truth, it was over quickly. Billie was dragged away, and bundled into the back of a police van that had materialised on the quayside. As soon as she was secure, the officers climbed on board, there was a brief exchange with Carter, and the van drove away.

Briony remained, tears of frustration streaming down her face.

She turned to Mila.

'What have you *done?*' she shouted, wiping her nose with the back of her wrist. 'Billie's been helping me! You haven't been listening to me! *You haven't been listening at all!*'

43

Ceci drove into Lorient to pick up Mila and Briony. Mila had never been so relieved to see her stepmother as she was that afternoon.

The wait had been fraught. After Billie's arrest, Briony had become hysterical, fighting Carter and Mila and screaming when they tried to calm her. Worried bystanders had tried to intervene. More than once, it had taken every ounce of Carter's charm, explanations and the showing of his Toronto police ID to reassure them that Briony was in safe hands.

'Weren't you supposed to give that back when you quit?' Mila asked.

'You should be grateful I still have it!'

By the time Ceci finally turned up on the quayside close to the sailing museum, the young woman's fury and frustration was mostly spent. Mila and Carter had been walking with her – it was harder for her to rant when she was on her feet – but now they were resting on a bench in the shade. For the last fifteen minutes, Briony had been slumped; hands between her legs, hair covering her face; a picture of misery. When Mila tried to comfort her, she'd shaken her hand away.

'Don't touch me!' she'd snapped.

Then Ceci arrived, heels clicking along the paving slabs, looking as glamorous as if she'd just stepped out of the pages of a magazine and clutching the bag that contained Briony's medication and a bottle of water.

The introductions were not amicable, but Ceci remained the epitome of calm.

'Perhaps you should take some of these tablets now,' she suggested to Briony.

'And turn into a zombie again? No way!'

Mila caught Ceci's eye. 'We could wait to see what the doctor says.'

'I don't need a doctor,' said Briony.

'We need to have you checked over, sweetheart,' said Ceci. 'Try to see it from our point of view. We're responsible for you now, and you've been a long time without medical care.'

'For one thing, *I'm* responsible for myself, for another, as I've told you a million times, there's *nothing wrong with me!*'

'Perhaps you're right. But where's the harm in having your opinion validated by a professional?'

Briony rolled her eyes – a typical, exasperated teenager.

'I *know* there's nothing wrong!' she snarled.

Even Carter's seemingly endless supply of good humour was being tested now.

He stood up, stretched and announced that he was going to the police station to help with the interrogation of Billie.

'Why do you need to be there?' asked Mila.

'To provide indispensable background information.'

'Surely, if the police need indispensable information, they'll call you.'

'Oh, let him be,' said Ceci, squeezing Mila's arm. 'He misses the force. He wants to be part of the drama; part of the team. It's good for him.'

Casual sexism from my own mother, said Sophie. *Carter gets to enjoy the macho buzz while you pick up the broken pieces of Briony.*

Before Mila could raise any further objections, Carter picked up his jacket, slung it over his shoulder and headed off. Mila found herself disproportionately annoyed by him abandoning the situation like this.

Ceci returned her attention to Briony.

'I've been speaking to your mother,' she said. 'She's delighted that we've found you safe, but obviously very worried about you too. I have my phone here. Would you like to have a quick word with her, to reassure her?'

'No,' said Briony.

'Later then, maybe.'

'I never want to speak to her again.'

'Briony has been making her views on her mother very clear,' Mila said.

'Why do you think I left home?' Briony asked.

'All right,' said Ceci. She considered the situation for a moment, and decided this was a battle not worth fighting. 'Never mind your parents for now. The important thing is that we get you to hospital. It's a very nice place – more like a hotel.'

'If you take me to hospital, they'll give me drugs! I went through all the fucking stress of cold turkey and now you want to get me hooked again.'

'I'd be grateful if you would refrain from using foul language, Briony,' Ceci said smoothly. 'It's bad for my blood pressure. And, for the record, doctors aren't allowed do anything that will hurt a person. They take an oath only to help, not harm.'

Briony was unconvinced. 'Mummy said if I argued with the doctors they'd lock me away. That's what's going to happen, isn't it? I'm going to be drugged *and* locked up *because nobody will listen to me.*'

She began to cry.

Frustrated as she was, Mila felt a rush of empathy.

She knew what it felt like to be ignored.

* * *

A short while later, Briony had been persuaded to sit in the passenger seat of Ceci's sports' car. She was a furious little figure, resentful and fearful. Ceci had put the hard top on; partly to protect Briony from the sun, but mainly to stop her getting any ideas about climbing out and running away when the car was stopped at traffic lights. The thought of losing her again, after all they'd been through, was inconceivable.

Ceci had loaned Briony a shawl to wrap around her shoulders because Briony had complained she was cold, despite the ambient temperature being in the low thirties. This in itself seemed an indication that the young woman really wasn't well. With sunglasses to protect her eyes, and bundled up as she was, Briony resembled a character from a Beatrix Potter novel – some eccentric, fussy, cross little creature, a she-mole perhaps. Mila sat behind her, hunched in the back seat, which was little more than a parcel shelf, wishing she was less tall.

From this position, Mila had plenty of time to observe Briony. Considering the physical, physiological and emotional upheaval she'd undergone, Briony seemed to be holding up pretty well. Mila was certain now that her initial suspicion there were elements of Stockholm Syndrome at play had been correct. Briony viewed Billie as her saviour, rather than an enigmatic, but misguided soul who had put her life in mortal danger. Some distance was needed, some calm space, before Briony would be able to see things as they really were.

They drove out of Lorient town and into the countryside. The traffic coming in the other direction was heavy; according to the report on the radio, vehicles were being diverted away from the predicted path of the latest wildfire. It was burning out of control, its progress being hastened by the wind. Briony did not understand the report, it being in French, but it made Mila uneasy.

'Do you think it's safe bringing our patient to this particular hospital,' she asked Ceci, in French, 'given the fire situation?'

'I'm sure it's fine,' said Ceci. 'The wind is expected to change direction this evening. The authorities are being super-cautious, that's all.'

Eventually Ceci turned the car into the hospital car park – the same private hospital where Carter's ex-wife and former *Bande Sauvage* member, Emmanuelle, worked. It was a fine building that had once been a chateau, now extended and converted. The old and modern parts of the building had been seamlessly melded to present a grand façade; Gothic towers, turrets and fancy, wrought-iron balconies tastefully marrying with the new, minimalist architecture. The surroundings were immaculately landscaped, carefully planted trees casting shade over pathways lined with lavender, the only colours in the gardens green and purple. It looked rather like the kind of hotel that might have both a secret garden and an infinity pool.

Briony gazed around, apparently unimpressed.

'This is one of the top-rated hospitals in France,' Ceci said, with some pride. 'You're going to be in good hands here, Briony.'

'How am I supposed to talk to anyone, when I don't speak any French?' Briony asked.

'One of the doctors is an old friend of mine,' Mila said. 'Her name is Emmanuelle. She's a good person. She lived in Canada for ten years and she's fluent in English.'

'There we are,' said Ceci. 'Communication isn't going to be a problem. I spoke to Emmanuelle on the telephone earlier, to brief her about you, Briony, and she's very much looking forward to meeting you. And I'm going to stay with you until you're settled, *ma chère*. You won't be on your own.'

'Settled? Why do I need to "settled"? You said they were just going to check me over.'

'Emmanuelle thinks it makes sense to keep you in overnight for observations.'

'For fuck's sake,' Briony muttered, 'you're all a load of fucking liars!'

Her voice was gruff.

It sounded rather like Billie's.

* * *

Emmanuelle had said she'd be there to meet them, when they arrived, but the receptionist said that unfortunately, Dr Jackson was tied up with an emergency. She suggested that Briony made herself at home in her room while she waited. Mila was ready for a break from Briony: fortunately, Ceci said she'd be happy to wait with the young woman.

Mila went back outside to stretch her legs, walking around the hospital grounds, enjoying the tranquility promoted by the delightful landscaping. The building and its gardens were surrounded by established woodlands. The foliage of nut trees bounced and jostled as squirrels ran along the branches. Mila couldn't help thinking how much fuel these woods would provide for the flames should the fire come this far.

Stop catastrophising, said Sophie. *Why must you always think the worst?*

This was one of Sophie's more valid complaints; she, Mila, acknowledged that she was inclined to picture worst-case scenarios. It was, she believed, a kind of insurance policy: be prepared for disaster and it might never happen.

She perched on the wall beside a solar-powered water feature and called Ani who picked up but said she was at the beach with her friends in the tone of voice that made it clear she didn't want to talk. After that, Mila called Luke, who didn't answer but who did, at last, send a text which read:

Will call later.

Finally, she called Carter.

'Hey,' he said.

'Hey. Are you still at the police station?'

'I'm just leaving. Where are you?'

'Outside the hospital. What's happening with Billie?'

'She's going to be escorted back to the UK to face charges.'

'Escorted by whom?'

'Welsh officers. They'll be over tomorrow.'

'Has she calmed down yet?'

'Hardly!' Carter snorted. 'What's happening at your end?'

'Briony and Ceci are inside the hospital waiting to see Emmanuelle who's tied up with an emergency.'

'If you don't need to be there, I could come and pick you up; take you back to Morannez.'

'That'd be great. I think they're in for a long evening.' Mila sighed. 'Briony's still protesting that she's not ill.'

'We'll find out the truth soon enough,' said Carter.

'We already know it, don't we?'

Carter was silent.

'What?' asked Mila.

'It's probably nothing.'

'What's probably nothing?'

'Ah, Mila... There was a case a few years back, in the States.'

'What case?'

'This woman. Wholesome as apple pie, an all-round good American mom. She was shot by her daughter's boyfriend. Turned out she'd been faking her daughter's cancer. She'd starved the poor kid, shaved her head, somehow or other convinced doctors to give her chemo...'

Mila was silent for a moment. She had a vague memory of the case Carter had mentioned – she'd seen a TV programme about it once.

'Are you suggesting that something similar might be going on here?' she asked cautiously.

'I'm not suggesting anything. But...'

'What?'

'I dunno. Listening to Billie being interviewed... She's 100 per cent adamant that Briony's mother has been using drugs to keep her in a chemical straitjacket. I'm certain she believes what she's saying.'

'Okay, maybe she does believe what she's saying, but believing something doesn't mean it's true.'

'No,' said Carter.

Mila detected the hesitation in his voice.

'Wouldn't Mr Moorcroft have had something to say about it if Briony suddenly started getting ill out of the blue?' Mila asked. 'Wouldn't he at least have had his suspicions?'

'Mrs M's from a medical background though, isn't she? She could have blinded him with science. And she spends every minute of every day with Briony... He's at work all the time, you said, sorting out his staff rotas.'

'No,' said Mila. 'It's not possible.'

'I thought it worth mentioning,' said Carter.

'Of course.'

But surely, Mila reasoned, *surely* there couldn't be any grounds to doubt Mrs Moorcroft's version of events? The case to which Carter had referred had been a one-off. It was well-known precisely because it had been so unusual. That kind of thing simply didn't happen to middle-class people who ran a cleaning business and lived in a house on an executive estate in a suburb of Cardiff. Mrs Moorcroft was the epitome of 'normal'. She wasn't some needy, desperate-housewife-type. She wasn't a narcissist who'd effectively ruin her only child's life in order to garner the attention she felt she deserved.

She was respectability encapsulated.

Wasn't she?

44

Carter said it would take him twenty minutes to get to the hospital, so Mila slid off the wall and went back into the main building.

Ceci was sitting in a plush, air-conditioned waiting room, talking on her mobile phone. She raised a hand to acknowledge Mila and continued talking.

'Yes, Mrs Moorcroft, the doctor's with Briony now. Yes. Yes. Absolutely. Of course.' She glanced at Mila. 'My colleague is waiting to speak with me. Why don't you go and make the necessary travel arrangements, and I'll call you back as soon as I have any news at this end? Wonderful! I'll talk to you later.'

She disconnected the call.

'Happy camper, I presume,' said Mila.

Ceci smiled. 'It's the most rewarding part of our work, isn't it? Telling a concerned relative that we've found their loved one, safe and well. I never tire of delivering good news.'

Mila nodded. 'Me neither,' she said.

'You still look worried, Mila. Is everything all right?' Ceci asked.

'Yes,' said Mila, pushing aside the unease generated by her conversation with Carter. 'Everything's fine. Carter's offered to pick me up and take me back to Morannez, so I can be there for Ani. Will you be okay here on your own?'

'Of course. I'll wait until all the tests are finished and make sure Briony is comfortable. I'll drive myself home.'

'It might be a good idea to have someone keep an eye on Briony overnight,' Mila said.

'You think she might do a midnight flit?'

'It's possible.'

'I don't think we can lock her in. But perhaps Emmanuelle could give her something to help her sleep.'

On the face of it, this was a pragmatic course of action. But the prospect of drugging Briony to guarantee her compliance after everything she'd said that afternoon – and after what Carter had said about Billie, was disquieting.

On the one hand, giving Briony sedatives was the sensible option. On the other, it could be regarded – almost – as a kind of abuse.

* * *

'Are you coming in?' Mila asked Carter when they arrived back at the sea house. 'There's some beer in the fridge if you fancy one. I'm going for a swim.'

She swung her leg over the back of the bike and jumped off.

'I wouldn't mind a swim too,' said Carter.

He took the key out of the ignition and pulled off his gauntlets.

Mila unclipped her motorcycle helmet and pulled it off over her head. She shook out her hair. 'You're welcome to join me. I could find you a pair of Charlie's trunks.'

'I'm wearing boxers,' said Carter. 'They'll do.'

'Okay.'

She put the helmet down on the dry grass beside the bike.

'Come on in,' she said. 'We'll get a drink first.'

Carter followed her into the house, through the back door that had been left ajar.

'Do you always leave the doors open?' he asked.

'It wasn't me, it was Anaïs.'

'Does *she* always leave the doors open?'

'We're supposed to lock the door and hide the key in the garden whenever we leave the house, but Ani's not very good at remembering, especially when she's with her friends.' Mila sighed as she looked around her. It looked as if a bomb had gone off in the kitchen: plates, cutlery, glasses and odds and ends of food were strewn about. The teenagers had clearly made themselves a picnic. 'The trouble is, when Ani goes to the beach, she regards it as not *really* leaving the house.'

She picked up a few items of crockery and moved them to the sink.

'Emmanuelle says it's an actual developmental thing, this teenage untidy phase,' said Carter. 'It's ubiquitous across cultures and it's perfectly normal.'

'Yeah? What exactly is the evolutionary benefit of young people being incapable of putting things away?'

'I dunno. But Harry's currently evolving big time.'

Mila smiled. 'I bet Briony Moorcroft never made a mess like this.' She considered for a moment and then said: 'She must've missed out on loads of the growing-up experiences. She never got to do any of the usual, rebellious things that young people do.'

'She's made up for it over the last couple of weeks.'

'Yes, she has.'

Mila ran a cloth under the tap, and started to wipe the table. She felt profoundly grateful that Ani was as she was: normal. She wouldn't want to change anything about her niece.

Nothing at all.

45

Mila collected together her towel and swimsuit from her bedroom and she took a second towel for Carter from the linen cupboard. When she came downstairs, she found him rooting through a pile of old papers and card she'd stacked for recycling.

'What are you doing?' she asked.

'Just looking,' he said. 'What is all this?'

Tell him it's none of his business, said Sophie.

'Junk I found amongst Charlie's stuff,' Mila explained. 'Some of those folders were in the kitchen drawers.'

'These are Toussaints' folders.'

'Yeah, but they're empty. I'm guessing they're old ones Sophie brought home to reuse, but she and Charlie never got round to creating a filing system.'

'You think they needed a filing system?'

'Why else would Sophie have brought the folders home?'

Carter shrugged.

'When I first moved in,' said Mila, 'their paperwork was in chaos. I kept finding random bills and letters from the tax department all over the place. I assumed Sophie meant to sort it out one day.'

'She and Charlie weren't the most organised people.'

'No.'

Mila passed the towel to Carter. He lay down the folders he'd been holding. On the front of the top one, written in black marker were two words: *Norah Anning*. The writing was Sophie's, distinctively flamboyant, like everything she did. The sight of it was enough to trigger a pang of loneliness in Mila.

'I don't know who Norah Anning is,' said Mila, making random conversation to stop herself missing Sophie. 'Some client of the agency, I guess. She must have been before my time.' She glanced at the clock. 'If we're going to swim, we'd better go now.'

She picked up the bottle of wine she'd opened and two glasses. Carter took the bottle from her. Together, they left the house, and walked down the sandy path, scattered with pine cones, through the woods that led to the little beach that the family had always used.

It wasn't a private beach, but few people knew about it, so it had always felt as if it belonged to them and their friends alone. Mila had happy memories of time spent there; long summer days swimming and relaxing with Sophie, building sandcastles with the young Anaïs. Charlie, with his unashamed public-school-educated Britishness, had organised the games. She remembered him so clearly: barefoot, trousers rolled up, cigarette in his mouth, holding a cricket bat in front of improvised stumps, giving instructions to the fielders.

Before that, of course, she had been here with the *Bande Sauvage* when they were all young and... well, not exactly carefree, but innocent in many ways. It was fortunate that they had not known what the future held. How could they have borne it?

Stop it, Sophie said. *Don't go all melancholy on me, Mila Shepherd. I had a wonderful life!*

And you threw it away, didn't you?

Mila looked at Carter, slightly ahead of her. She looked at his broad shoulders, and the shape of his arms, one hand holding the neck of the wine bottle. She looked at his hips and the way his jeans were baggy around the knees, and she saw his bow-legged gait and remembered that he had always walked like that, with something of a swagger that she'd always, secretly, admired. This, she realised, was something she could never confess to anyone.

Except me, Sophie said smugly.

I never told you that.

But I knew.

Really? You knew how I felt, and you still got involved with Carter? Even though you didn't really want him?

I didn't set out to hurt you, Mila.

Mila frowned. Was it true? Had Sophie known she held a torch for Carter? She couldn't be sure.

A pause. Then Sophie asked slyly: *Do you still want Carter?*

I'm engaged to Luke.

That's not what I asked.

Mila walked on, through the heat of the afternoon.

She followed Carter past the group of menhirs known locally as 'the wedding party'.

He looked back over his shoulder. 'Do we still have to touch all seven stones for good luck?'

'We do,' said Mila, quietly thrilled that he remembered the tradition. She followed him as he walked between them, her hand reaching out after his. The ancient granite was warm beneath her fingertips. It felt exactly the same as it always had.

They could hear Ani and her friends before they reached the beach.

Mila waved to Ani, who gave the briefest of acknowledgements. The youngsters were playing with a frisbee and Mila didn't want to intrude or embarrass Ani, so she dropped her towel close to the wiry grass that rooted amongst the dunes, and Carter did the same. She changed into her costume, and he undressed. Mila took care not to look at him. Normally, she would have run down to the sea, but because Carter was there, she walked sedately, not quite knowing what to do with her arms.

How good the cooling air felt against her skin. How cleansing.

They entered the sea together, but Carter immediately went ahead, diving into the waves. Mila walked slowly, enjoying the incremental sensations of immersing herself in the sea; the cold water lapping around her ankles, the wet sand, ripples made by the incoming tide, making lines beneath the soles of her feet, the sensation of the waves slapping her stomach as she went in deeper. At the moment when she gave in to the cold and dived into an oncoming swell, she gasped, the water holding up her body, making her weightless and free.

She'd been anticipating this wondrous cold for what seemed like an eternity of heat. She swam out as far as she was comfortable and then lay on her back and floated with her arms extended to either side, enjoying the rhythm of the water moving beneath her, raising her and then letting her fall again, the sunlight glorious in her eyes, shattered into fragments by her lashes. Carter was further out still, swimming a business-like crawl in the deeper water.

Mila could hear the teenagers' laughter from the beach; some of the boys had voices that sounded deep as men now; others hadn't broken yet. They shouted, she knew, because they were shy. It was a strategy to cover up their lack of confidence.

That thought made her think of Billie. She, perhaps, was the same. She was physically large, but perhaps the swearing, the violence, was a smokescreen.

No, she told herself. *Don't you start feeling sorry for Billie Dexter.*

The following thought was of Briony and Mrs Moorcroft. Only one of them could be telling the truth, the other must be lying. Either Mrs Moorcroft was telling the truth, and Briony was seriously ill and needed the drugs she'd been taking to survive, or Briony was telling the truth, and she was being drugged by her mother in a bid to convince the world that she was ill when she wasn't.

But *why?*

Why would anyone do that to their own child?

* * *

When Mila came out of the water, she walked past Ani's group, settled now, on their own towels, drinking Coke and eating the sandwiches they'd prepared in the sea house kitchen. Music was playing out of somebody's phone. They were cheerful and rowdy, teasing one another; full of laughter. This was exactly how the *Bande Sauvage* would have looked to any adult who saw them on the beach almost three decades earlier.

Ani's hair was wet. She was wearing a bikini, and her skin was tanned; her limbs long and coltish, her wrists and ankles slender. Mila was, momentarily, stunned by the beauty of her niece, and also by how young she looked, and how natural; a creature of the sea and beach; nature's child.

She remembered the old song, 'Boys of Summer', that Sophie had been mad about one year and sang all the time until Mila had to beg her to stop. But Sophie had misheard the lyrics. She thought Don Henley was singing about a poisoned summer. Her mistake had tainted the nostalgic words for Mila ever since.

Ani didn't know any of this. She was holding half a baguette stuffed with cheese and olives between her hands. Her mouth was full.

'Hi!' she said to Mila around the food, and Mila said, 'Hi!' back in a cheerful voice.

It took every ounce of self-control she possessed to stop herself throwing her arms around her niece and telling her how she adored her.

She walked back to the dunes, picked up her towel, wrapped it around her shoulders and sat on the sand to dry off.

Gaslighting, said Sophie.

Shh, Sophie.

Think about it. Someone in this case is gaslighting.

Mila was familiar with this concept, a means by which one person manipulated another, and also, sometimes, the world around them both, to make lies appear to be truths, and vice versa.

It was a peaceful evening and she didn't want to think about gaslighting in relation to Briony Moorcroft. She didn't want these niggling thoughts to be in her mind, but it was too late. They were there.

Carter came out of the sea and walked up the beach. The sinking sun was painting one side of his body gold. The beach and the sea behind him were particularly beautiful at this time, the border between day and night.

Mila pulled her knees up to her chin and concentrated on drawing a pattern in the sand with her finger so that her eyes wouldn't inadvertently see Carter's body: the musculature of his chest, the tight, wet curls of his body hair, or the shape of his genitals, which she knew would be perfectly visible beneath the wet boxer shorts.

'Hey,' he said, dropping down beside her, spraying her with droplets of water.

'Did you enjoy that?'

'It was fantastic.'

He reached beside him for the wine bottle, unscrewed the lid and poured them both a glass.

'Here,' he said, passing one to her. They chinked. 'To a good day's work well done and a happy ending. Briony Moorcroft safe in hospital under the care of my hugely competent ex-wife and Billie Dexter locked up by the excellent Lorient police force.'

He lifted the glass to his lips, but paused before drinking.

'What?' asked Mila. 'What are you thinking?'

'It's Billie,' he said. 'Something I need to check out.'

46

After Carter had left the sea house, Mila tidied up, and made a salad for supper. Then she sat on the back doorstep and searched the internet for the case of the American woman who had been shot by her daughter's boyfriend, the case that Carter had mentioned earlier.

She found it soon enough. It had attracted a huge amount of media attention at the time, probably because of its weirdness. Several books had been written about those involved; there'd even been a film and a television mini series.

The daughter had, like Briony Moorcroft, been famous for being ill. Only this girl had been a mega-celebrity in America. Her mother had manipulated the health system to back up her lies about her daughter's various, complex medical conditions. The two of them had been given all kinds of perks: a new car; backstage passes to Disney; some kind-hearted souls had even built them a new home.

There were other similarities. The American girl was, like Briony, small for her age and child-like as a teenager. Her mother had used various strategies to avoid her lies being detected. She changed doctors often, and claimed, when challenged for proof of her daughter's condition, that her medical records had been lost. Eventually, the young woman met a man online and between them they came up with the plan to kill the mother to free the daughter from her abuse. Both the daughter and her male friend were currently in prison, locked up for murder. The daughter was quoted as saying she was happier now, because at least she was being allowed to live a 'normal life'.

Mila pressed her fingers into her temples.

Inside her head, Sophie whistled.

It's so messed up, she said.

Isn't it just?

In the case of the American girl, it was a paediatric neurologist who questioned the diagnosis of muscular dystrophy which her mother was propounding.

According to the article Mila was reading, it was this same doctor who first put forward the theory that the mother in this case had Munchausen Syndrome by proxy.

Mila had heard of this, but didn't know much about it. Again, she asked the internet for help.

She discovered that basic Munchausen Syndrome – or factitious disorder – was a condition in which people faked symptoms of illness, or deliberately brought them about, in order to attract attention and sympathy. The lengths to which people would go to convince medical professionals they were sick were shocking: poisoning themselves, cutting themselves, rubbing dirt into existing wounds to create infections, eating faecal matter to bring about gastric problems.

Munchausen Syndrome by proxy was the same condition, only this time a different person – often, but not always, the mother – inflicted the fake symptoms onto a third party, usually their child, or else caused real symptoms in order to trigger a diagnosis.

The psychological foundation for the behaviour was the same – a desire to attract attention and sympathy. Being the parent of a very ill child invariably inspired an outpouring of heartfelt emotion, and a rush of other people wanting to help. It meant, Mila realised with a sinking heart, that the mother of a child in this situation would be invited to all the fundraising events, and 'celebrations' to which the sick child was invited. She would also be able to enjoy donated holidays and other gifts and treats. For a mother with Munchausen Syndrome by proxy, having a child like Briony would be like a narcotic addict having unlimited access to heroin.

The behaviour of such a mother was the polar opposite to the maternal ideal. A mother was supposed to nurture and care for her child. She was supposed to do all she could to keep the child in good health, not deliberately make it ill.

On rare occasions, Mila discovered, the 'sick' child, who in fact usually had nothing wrong with them, was killed by their parent.

Shit, thought Mila. *Shit, shit, shit.*

She stood up and paced around the sea house; there wasn't enough space for the pacing she needed to do to alleviate her anxiety, so she went outside and walked around the garden. Swallows were hunting in the gloaming. The bats would be out soon. The evening air smelled faintly of smoke, but the temperature was cooling and Mila sensed that dew would be laid down in the grass tonight.

What if Briony was telling the truth, she wondered.

What if they'd got it all wrong?

47

Mila's phone rang. It was Luke.

She answered instantly. All her previous tetchiness had dissipated. She wanted to tell her fiancé that she was sorry for being so absent, that she'd been thinking of him, that she loved him, that she was exhausted and confused, that her head was in a mess, that she was desperate to see him, that she wanted to marry him and be his wife and live with him and share his bed.

She wasn't 100 per cent certain that all those facts were true, but her overriding instinct was to make things right. There was so much horribleness in the world, so much weirdness, so many strange, damaged, damaging people, and Luke was an honourable man with a kind heart. He might wind her up the wrong way sometimes, but he was definitely one of the good ones and, as such, she should value and appreciate him.

'Hi,' was all she actually said, but perhaps the genuine warmth in her voice transmitted to Luke because he said: 'Hi,' too and didn't add 'at last', or make any other kind of comment to set the conversation off on a snarky footing. 'It's nice to hear your voice,' Luke said, but not in a sarcastic way and then he waited for Mila to speak.

She didn't know where to start. So much had happened since she last spoke to him and there was so much going on inside her head. Instead of trying to explain, she stuck to the British convention and asked about the weather. 'Is it still hot in Bristol?'

'Stifling. People are getting drunk and taking off their clothes and jumping into the docks.'

'Oh no.'

'Oh yes.'

'I hope they're keeping their mouths closed.'

He laughed. 'If the heatwave carries on, I'll be tempted to jump in myself.'

'Don't,' said Mila. Then she added: 'Although Carter and I went swimming this evening and it was lovely.'

'You and Carter?'

'Yes.' Shit, why had she told him that?

Luke didn't know that Mila had once loved Carter because she had never seen any reason to tell him. Dead Sophie could insinuate all she liked, but there was nothing now between Mila and Carter beyond friendship. Yet, Mila habitually edited Carter out of the stories she told Luke. It wasn't that she had anything to hide, but still she was compelled to distort the truth. She didn't know *why* she didn't tell Luke that Carter regularly gave her lifts on his motorbike for example, but she didn't.

She felt awkward now, as if she'd betrayed Luke somehow, when she hadn't.

Oh, what is wrong with me? she thought.

'Sea swimming? That sounds great,' said Luke. His voice had changed ever so slightly.

There was a silence, then they both spoke together, she asking him about his case, he asking about hers.

'You go first,' said Luke, and Mila told him briefly about the events of the day, about how it had shifted from a search for an abducted girl into a possible murder case, which had then resolved itself and now there was an actual chance that Billie's motivation had genuinely been to help Briony, rather than harm her.

'Even if the two of them are mistaken about Briony, and she is really sick, it seems Billie's intentions were good,' Mila said. 'Misguided, but altruistic.'

'Munchausen by proxy does happen,' said Luke, 'and more than you'd think. I worked on a case, ages ago. It was an outwardly respectable family. They were middle-class, lived in the kind of house the *Daily Mail* would approve of. The woman was educated, well-spoken, nobody had a bad word to say about her, and she gave every appearance of being a devoted mother. But it turned out she'd been poisoning her kid with salt. It only came to light when he was admitted to hospital in a coma.'

'But, this is what I don't get, Luke, *why* would she do that? She wasn't after tickets to Disney, presumably.'

'No, no. It was purely for the attention and the approbation. So that everyone would know she had a sick child and think she was a star for taking such good care of him.' He paused. 'In that respect, it's a typical personality disorder; an inadequate individual needing to provoke attention to fill up some massive great hole of insecurity within their psyches.'

'No matter how successful their lives apparently are.'

'Exactly.' He paused. 'Would that description apply to the mother of your girl?'

'Mrs Moorcroft? I don't know much about her. She told me she used to be a nurse...'

'People with Munchausen by proxy usually have in-depth medical knowledge. They couldn't do what they do without it.' He paused. 'But you don't know for sure yet that this is what you're dealing with?'

'No. We won't know either way until we hear back from the hospital.' Mila stopped talking to wave to Ani and her friends who had emerged from between the trees, coming back along the track towards the sea house. 'Anyway, that's enough of the Moorcrofts for now. Tell me about your case. How's it going? Are you any closer to wrapping it up?'

He told her. It was protracted and brutal and bloody and compli-cated, and it was weighing him down. Mila knew how much it took out of her fiancé, dealing with hardcore crime every day. She knew that what he needed was to be able to come home to a supportive partner who would listen to him while he unburdened himself. He needed someone to encourage him to exercise; to go for a drink with him; to suggest a spontaneous outing to one of the local restaurants; to provide some lightness in his life; some fun.

He needed her to be with him. He needed her back in Bristol.

48

Some of the teenagers called goodbye and faded away into the evening. Ani asked if her closest friends could sleep over and Mila said of course they could. After dinner, the girls disappeared up into the bedrooms, and Mila locked up and closed the shutters but left the windows open for the air. She put some pillows onto the sofa and spread a sheet to lie on. From above her, she could hear music and laughter, but it was muted, not loud enough to disturb her.

The sofa in the sea house was old, big, squashy, comfortable, and the living room was cool. The fresh breeze that had been skipping over the waves of the ocean came through the narrow gaps in the shutters like dozens of tiny zephyrs. It sang a lullaby in the branches of the trees in the wooded area between the sea house and the beach. It brought down the temperature a fraction, but the wind was the enemy of those trying to put out the fires.

The sea house felt safe, but on the radio, the head of the Finistère Firefighters' Association said more resources were needed for the force to combat wildfires that were increasing in number and ferocity. The presenter spoke to a woman farmer who had lost crops and livestock. She described the silence of the blackened moorland close to her home; there was, she said, none of the usual clamour of insects; no birdsong.

Mila couldn't bear to listen further. She turned off the radio, and sat up for a while, reading articles on her computer, going down various Munchausen rabbit holes. The more she learned, the more she was both fascinated and disturbed. Human beings were such strange, complicated, perverse creatures. And the difference between normal and psychologically dysfunctional seemed to be no more than a matter of scale. Telling a few untruths here and there, was commonplace behaviour, necessary, in fact, to oil the mechanisms of a society, but there was a line that those with personality disorders crossed.

Billie Dexter's bullish approach to life appeared destructive, but it was straightforward. If any of what she had said about Mrs Moorcroft turned out to be true, then Briony's mother was going to be far harder to deal with.

Before she settled down, Mila carried out one last internet search, for the word 'Tadcu' that she'd seen tattooed on Billie's neck.

It turned out to be a South Wales colloquialism. It meant 'Granddad'.

* * *

Mila did not sleep well. In her restless state, she imagined she heard a car driving up the track to the sea house. Tangled in her dream, she found herself at the window, looking out at the Moorcrofts, who were demanding to see their daughter. Behind them was a bitter-faced man, with a long white beard, and pointy ears, who Mila – although she had never seen the man – recognised as Billie Dexter's grandfather. He was surrounded by an army of garden gnomes come to life, wielding pitchforks and blazing torches.

She woke in a panic to find everything that she thought she'd seen and heard wasn't real. She was still on the sofa, her legs wound in the thin cotton sheet. Berthaud was playing with a spider on the floor, her body shape illuminated by stripes of moonlight falling through the slats of a shutter onto the floorboards. The sea house was quiet; the only sound was the soft sighing of the breeze in the leaves of the trees beyond.

'Idiot,' Mila told herself. 'Gnomes! For goodness' sake!'

She plumped her pillow, straightened the sheet, tried to settle.

Her thoughts drifted to the sea; to the wreckage that Monsieur Bolloré had spotted amongst the rocks. She closed her eyes and tried to work through the consequences of the only two outcomes: that the wreckage be identified as being *Moonfleet*, or it turning out to be unconnected.

And then, before she knew it, she was back in the boathouse at the far end of Lydia's garden, in Maidenhead, and the river water was lapping up against the wooden frets – Mila could smell it, foul and warm – and there was Sophie's body, face down, with her hair floating around her. Her hair and her skin were greenish in colour and her fingers were horribly swollen, drifting lifelessly on either side of her head.

Mila woke again, with a start.

This was hopeless. She was not destined to sleep. She would get up and make the most of this unscheduled early start.

She pushed off the sheet and crept up the stairs, stepping as carefully as she could on the soles of her bare feet to avoid the creakiest of the treads. Light was already coming through the little window on the landing, the glass light-catchers that Sophie had hung in front of it making colourful spangles of brightness on the lumpy old wall opposite. Mila had also hung up a string of glass beads she'd found stuffed into a sock amongst the assembled bric-a-brac in Charlie's wardrobe. The combined effect now was so pretty and so cheerful that the horrors of the night immediately subsided. Mila felt a rush of affection for this house, this place. It was home. It was safe; she belonged here.

Carefully, she opened the door to her bedroom and looked inside. It was dark in that room, the shutters kept out all but a few narrow strips of light, but Mila could see a tumble of young girls asleep on the bed. She closed the door again and carefully opened the door to the other room. This room, Ani's bedroom, was strewn with clothes and make-up and it smelled sweet; of vanilla and pear.

Ani was sharing the bed with her best friend, Pernille. They were lying together, facing one another, Pernille's hand on Ani's waist. They reminded Mila of the dolls in Briony Moorcroft's dolls' house. Two friends; close as sisters: exactly as Mila and Sophie once had been.

Mila went downstairs again. She put the coffee-maker on to boil and was forking tuna into a saucer for Berthaud when her phone buzzed. It was Carter.

'You awake?' he asked. He always asked this when he called at some unsociable hour.

'I am now,' said Mila. It was her stock reply.

'I thought you'd want to know that the police have finished excavating the disturbed ground behind the sheep shed at the commune. All they found were soiled towels, sheets and other crap. Billie said she'd buried them because she couldn't burn them because of the ban on fire-lighting. Also, the remains of various credit cards and other bits and pieces that she'd stolen.'

'So what will happen to Billie now?'

'She's been moved to Morannez police station where the Welsh contingent will come and pick her up.'

'Okay.'

'Meanwhile, I'm trying to get hold of the director of the facility where Billie was treated for her addiction. I want to check out if some of the stuff she's been saying is true.'

'What about the Moorcrofts?'

'They're flying into Brest this morning. Their plan is to collect Briony and drive home together in the van. Billie had the key about her person when she was arrested. I've got it now.'

Mila hesitated. 'We shouldn't hand Briony back to her parents until we're certain she's going to be safe with them.'

'I agree,' said Carter. 'Which brings me to the reason I'm calling so early. Emmanuelle wants to see us together – you, me and Ceci – before she goes into work. The most convenient place to meet, if it's okay with you, would be the sea house in about forty minutes' time.'

49

Mila was showered and dressed, but she hadn't put make-up on and her hair was still damp when she saw Emmanuelle Jackson walking across the garden. Emmanuelle looked impossibly elegant, with her silky black hair in a long bob, the burnt orange colour of her linen dress accentuating the warm tones of her skin. She was wearing chic designer sunglasses even though the sun wasn't that strong yet.

Mila remembered Emmanuelle as a teenager. She'd been the leader of the *Bande Sauvage*, the one the others looked up to. She'd been a little older; more confident. And she'd been strong, not a street-fighting kind of toughness, born of being brought up in poverty, like Melodie Sohar – Melodie Valette, as she'd been then – but a strength instilled by the role-modelling of her mother and compounded by intelligence.

Mila met her at the door and they kissed one another's cheeks in the French way.

'Hi!'

'Hello, Mila. It's good to see you.'

'Shall we sit inside or outside?' Mila asked. 'Either way, we'll have to keep our voices down because my niece is having a sleepover.'

'Outside,' said Emmanuelle, 'it's too beautiful to be indoors.' She looked around her. 'I haven't seen any smoke this morning.'

'I think we're okay here.'

'Although this latest fire seems to be jumping about all over. The wind keeps changing.'

'It's a nightmare for the authorities.'

Mila brushed fallen leaves and cobwebs off the old, wooden garden seats and invited Emmanuelle to sit at the table. Then Mila brought out the coffee tray and returned for a second tray of plates, cutlery and other breakfast accoutrements.

Berthaud was making the most of the morning cool and hunting amongst the long grass, sending up moths and emerging with her coat covered in seeds. The resident blackbird was singing joyfully from the branches of the old hawthorn.

'I haven't been to this house for ages,' said Emmanuelle, helping Mila unload the trays. 'Not since the *Bande Sauvage* days.'

Her fingers moved to the triskele tattoo on the inside of her wrist. Mila saw, and felt the old teenage loneliness, haunting her still.

Emmanuelle continued: 'I remember having sleepovers here with Sophie when we were teenagers.' A pause. 'You must have been here sometimes too, Mila.'

There was no malice intended in that last comment, but Mila, ever sensitive to the fact that her role in the *Bande Sauvage* had only been incidental, was stung anew.

Originally from the nearby town of Quimper, Emmanuelle had, at first, been almost as much of an outsider as Mila, although she'd quickly established herself as the key player. Her mother, Bathsheba, was a singer who performed during the summer months at the beach bar and the holiday park during the week. On Saturdays, Bathsheba Aubert put on a sequinned gown and was the star of the cabaret at the Grand Hotel in Bloemel-sur-Mer. All three businesses were owned and operated by the Girard family. Arnaud and Guillaume Girard, were, as a consequence, closest to Emmanuelle, the three of them spending the most time together simply because of logistics.

One year, Mila remembered, there'd been discord between Emmanuelle and the Girard boys. She couldn't recall the details, but it had been on account of a falling out amongst the adults. Was Bathsheba alleged to have stolen from Monsieur Girard? Or had he propositioned her? Perhaps neither of those was correct, but there'd been something, and Emmanuelle had left the town early that year, with her mother.

They were ostensibly equals now, Mila and Emmanuelle; adults living their own lives. Yet Emmanuelle was better educated and more highly qualified, she had an important job, even her clothes sense was superior. Everything about her was still an improvement on Mila, or that was how it felt.

Strange how the old insecurities were still so close to the surface.

Strange too, Mila thought, that of all the *Bande Sauvage* girls, it was Emmanuelle who had ended up marrying Carter Jackson. She recalled how, when she first heard the news, she'd assumed their relationship was a rebound: Carter turning to Emmanuelle after he'd been rejected by Sophie. At the time, it had felt like a double rejection to Mila: not only had Carter not turned to her, but he'd chosen Emmanuelle, someone with whom he ostensibly had little in common, beyond their shared Black heritage. But the marriage had been a good one. Carter and Emmanuelle had settled in Canada, where they'd established successful careers and raised their son. Mila didn't know why they'd decided to separate. Carter had never spoken of it and there was no apparent animosity between the pair.

Now Emmanuelle smiled warmly. 'It's good to see you, Mila,' she said. 'Carter's told me how you stepped in to look after Sophie's daughter, and how you help out at the agency too. It can't have been easy for you. I understand you've been an absolute star.'

Mila didn't know how to respond to this praise. It wasn't entirely justified because, truthfully, she hadn't had much choice in the matter. Sometimes her new roles – roles she had never asked for – felt like a privilege. Other times, they'd undoubtedly been a burden.

'What about you? Are you glad to be back in Brittany?' she asked, to deflect attention. 'Is Harry settled? He's what? Fourteen now?'

'We're both good. I didn't know how it would pan out, but you know what? It's been great! I like my work, the people are wonderful and Harry's settled right in. He's really into kayaking and football. He sees more of his father now that we're divorced and living in Brittany than he did when we were married and living in Toronto and Carter was working all hours. It's less stressful, and I get to spend time with my mother.'

'Of course. How is Bathsheba?'

'She's fine. She has an apartment in Bloemel, and still acts the diva. She won't go out unless she's fully made-up and dressed like a film star. You must come over one day and we'll all have lunch.'

Before Mila could respond to this kind invitation, she heard the sound of engines approaching: Ceci in her convertible, followed by Carter on his motorbike, the noise reverberating through the morning air. Emmanuelle's attitude immediately changed. She smoothed her dress, and straightened her shoulders.

'Here they are,' she said. 'We can get down to business.'

50

When the coffee was poured, the four adults sat down around the table.

Ceci had brought croissants, madeleines and apricot pastries, still warm from the Morannez boulangerie and Mila provided a pot of Madame Abadie's home-made apricot jam. They each helped themselves to breakfast.

Mila observed Carter and Emmanuelle. She thought she detected a slight undercurrent of tension between them, but they were politely friendly with one another.

'We're all anxious to hear your opinion as to the state of Briony Moorcroft's health,' Ceci said to Emmanuelle, once the pleasantries were over.

Emmanuelle wiped her fingertips on a napkin and said: 'Before we start, Mila, Briony told me her mother gave you some of the drugs she was taking every day.'

'She did,' said Mila.

'Could I see them?'

'They're in the glove compartment of my car,' said Ceci.

Mila retrieved the bag containing Briony's medication and gave it to Emmanuelle, who took the contents out, one by one, and lined them on the table. She looked at them, frowning.

'This,' she said, pointing to one of the boxes, 'is Fentanyl. It's a synthetic opioid used to treat chronic pain. As an analgesic, it's fifty times stronger than heroin. And this, Oxycodone, is a similar, highly addictive drug that's frequently abused.'

Carter's phone rang.

'Excuse me,' he said, 'I need to take this.' He stood up and walked a little way distant to answer.

'But Briony does have an unusual mixture of life-threatening illnesses, doesn't she?' Mila asked Emmanuelle, doubt rising inside her like bile.

Emmanuelle shook her head.

'We've scanned her,' she said. 'We've examined her. We've taken bloods. We haven't had all the results back yet, but there is nothing obviously wrong with Briony Moorcroft. She's malnourished, and has poor muscle definition, but that's because she's not active. Her teeth are in a terrible state and she suffers from chronic constipation – these are side effects of the drugs she's been taking. Her amenorrhea, in my opinion, is a result of hormonal imbalances caused by her lifestyle. In a nutshell, she's presenting as a healthy-ish, nineteen-year-old who hasn't been getting enough good food, fresh air or exercise.'

'Mon Dieu,' Ceci murmured.

Mila had been prepared for news of this kind, she'd been half-expecting it, but hearing it from the doctor was still shocking.

An image of Billie, face-down on the ground after her arrest in Lorient sprang to mind: Billie protesting that she'd been telling the truth.

'Cancer can be hard to spot, can't it?' asked Ceci, also struggling to come to terms with what Emmanuelle was saying.

'It can. And we'll need to wait for the other test results to be absolutely confident that Briony is clear. But...' Emmanuelle said, 'I'm often dealing with people who have cancer. You learn to recognise the subtle, physiological signs. I can't be certain, but in my opinion, Briony Moorcroft does not have cancer, nor does she have any kind of autoimmune condition.'

Ceci and Mila exchanged glance.

Carter finished his call and returned to the table. 'What have I missed.'

'Emmanuelle's professional opinion is that Briony Moorcroft is not seriously ill,' said Mila.

'Jesus.'

Carter looked to Emmanuelle, who nodded her assent.

'These drugs,' Emmanuelle indicated the array of packages laid out on the table in front of them, 'aren't cancer drugs. They're a combination of opioids, benzodiazepines, and this one' – she lifted a box of tablets – 'is usually prescribed to treat conditions such as narcolepsy. I can't imagine any circumstance where a regular doctor would use this cocktail of medication to treat... well, *anything*.'

'Is there any reason at all why someone would give these drugs to someone else?' Mila asked.

'To control them. To take away pain. To make them live in a hazy world in which they were never fully participating.'

Ceci pressed the tips of her fingers together. 'So, do you think we're dealing with medical negligence?'

'It's not negligence,' said Emmanuelle. 'What's been done to Briony Moorcroft is deliberate. Someone has prescribed these drugs for her, and someone's been giving them to her, and that someone, she's told me herself, is her mother. I don't believe there ever was a doctor who diagnosed cancer and this imaginary autoimmune disease. It's all a fantasy dreamed up by Mrs Moorcroft. She's turned her daughter into a zombie.'

Briony had used that word too.

'But how is Mrs Moorcroft getting hold of these drugs?' Ceci asked.

'She might have obtained the medication illegally,' said Emmanuelle. 'She might have sourced it on the dark web. You can buy anything if you know where to look.'

'I don't think Mrs Moorcroft would know what the dark web was,' said Mila.

'Or she might be faking the prescriptions herself somehow.'

'She does have a medical background.'

'There we are then.'

'Would it really be possible to keep a deception going for all this time, without any genuine doctors being involved?'

'Doctors have been involved,' said Emmanuelle. 'Briony has been admitted to accident and emergency numerous times. But those doctors weren't looking for the cancer, they were treating the presenting problem: seizure, vomiting, whatever. When Mrs Moorcroft thanked them via the media after Briony's subsequent recovery, it was *she* who mentioned Briony's life-threatening illnesses and that was how the myth was perpetuated.'

'It must have been exhausting,' said Ceci, 'managing so many lies.'

'It is a classic case of Munchausen Syndrome by proxy,' said Emmanuelle. 'Briony was lucky that she had a friend who recognised what was going on and was willing to take risks to help her. Billie had the right idea about removing Briony from the situation she was in, and getting her off the drugs, even if her methods were unconventional.'

'She tied her to the bed,' said Mila, 'in the burning heat, in a sheep shed.'

'Yes, she did. And I would never advocate unsupervised withdrawal, like Briony's just experienced, for any addict. It's potentially very dangerous. But Billie's research must have been meticulous. She told Briony exactly what to expect, *she* knew what was coming, and she looked after her friend competently.'

Carter cleared his throat. 'I've just been speaking to the doctor who treated Billie in rehab,' he said. 'She says Billie expressed an interest in training to work with young people with addictions. The last the doctor heard, Billie was teaching herself to read so she could study addiction psychology.'

Mila realised how everything that Billie had done, all the behaviours they had assumed were destructive, could be regarded as heroic when seen in this alternative light. She felt a pang of deep shame at the assumptions that had been made about Billie Dexter, and the way she'd been treated.

'We need to help Billie,' she said.

'Unfortunately, Billie has broken a good many laws,' said Ceci.

'We can't stop her being taken back to Wales,' said Carter. 'She's going to have to face the music.'

'We have to do something!'

Emmanuelle finished her coffee and looked at her watch. 'I need to be off,' she said. 'The fires are making my commute tricky. But I'd just like to make one more point. Which is that people who *pretend* they or their loved ones are sick are not only playing the system, exploiting the kindness of those who want to help them and wasting the time, energy and resources of beleaguered health professionals, they're also, effectively, belittling those people who are genuinely suffering. Those people who *do* have serious illnesses don't have a choice about it, nor do the people who care for them. They would never, *ever* willingly put themselves in that situation. It makes me furious that, for some people, this is a kind of... I don't know... *fetish*.'

Ceci reached out, took Emmanuelle's hand and squeezed it. 'Thank you for doing this for Briony,' she said.

'You're welcome. The most important thing now is to protect her from her parents, especially her mother.'

'They're flying into Brittany this morning.'

'Put them off if you can. If you can't, keep Briony well away from them. Does she have any friends or relatives she could stay with?'

'Only us,' said Ceci.

'I'd be happy to release her into your care, Madame Toussaint.'

Ceci frowned. 'But Mr and Mrs Moorcroft know we're based in Morannez. It's not a large town. If Briony was here, it might be difficult to keep them apart.'

'Then we'll keep her in the hospital for another day or two,' said Emmanuelle. 'She'll be perfectly safe there.'

51

Mila could hear voices coming from the upstairs of the sea house. The girls were awake. Soon, they'd come galloping downstairs, hungry and refreshed, full of laughter, eager to embrace the day ahead. Thank God none of them was in a situation like Briony Moorcroft. Thank goodness, Mila thought, that their lives were normal. Only, of course, Ani's life was far from normal, with her mother dead and her father missing, and remembering these things and the unself-pitying way Ani dealt with her lot made Mila's heart swell with love for her niece.

If ever Ani was in trouble, Mila could only hope that she would have a friend as committed and courageous as Billie Dexter.

'So,' said Ceci, who was fond of making lists, 'we need to prioritise what we have to do next. Number one: what are we going to do about Mr and Mrs Moorcroft?'

Carter checked the time on his phone. 'Their plane is due in at Brest at eleven, so they'll be at Cardiff airport by now. I guess you could call them. Or would you rather wait and talk to them face-to-face?'

'I'd rather not see them, if it can be avoided,' said Ceci. 'Perhaps I can stop them coming.' She picked up her phone and dialled, listened for a moment, then mouthed: 'Voicemail'. She put on her phone voice and spoke into the receiver. 'Hello, Mrs Moorcroft. This is a message from Cecille Toussaint to update you on the situation here in Brittany. We had a meeting with Briony's doctor this morning and Briony is fine, none the worse for her adventures. However, the medical team has some serious concerns about Briony and the drugs you've been giving her. It's going to take a little time to establish the full truth. It seems sensible for Briony to remain in hospital until we can see a clear way forward. You may not pick up this message until you arrive in Brest, in which case I'd respectfully ask that you and your husband check into a hotel, and we'll be in touch later in the day. Thank you.'

She disconnected the call.

'Was that okay?' she asked Mila, which was un-Ceci-like. Ceci usually had the confidence of a bull elephant.

'It was perfect,' said Mila.

'Mrs Moorcroft's going to know that we're onto her when she hears that message,' said Carter.

'Do you think she'll come clean?' Mila asked.

'I think it's more likely she and her husband will go on the offensive. We could be in for a rocky ride,' Ceci answered.

Above them, there was a clatter as the bedroom window shutters were thrown open. Billie Eilish was singing, accompanied by enthusiastic French teenagers.

'Life goes on,' said Ceci brightly. Mila glanced at her, and recognised that she was using bravado to mask her own anxiety. This was unsettling to Mila, who had always regarded Ceci as bombproof. She didn't like to think of her formidable stepmother experiencing insecurities.

'What's your plan for this morning, Carter?' Ceci asked.

'I'm going to ride into Lorient and fix the tyre on the Moorcrofts' van.'

'You're going to help them?'

'I let the tyre down,' said Carter. 'I should pump it back up again in case it all turns sour and they accuse us of criminal damage. They'll need the van to be working to get home.'

'If it makes them go away more quickly, then it's a good idea,' said Ceci.

Ani came out of the house wearing one of her father's old T-shirts.

She danced barefoot across the lawn, holding Pernille's hand, and reached across to her grandmother for a kiss. 'Hello, Mamie.'

'Good morning, angel. It's so good to see you. Here! I brought extra pastries and croissants for you and your friends. Take them inside, will you? And the jam, before the flies get to it.'

'Delicioux!' said Pernille. 'Can we take them upstairs?'

'Whatever you want, *ma chère*.'

The girls gathered the food together and disappeared again.

Mila watched them. She missed the days when her own life was like theirs. All she wished for Ani was simple good health, uncomplicated love and straightforward happiness; for mornings like this one.

52

After the others had left, Mila took her laptop outside, sat on the swing seat and went back through the notes she'd made after her original meeting with Mr and Mrs Moorcroft, at their home in Carnarth. When she'd found the name of the hospital where Mrs Moorcroft had said she'd worked, the Llinas Powys, Mila looked it up and saw that it did have an orthopaedic clinic, as Mrs Moorcroft had said. She checked the staff list and recognised one of the administrators: a woman she'd worked with in her time at Frenchay Hospital, in Bristol, before its closure – Liz Rashidi.

Mila began to draft an email, reintroducing herself and asking her old friend if she could call her for a quick chat about a person of interest, when she was interrupted by Carter on the phone. She could tell from the traffic noises in the background that he was pulled over at the side of a road somewhere.

'Everything okay?'

'I'm trying to get to the police headquarters in Lorient, but the roads are closed.'

'Fire?'

'Yep. They're directing people away from the affected area.'

'Can't you try the back lanes?'

'I can, but that's not why I called. I just spoke to Arnaud Girard. The weather's perfect to go out to the Quiberon peninsula this morning to check out the wreckage. He and Monsieur Bolloré are going to head out of Morannez harbour in about forty minutes. There's no way I can make it back in time. If you want to go with them, you'll need to leave now.'

* * *

Dressed in shorts and a T-shirt, with a swimsuit underneath, a sweatshirt tied around her waist, her bare arms and legs slathered in factor fifty, Mila went to find the girls. They had moved downstairs into the living room and were huddled together watching a video on Ani's tablet.

'Are you going out?' Ani asked.

Mila had already decided that an honest approach was the best one. 'Arnaud Girard is putting out an inflatable this morning to try to get close to the wreckage Monsieur Bolloré spotted.'

'Today?'

'Now. The tides are just right apparently.'

'Who's going?'

'Arnaud Girard, me, Monsieur Bolloré, maybe one of his daughters.' Mila smiled as reassuringly as she could.

Ani's friends had gone quiet, listening to the conversation.

'What will happen when you find it?'

'If it is *Moonfleet*, then we'll let the coastguard know and... well, I don't know what the process is, Ani, but I guess the authorities will launch an investigation into how it got there.'

'Okay.'

'Will you be all right?'

Ani looked around her. Her girlfriends were all watching her with concern and affection. Pernille put an arm around Ani's shoulder and pulled her close. She kissed her square on the forehead.

'We'll look after her, Mila,' Pernille said.

'Girlfriends are a girl's best friend,' said one of the others.

And Mila knew then that Ani would be fine.

53

Mila got on her bike and cycled down the track and onto the lane that led into Morannez and towards the harbour. Here, the sky was a perfect blue colour; it was almost impossible to comprehend that just a few miles away, fires were raging out of control. The wind was taking the smoke away from Morannez.

The sea, when Mila glimpsed it between the trees, was blue too. The air had lost its early-morning freshness, but it wasn't burning hot yet. Birds were singing in the trees, and, for the first time that year, Mila had the sense of autumn encroaching; an instinct rather than an observation.

She heard distant sirens as she cycled down into the harbour, fire engines, no doubt. Those firefighters deserved medals. She slowed the bike, and spotted Arnaud Girard with Solene and Monsieur Bolloré, standing at the top of the ramp. They were holding onto the sides of a robust inflatable boat, an enormous outboard engine attached to its rear.

Mila secured her bike in the rack, waved to Solene and headed over.

Monsieur Bolloré muttered a greeting around the cigarette stump that was burning between his lips.

Arnaud said: 'Good morning, Mila.' He was barefoot, with his trousers rolled up to the knees, and was going in and out of the shallow water at the top of the ramp checking various components of the dinghy. His ankles were hairy and tanned. He was not a large man. Mila recalled that he'd been a slender teenager, smaller than the other boys; quieter. He took after his mother, Monique, a beautiful woman, a former fashion model, with a mannequin's small bones.

'Carter not coming?' Solene asked brusquely and with a twinge of hope in her voice.

'No, he's stuck somewhere between here and Lorient on account of the fires, I'm afraid. You'll have to make do with me.'

'Fair dos,' said Solene.

'Are you okay with boats, Mila?' asked Arnaud.

'Fine,' she said, although her experience was predominantly limited to ferries. Once, for Luke's birthday, she'd booked a voyage around Bristol Docks aboard the replica of *The Matthew* caravel – the ship that John Cabot had sailed from Bristol to Newfoundland in 1497. And there'd been an excruciating outing with Patrick aboard a mackerel fishing boat during a visit to his homeland of Ireland. Mila had been ten and had not realised that the mackerel would not be returned unharmed to the depths after their capture and had spent the trip crying inconsolably as the fish writhed dying in the drum at the base of the boat. In an attempt to make her feel better, the boatmen had taken to whacking them on the head to hasten their demise, which had upset Mila even more. She could still remember the scorn on the face of the fisherman's daughter.

When Mila was a child, and her parents were still married, they sometimes hired pleasure boats from Marlow, in which they motored up and down the sections of the River Thames close to their home. Lydia had loved those outings. If Patrick ever said: 'What shall we do today?' Lydia always wanted to hire a boat. She liked to look from the river up into the gardens of the houses, like hers, built along the banks.

And, of course, there'd been the dinghy trips out to the islands the *Bande Sauvage* had made as teenagers.

But all these memories, good and bad, were as nothing when it came to remembering what had happened to Sophie, the last time she went out onto the ocean.

Mila shuddered.

'Mila?'

Arnaud was waiting for her response.

'Yeah, I'm okay with boats,' Mila said.

'Okay,' said Arnaud. He picked up a life jacket and tossed it to her. 'Wear this please, just in case.'

Mila put the jacket on. It was old and cracked, and smelled musty. She tried not to picture herself bobbing on the huge Atlantic waves, her chin sticking out above the orange flotation device like an egg in a cup. Sophie hadn't been wearing a life jacket when she drowned. She and Charlie never bothered with them. Mila felt a twinge of pain; half annoyance at their selfishness, and the terrible example they were setting for their daughter and half sadness, at their loss.

Whoever had worn this jacket last must have been smaller than she was. She couldn't do up the straps. Solene, with her big, strong hands and sturdy wrists, helped her. Mila felt useless.

'Leave your bag here,' Arnaud said. 'It'll get wet otherwise. And unless your phone's salt-waterproof, I'd leave that too.'

'I was going to take some pictures,' Mila said. She'd known that Carter would be interested, and she wanted some available if Ani asked.

'If it's possible to take pictures, I'll take them,' said Arnaud. His tone was brisk.

Mila took her phone out of her pocket, put it in the canvas rucksack that had been hooked over her shoulders, and gave the bag to Arnaud, who passed it to another man, an employee of the Girard family, who was hovering nearby.

'Now, please get into the boat,' Arnaud said.

He took Mila's hand, and helped her climb onto the craft. It wasn't easy. The thing rocked and lurched as her weight shifted. The floor was rigid, the frame made solid by an inflated skeleton. Mila was to sit at the back, and to the side. Arnaud told her to hold onto the straps. It occurred to her that without her phone, she would be completely in the hands of this man, a member of the family that was rumoured to have connections with the underworld. A chill ran through her.

This was quiet Arnaud, she reminded herself, not reckless Guillaume.

You could still get out, Sophie whispered. *You don't have to do this.*

But Mila knew that she did.

Solene got in next, sitting parallel to Mila, followed by a young man wearing a polo shirt with the Girard-brand logo – a letter G drawn to look like an anchor – over the heart.

'This is Hugo,' said Arnaud, 'he's our skipper today.'

'Hi,' said Hugo.

'Hi,' the two women echoed.

Arnaud climbed into the front of the boat, and lastly came Monsieur Bolloré, unsteady but waving away assistance with the hook at the end of his left hand. He sat next to Arnaud, looking as uncomfortable in his life vest as Mila was in hers. His cigarette was still burning.

'Okay,' said Arnaud. 'Let's do this.'

To start with, progress was slow. Arnaud, Solene and Hugo paddled the craft out of the harbour, weaving carefully amongst much larger boats. The sensation was similar to being on the middle lane of a motorway in a small car with lorries on either side. Mila was afraid one of the bigger boats would set off without realising the inflatable was there. But soon the craft was nosing out between the great stone curve at the end of the protective jetty, with gulls coasting around, calling like a Greek chorus.

Only when they were out in the open sea did Hugo start the engine, and the boat began to move forward; slowly at first and then gaining momentum, until it was zipping over the waves.

The noise of the engine and the wind and the bouncing of the boat meant there was no opportunity for talking. All Mila could do was hold on tightly and try to enjoy the sensation of flying over the surface of the sea. The spray whipped into her face, saltwater stinging her eyes and wetting her hair and clothes. The world became a blur, a mix of blue and white and sunlight. There seemed to be more oxygen in Mila's lungs, more light in her eyes, more sound in her ears. Her blood pumped and her lungs grabbed at the air and she was glad that she'd tied back her hair.

This is what it was like, Sophie said, *this is why I loved sailing*, and Mila, engrossed in the experience, replied: *I get it! I understand!*

Hugo was skilled at controlling the rudder, and soon they were a long way out, with the horizon to Mila's left, sea and sky merging at a zipline of pure light, and the dark, rocky finger of the Quiberon peninsula reaching out like the blade of a knife before them.

At Monsieur Bolloré's signal, Hugo slowed the craft.

Arnaud pointed to a grey cloud hanging over the mainland.

'Another fire?' Mila asked.

'A new one,' he said, 'southwest of Lorient.'

That explained the road closure and the sirens Mila had heard earlier.

Monsieur and Solene had a brief, muted conflab, then Monsieur turned to Hugo and muttered instructions, gesturing with his hook.

Hugo said to Arnaud: 'He says we need to aim for the rock on the cliff in the shape of a bullfrog.'

Arnaud lifted a pair of binoculars slung around his neck, and held them to his eyes. 'That rock there?' he asked.

'Yes,' said Monsieur Bolloré. 'That's the one.'

54

There was a swell, breakers rolling in from hundreds, perhaps thousands, of miles away. The inflatable climbed and fell. Beneath the water, Mila spotted shoals of tiny silver fish, and larger, darker shadows moving sinuous and sinister in the deep. The sun was strong on her bare skin, the tiny hairs on her arms and thighs crusted with salt crystals left behind by the evaporation of the spray.

They came closer and closer to the rocks at the side of the peninsula. The sea was moving both ways now, travelling towards the outcrop, breaking against it and retreating in the other direction. There was a good deal of splashing as the waves smacked into one another. White foam on the surface. All the deep beneath. The tilting and lurching of the inflatable was difficult to predict. Mila's shoulders, tense with holding on, were beginning to ache. She couldn't see any sign of yellow debris.

Monsieur Bolloré had, somehow or other, managed to light a new roll-up, and every second or third breath, Mila caught the taste of smoke in her mouth. He was calling instructions, pointing.

Solene leaned forward, adding in her opinion.

'That way!' she was saying. 'That's where we went before! We followed the channel between the rocks. Be careful!'

Looking over the side of the craft, Mila saw the great jagged outcrops that lay beneath the surface like jaws. The inflatable was only just clearing the tops of the rocks; they'd be a nightmare for any hulled vessel.

'Goodness knows how you got your boat through this,' Arnaud said, admiration in his voice.

Monsieur Bolloré's eyebrows, bushy and dark, furrowed further. 'It wasn't easy,' he said, around the cigarette clamped between his lips.

'It was even calmer than this the day we first came,' said Solene.

Mila looked to the foot of the cliffs; there was nothing to indicate they were in the right place.

'There!' said Solene, half-standing, tilting the inflatable. 'See where the water is flat, that pool, that's where we need to be.'

'Slow down,' said Monsieur Bolloré, even though the craft was barely moving; when a wave pushed against it, Hugo made subtle adjustments until it seemed as if it was making no progress at all.

They inched across the flat calm of the pool surrounded by rocks. There was a line of stone behind them, forming a barrier between the wide sea and the landmass of the peninsula. Mila realised how well hidden they were; entirely concealed by the rocks from anyone at sea, and the cliffs overhang made them invisible from the peninsula. It occurred to her that if you happened to be in a small boat when a storm blew up, this would be an ideal spot to shelter. And also, to hide.

The inflatable moved slowly forward.

And then Arnaud said: 'I see it.'

Mila saw it too.

It was the butter-yellow hull of a small sailing dinghy. It did not appear wrecked, from this distance, so much as jammed up between two rocks, caught between them, firmly wedged.

The inflatable rocked from side to side, but the small yellow dinghy stayed still, even as the water sloshed and lapped about it.

Arnaud held the binoculars to his eyes even though they weren't far from the craft. Then he lowered them again, and he turned so that he was facing Mila.

She realised then that she'd hardly ever seen him without his sunglasses, but she recalled how he used to be as a teenager; a thoughtful young man; serious even. Now he looked at her with dark-lashed eyes, clear brown in colour, eyes full of genuine sorrow.

'It's Charlie's boat,' he said quietly. 'It's *Moonfleet*.'

55

'Can I see?' Mila asked.

Arnaud lifted the binoculars from around his neck and passed them to Mila. She held them to her own eyes. It took her a moment to work out how to look through them, and she struggled to hold them steady, but when she managed to do this, she could clearly see the 'M' and the two small 'o's painted onto the side of the yellow hull. Beside the letters was a stencil of a crescent moon with the tip of its lower point piercing a windswept cloud. There was no doubt that it was Charlie and Sophie's boat.

It had been here all this time, caught between the rocks.

Had Sophie been here too? Mila wondered. Had she and Charlie come to this place deliberately, to try to escape the storm? Had the boat got stuck, and had they fallen into the sea, as they tried to make their way across the rocks, to the land mass of the peninsula? Was this the exact spot where Sophie had died?

While she had the binoculars, Mila looked around, beyond the wreckage. Behind the line of rocks in which *Moonfleet* was trapped were more rocks, a tumbled, chaotic mass at the foot of the cliffs. It would be impossible to climb up from this spot. On a day like today, when the sea was calm, it might be possible to swim a little way along the peninsula, to a more accessible place, if there was one. But when the weather was bad, there really was no place to go. This would be a safe haven, but it would also be the end of the road. You would be stuck. Trapped. Invisible.

The thought made her dizzy.

She passed the binoculars back to Arnaud. He stood up, legs apart, balancing as he looked around. Then he pointed. 'There's a cave.'

'Where?'

'There, behind the stones.'

Mila shielded her eyes with her hand to look and he was right. A little way up from the base of the cliffs was a dark circle that surely had to be the entrance to a cave, hollowed out of the cliff by the sea.

'I can't see how you could get to it,' Mila said.

'You'd have to swim,' said Arnaud, 'then climb up the rocks.'

Mila nodded. Again, it would be feasible only on a day like this one, flat, calm, and at certain tide times.

Arnaud passed the binoculars to Monsieur Bolloré, and took off his life jacket.

'Are you going to try to reach it?' Mila asked, taken aback.

'I'm going to see if it's possible.'

'Arnaud...'

'It's okay. I'm a good swimmer. I won't take any stupid risks.'

He stood up, unzipped his trousers and let them fall down. Beneath, he was wearing a pair of black swimming shorts.

He wants to see if Charlie's in the cave, said Sophie. *You should go with him.*

If Charlie is there, thought Mila, *then he's dead.*

'Arnaud, I don't think this is a good idea,' Mila said. 'We need to tell the authorities that the boat's here and leave the recovery work to the professionals.'

'I'm going to have a look,' said Arnaud, 'that's all.'

He pulled his shirt over his head.

'But you might contaminate the evidence.'

'Evidence of what?'

Mila couldn't say.

Arnaud, in a single, elegant movement, slid off the boat into the water, disappearing beneath its glassy surface. The inflatable rocked in the opposite direction as the balance of weight shifted.

He emerged a moment later, a few metres away.

Fuck it, thought Mila, losing her fear. This was the wreckage of her family's boat. If anyone was to do any exploring, it should be her. And also, she realised in the next thought, this might well be the only chance she ever had to look inside that cave. She might never have another opportunity to return to this place, the place that was probably the last thing her stepsister saw while she was alive; the place where she, in all likelihood, took her last breath.

She had her life jacket and shirt off in an instant.

'Not you too!' said Solene.

'Yep,' said Mila. She got her shorts off as fast as she could, before anyone could stop her, and slipped into the water. It was cold, colder than the water that she swam in off the beach at Morannez, and it shocked her. She hung onto the side of the inflatable until she had caught her breath and then she swam around the craft, following Arnaud's head, a dark silhouette against the glimmer and flash of the light on the rippling waves of the pool.

Arnaud swam carefully around the rocky outcrop in which *Moonfleet* was stuck.

The shards were close to the surface; Mila scraped her ankle and blood bloomed in the water. Damn! She should have been more careful. Arnaud was being super-cautions and he was right. It would be easy to panic and rip the skin of her legs to shreds.

Again she thought of Sophie. If she'd been in the water here during the storm, she'd have no chance of avoiding the dangers beneath the surface. She'd have been helpless. Mila had not attended the inquest into Sophie's death and she hadn't been party to the coroner's report. She knew Sophie had drowned, but she didn't know if her body had also been battered and bruised, which it would have been, surely, if she'd been in the sea here.

It would not be difficult to check.

Arnaud had made his way into a channel, barely wide enough to accommodate a human body, between the outcrop and the main cliff wall. 'Hey! Mila,' he called, 'come and see this.'

She made her way slowly towards him, using her hands to pull herself between the rocks until she saw what he had found. Reaching down into the water was an ancient, metal ladder. It had been bolted into the wall, and the heads of the bolts had rusted so badly they were like one with the old stone.

'Will you look at that!' Arnaud said quietly. 'Charlie and Sophie must have known about this place. They came here for a reason!'

Mila didn't know why he was whispering, but she felt the same need for subterfuge. 'We ought to leave it to the authorities,' she said again.

'Don't you want to see what's up there?'

She did.

'We won't touch anything, okay? We'll just go up and look.'

'Okay.'

Arnaud climbed first, helped by the light swell of the waves. Mila watched his slender legs, the hairs black and fine against the tan of his skin, as they ascended. At the top, he pulled himself up and into the darkness of the recess. Then he reached down his hand towards Mila.

'I'm okay!' she said, both hands on the side of the ladder. It was rusty, flakes of disintegrating metal came away into her palms.

She reached the top, and heaved her body onto the lip of the rock. The temperature was several degrees cooler than it was outside and the rock was covered in guano. It was already all over Mila's hands.

'Can you see the others?' Arnaud asked.

Mila leaned out, but she couldn't see the inflatable. The topography of the cliff ensured the lower part of the cave entrance was absolutely concealed.

She turned to the interior. It was dark as the grave, and cold, and it had the primeval smell of weed, and wet sand. The sound of the sea echoed from its reaches.

The floor sloped steeply upwards. Arnaud glanced at Mila, and then went forward on his hands and knees, moving slowly and carefully. Mila followed. It only took a few moments for the light to all but disappear, and as they climbed, the passage turned, like the spiral inside a shell, and as soon as they lost the opening, the temperature dropped further and their pitch-black world became quiet and claustrophobic. Arnaud was feeling his way forward. Mila bumped into the back of him.

'Sorry,' she said.

'Hold on,' said Arnaud. 'There's a light on my watch. It's not great, but better than nothing.'

A moment later, a thin but clear beam of torchlight sprang out from the area of Arnaud's wrist. He moved his arm to run the beam over the rock walls, like a laser scanner. The cave was far larger than Mila had imagined it to be. Bats were hanging from the crags in the roof.

Arnaud swung the tiny light around, zigzagging downwards. Some ancient graffiti was scratched into the old stone. *AT loves SE, 1927.* 'I expect it was an old smugglers' den,' said Arnaud. 'Probably used to store booty looted from the ships that had run aground on the rocks. You could keep stuff safe and dry in here for years.'

'Do you think they knew about it?'

'Charlie and Sophie? Yeah, they must have. They couldn't have ended up here by accident. They didn't mention anything about it to you?'

'Nothing. Never.'

'They probably thought they could come and see out the storm here.'

'Maybe.'

Arnaud was still moving the light, coming gradually lower. Metal rings had been bolted into the wall. Mila could imagine ropes threaded through them, and barrels and crates of pilfered flotsam stacked in the cave. Perhaps these were the remains of an old pulley system.

At the back, higher up, was a crumpled tarpaulin and several small, bright yellow buoys of the kind fishermen used to mark where they'd dropped their lobster pots. One of the buoys was marked: Mila strained to read the lettering: N perhaps, and O. No?

Suddenly, Arnaud yelped as if he'd been stung and stumbled backwards, knocking into Mila and almost sending her sliding back down the slope.

'What happened?' she squeaked, her heart pounding.

'Did you see it?'

'See what?'

'Perhaps I was mistaken,' said Arnaud. 'Merde!'

The light had gone off on his watch. He fiddled with it, turned the light on again, and directed it towards the incline, in front and to the left of where he and Mila were crouched.

And this time Mila saw what he had seen.

First, she saw the soles of a pair of trainers, the heels together on the floor, with the toes slightly apart.

Then Arnaud moved the light a little further up and this time it was Mila who gasped.

Beyond the trainers, the decomposed remains of a human body lay on the slope before them.

56

Arnaud swung the light away from the corpse. Mila could hear his breathing, quick and shallow, as well as her own. The desire to escape was tangled up with the horror of what they had just witnessed.

'It's okay,' said Arnaud. 'It's okay, we're all right, we need to stay calm.'

'I am calm,' Mila said, although that wasn't true; she was feeling terrified, panicked, afraid of somehow becoming trapped in the cave with the body.

Ohmygod, she thought, *ohmygod, ohmygod, is that Charlie?*

'Let's get out,' Arnaud said, disguising his own disquiet with a shield of authority. 'Go backwards, Mila, carefully. Don't rush. Keep your head low.'

'I'm not an idiot,' she muttered, ashamed of her tetchiness, because Arnaud was only trying to look after her welfare. The darkness was wrapped around her, tight as a tourniquet. Someone had died in this cave and she didn't want to die here too. She stumbled in her hurry to back out on all fours, scraped her elbow, bit her lip to stop herself crying out in frustration. At the back of her mind was the knowledge that she and Arnaud were comprehensively destroying any evidence there might have been to help decipher the events that had led to this person's death.

They reversed together, helping one another, dirt digging into the palms of Mila's hands, and the skin of her knees. This time, she was glad when their elbows and hips accidentally touched. If something happened to Arnaud, she knew she would struggle to find her way out. She was afraid he might fall down a hole that they could not see, or disappear for some other reason, and she could not bear the thought of being in the absolute blackness alone.

Soon, they heard the sounds of the sea again, and the gulls. The temperature lifted a little. A welcome light infiltrated the darkness, and now they could see where they were going, they turned round and went forward, half standing. It was bliss to emerge into the warmth of the air.

Mila had no idea how much time had elapsed since they had first climbed up into the cave – it couldn't have been very long. From the perspective of the three people who remained in the inflatable, it was long enough to cause concern.

Monsieur Bolloré was bellowing their names.

'It's okay, we're here! We're all right!' Arnaud called. 'I know you can't see us, but we're fine.'

Arnaud looked at Mila, her eyes screwed up against the blinding brightness of the daylight, the ends of her hair and her swimsuit still damp. Her knees, calves, feet and hands were filthy; so were his.

'Are you okay?' he asked quietly, putting a hand on her shoulder. The touch made her jump; she was so pumped with adrenaline. His skin was gritty and she didn't want to think about gull shit and bat shit and whatever else might be on his palm.

'Yes,' said Mila, 'just let me have a few seconds.' She didn't want to go down the ladder and into the water, glassy and sparkling with sunlight, while she was feeling so shaky. She tried to slow her breathing, tried to calm herself.

'Did you find anything?' Monsieur Bolloré called.

'It's him,' Mila said, under her breath, urgently, to Arnaud. 'The body. It's Charlie.'

'You don't know that.'

'I can. I recognised him. Even like that. I know it's him.'

'No,' Arnaud said more forcefully. 'Those remains, those bones, they could be anyone.'

Mila half turned towards him. She wanted to put her arms around him, so that he might reciprocate – selfishly, she craved the comfort that a human touch would bring. But she couldn't reach out to him, not as she was, naked save for a navy-blue swimsuit, covered in filth and the cut on her leg trailing blood down her calf and around her ankle. She was shivering, although she wasn't cold.

'What are you doing?' Solene yelled. 'Why aren't you coming back?'

'We are coming!' Arnaud called. 'Just a minute!'

Arnaud was reflecting Mila's anxiety, and she his. This was something they would always share. Whoever's body was in the cave, they had found it together. Nobody else would ever know how it had felt to be there. It was an awful connection.

* * *

Back on the inflatable, they told the others what they had found. Solene wanted to see for herself.

'No!' said Arnaud. 'You mustn't go there.'

'But you've seen! I want to see!'

Arnaud was pulling his T-shirt over his head. The fabric was sticking to his wet skin.

'There's nothing to see,' he said. 'Just a pair of trainers and some bones.'

'And the tide is going out,' said Monsieur Bolloré. 'If we don't move soon, we'll be fucked.'

'Let's go,' said Mila, 'quickly, please.'

She was desperate, now, to be away from this deadly pool, seawater slapping gently against the vicious rocks, and the dark cave above with its macabre secret.

There must have been something in the tone of her voice, because Solene, who had been poised to launch another argument in favour of her being permitted to go into the cave, backed down at once.

* * *

Back at Morannez harbour, Arnaud found a jacket in his car for Mila to put on over her damp clothes. She was aware of the water stains on her shirt and shorts, but was too preoccupied with what she and Arnaud had found in the cave to care about her appearance. She couldn't get rid of the image of the human remains lying on the cave floor, like something glimpsed in the brightness of a lightning flash and imprinted on her brain.

Already she was worried about what she would say to Ani. How would she explain this development to her niece? How could she be honest and still sensitive? How could she describe what she'd seen in a reasonable manner when her own mind could not process the horror.

First there were practicalities that had to be dealt with.

Together with Monsieur Bolloré, she and Arnaud went to the coastguard's office and they sat, side by side, on wooden chairs to report their finds and answer his questions. Arnaud seemed the most relaxed: he sat, legs slightly apart, his right ankle resting on his left knee, the foot, back in a deck shoe now, jiggling. Mila sat beside him, struggling to appear composed and rational when inside she felt as if she was falling apart. Monsieur Bolloré was his usual verbose self, although even he seemed to have been knocked sideways by the discovery of the body.

The coastguard was a middle-aged, practical man. He had clearly encountered his share of maritime catastrophes and did not seem surprised by anything. His questions were straightforward. Monsieur Bolloré and Arnaud answered, Mila did not have to say a word.

The fisherman showed the coastguard exactly where the wreckage was located on a map of that part of the Atlantic Ocean, tapping the spot with the tip of his hook. Arnaud described the ladder and the geography of the cave. The coastguard took their contact details but for now, they were free to go about their business.

'The police will be in touch with you,' the coastguard said, 'but it might take a while. They're all tied up with the evacuations today.'

'Evacuations?'

'Because of the wildfires,' said the coastguard. 'The wind is changeable so the path of the fires is unpredictable. They're having to clear domestic and commercial properties that might be in danger. People will say they're being over-cautious, but better safe than sorry. Nobody wants anyone else to be hurt.'

'Haven't storms been forecast?' asked Arnaud.

'Rain's coming, but not quickly enough.'

They left the office, Monsieur Bolloré lighting another cigarette. Arnaud returned Mila's bag, and they shook hands as they said 'good-bye', formally, as if they were business acquaintances, and not old friends who had just made the most distressing of discoveries. Mila then fetched her bike and cycled back to the sea house.

She was alone. Ani had left a note to say she'd gone to her grand-mother's apartment.

Mila showered and changed into a long, cotton dress. Padding through the house barefoot, she picked up Berthaud and nuzzled her face into the cat's fur. When she closed her eyes, she saw the human remains clearly.

The corpse could be anyone.

It could easily *not* be Charlie.

Mila tidied the kitchen. Then she poured herself a small glass of sweet Monbazillac wine. She sat on the swing seat in the sun, with her damp hair piled up on her head and the cat on her lap, and she tried to order thoughts that were jumbled and chaotic; a deck of cards tossed in the air and falling randomly.

Nothing felt right.

57

Carter called.

'Hey,' he said.

'Hey.'

'Arnaud told me what you found in the cave.' A pause. 'That must have been a shock.'

'I think it's Charlie.'

'You can't know that, Mila.'

'I know I can't. But I think it is.'

Carter said: 'Fair enough.' He had always acknowledged the validity of instinct and intuition; had even taught Ceci to take hunches seriously. It was a quality, Ceci had told Mila, not a weakness. Now he asked: 'Are you okay, Mila?'

'Yeah, I'm fine. Is everything okay with you?'

'I just found out they've evacuated the hospital.'

'The hospital where Briony is?'

'Yes. It's directly in the path of the fire.'

Mila took a deep breath. 'But Briony will be okay. Emmanuelle will look after her, won't she?'

'Emmanuelle didn't make it into work this morning. They wouldn't let her through the cordons.'

'Oh.' Mila put down her wine. 'But they'll be super-careful at a hospital, especially with someone like Briony, who doesn't speak French.'

'I guess.'

'Where did they take her?'

'I don't know. That's what I've been trying to find out.'

'It can't be that difficult to track her down, Carter.'

'Nobody I've spoken to knows where she is.'

For a moment there was silence at the other end of the line.

'I don't like it,' Carter said at last. 'I have a bad feeling about the situation. The Moorcrofts have been in Brittany for hours but Ceci hasn't heard from them either.'

'What about Billie?'

'She's still in custody. The Welsh police are stuck on the wrong side of a roadblock inland.'

'So she's safe?'

'Yeah.'

'I'd like to talk to her, Carter. Could you clear that for me with the Morannez police?'

'Is that really a good idea?'

'Please. Just call them and tell them I'll be over shortly.'

Carter sighed. 'Okay, okay.'

'What are you going to do?'

'Concentrate on finding Briony. I'll be in touch.'

Carter disconnected and Mila returned to the email she'd started drafting earlier, to her old friend and colleague at Llinas Powys Hospital.

Dear Liz,

she wrote.

This is Mila Shepherd, we used to work together in the Burns Unit at Frenchay Hospital a long time ago.

I currently do some work for an agency which specialises in

finding lost people. We've been dealing with the case of a young woman called Briony Moorcroft.

Briony has been assessed here in Brittany by a medical team who believe her mother, Gwyneth, has undiagnosed Munchausen Syndrome by proxy.

Gwyneth Moorcroft has been sourcing prescription drugs for Briony, and as she used to work at Llinas Powys and would know her way around the system, we suspect they might be coming from there.

The Moorcrofts own a cleaning business. If they have the contract for cleaning the hospital, that might be how she's gaining access.

If you think there's even the slightest possibility that I'm right, would you let me know asap? My mobile number and that of the Toussaints agency's landline are listed below.

Many thanks, Liz.

All my best,

Mila.

Mila pressed 'send'. Then she called Ceci's friend, Joe Le Taxi, and asked him to come and pick her up and take her to Morannez police station.

She could have cycled, but she didn't want to waste a single second.

58

Billie was slumped on a chair that had been placed on the other side of the table in the room in the police station. Her arms were crossed over her chest, her legs stretched out in front of her. Mila observed how heavily her forearms were tattooed, and how they bulged with muscle. She also noticed a criss-cross pattern of scars dissecting the tattoos. Mila had seen scars like those before. At some point in her life, Billie Dexter had cut herself – a means of managing insecurity and pain.

Billie did not move when Mila came into the room, only her eyes followed Mila's progress from the door to the empty chair on the opposite side of the table.

'Are you going to behave yourself, Billie?' the female officer who had showed Mila in asked in English.

'Do I look like a fucking toddler?'

'There's no need to be rude.'

'Respect me, and I'll respect you back.'

The officer's lips made a line. 'I'll bring some coffee,' she said, and she left Billie and Mila together, alone.

Billie was wearing the same clothes as before and she appeared tired. Her hair needed washing and there were dark circles under her eyes. She smelled strongly of sweat and dust: the odour of police cells.

Mila pulled out her chair and sat down. Billie watched, apparently disinterested but, Mila suspected, taking in every detail.

'Have you come to make sure they get me out of France and banged up back where I came from?' Billie asked.

'That's not why I'm here, no,' said Mila.

'Come to gloat at the weirdo, have you?'

'I'd like to help you, Billie, if I can.'

'Bit late for that, innit?'

'I hope not.'

Billie fell silent. She glowered at Mila.

Mila cleared her throat. 'First, though, I wanted to let you know about Briony,' she said.

At the mention of Briony's name, Billie became more alert.

'We took her to hospital,' Mila said. 'A doctor friend of ours checked her over and she, the doctor, told us that you were right, Billie. Someone – one of her parents, most probably her mother – has been giving her drugs to treat diseases that Briony doesn't have.'

Billie shrugged as if she didn't care, but Mila noticed the line of her lips soften. It must be a relief to know that her instincts had been correct.

'Also,' Mila continued, 'the doctor said you did a good job looking after Briony. You did all the right things. You should be proud of yourself.'

Billie's looked down at her hands, began picking at the cuticles.

The officer came with two cardboard cups of coffee. It looked black and tarry, but smelled good.

'Thank you,' said Mila.

'I'd fuckin' kill for a decent mug of tea,' said Billie.

Mila picked up her coffee and took a sip.

'How did you know?' she asked.

'About Briony? It was obvious.'

'Everyone else missed it.'

'When I was in rehab, I learned about addiction.'

'Who taught you?'

'My shrink. Doctor Khadra.'

'Carter spoke to her. She told him you were interested in psychology.'

Billie sat up straight and leaned forward, her whole demeanour changed.

'Doctor Khadra didn't treat me like a moron. She said me being how I was, wasn't my fault.'

'No,' said Mila quietly, thinking of the grandfather, the golf club, Billie's tattoo.

'In her opinion, see,' Billie continued, 'I'd been damaged. My "trust issues"' – she made the quote marks with her fingers – 'were down to people making promises they never kept. Said that I'd learned coping strategies in childhood that were hard to shake off. Said all the things that everyone told me I was weren't true.'

'What did people say about you?'

'That I was useless, born bad, a waste of space.'

Mila recalled the woman outside the flats on Splott Terrace, who had spoken about Billie as if she wasn't quite human.

'Doctor Khadra gave me some books,' Billie continued. 'I wasn't a good reader back then, but I'm better now. The books explained a lot – about me and about other people.'

'It's the hardest thing in the world, understanding other people.'

'Nope,' said Billie, 'it's not hard. It's just most people can't be arsed to imagine what it would be like to walk in other people's shoes.'

'Yes. You're right.'

Billie took a sip of coffee and pulled a face. 'Tastes like shit,' she said.

'I'm sorry we made assumptions about you, Billie,' Mila said. 'We were wrong to do that.'

Billie shrugged. Mila took that as acceptance of her apology.

'Tell me what you thought when you first met Briony Moorcroft,' said Mila.

'I'd seen her around. She's famous in Carnarth.'

'But you hadn't spoken to her until recently?'

'Not until I started working for her dad.' Billie smiled, like someone remembering an event from long ago. 'Briony spent a lot of time, and I mean *a lot* up in her bedroom, watching people come and go in and out of the park. After we'd been waving at each other for a while, she started coming downstairs when I was dropping off my cleaning stuff. Sometimes Mrs Moorcroft left us alone.'

'Okay.'

'I could see something was wrong. Her eyes would be kind of half closed and she'd be slurring her words. I looked up some of the drugs she was taking and they didn't make sense, I mean not for what was supposed to be wrong with her.'

Mila nodded.

'What was I supposed to do?' Billie asked. 'Nothing? Let her keep controlling Briony like that?'

'Her?'

'Briony's mum.'

'You didn't think about trying to get some professional help?'

Billie snorted. 'Imagine what would've happened if I'd walked into the doctors' surgery and started making accusations about Mrs Moorcroft. Me with my record and that.'

Mila did imagine what would have happened and realised that of course that would not have been an option.

'Weren't you afraid that you might have been wrong about Briony?'

'Yeah. But I was prepared.' Billie looked down at her hands. 'When Bri was withdrawing, she was pretty sick. I was shitting myself.' She smiled. 'So was she. But she came through. I wouldn't wish what she went through on my worst enemy, mind.' She looked at Mila. 'You'd better make sure she doesn't go back to that woman.'

'She won't.'

'I mean it,' said Billie fiercely.

'I mean it too,' said Mila.

'I'll be locked up. I won't be able to protect Briony. And Mrs Moorcroft will pile the guilt onto her,' said Billie. 'She'll be all "Oh, darling, I was only trying to do the best for you." And Briony has a soft heart, and she'll feel sorry for her mum and agree to go home. But the minute Mrs Moorcroft's got her back, it'll all start over again.'

The door opened and the officer's head appeared. 'The Cardiff police are here to collect Billie,' she said. 'I have to ask you to leave now, Madame.'

Mila acknowledged this, then she leaned towards Billie. 'We're not going to abandon you either,' she said. 'You're going to have to face some charges in the UK, but my colleagues and I will help you. We'll look out for you. You're not on your own.'

'I've always been on my own,' Billie said.

'Madame,' said the officer.

Mila stood. 'I have to go.'

Billie slid back down into the chair. She recrossed her arms. The expression on her face was one of utter misery.

59

That evening, a fresh, new wind blew in from the west. It should have been a relief after the heat but Mila couldn't enjoy it because she was consumed with anxiety about Briony Moorcroft.

She didn't know where Briony was, and she didn't know where Carter was either. They'd spoken after she'd left the police station, but now he wasn't answering his phone. If he had found Briony, and she was safe, he'd have been in touch.

Ceci was desperately concerned too.

There'd been no word from Briony's parents. Nobody knew where they were or what they were doing. Ceci had tried to call both Mrs Moorcroft and her husband a dozen times, but either their phones were switched off, or they were diverting all calls to voicemail.

Emmanuelle had been enlisted to help find Briony. She'd spoken to colleagues, who reported that the hospital had had to be evacuated with urgency late in the morning, when the wind had picked up and the speed of the fire's progress had accelerated. The threat to the hospital and the safety of staff and patients had been immediate and severe. There had been no grand plan, no methodology; the evacuators had been focussed on removing the patients from danger and getting them out of the path of the blaze as quickly as they could.

Patients had been distributed far and wide: some to alternative hospitals, others to clinics and even hotels. They had travelled in minibuses, taxis and the staff's private cars. Some had been discharged, temporarily, and had gone home.

No single person had been in charge of checking where the patients were going. Only now were administrators trying to locate all those who had been inside the building at the time.

Carter had already followed a handful of dead-end leads. When Mila and he last spoke, he'd said his only option was to work his way around the various locations where he knew patients had been taken, searching for Briony himself. It was a time-consuming and laborious task, and there was nothing Mila could do to help.

When Mila's phone rang, she jumped. It was Ceci.

'I've checked with the airline,' Ceci said. 'Mrs Moorcroft didn't board the plane this morning. Her husband travelled alone. Perhaps he had an inkling about his wife's disorder, and when my message confirmed his fears, he sent her home and came to collect Briony himself.'

'Is he still not answering?'

'No. Wouldn't you think he'd want to talk to us and find out what we know?'

'He must be upset,' Mila said. 'I mean, I know you didn't spell it all out, but he's had time to think through the implications of what's been going on and it's a pretty horrific situation for him to be in.'

'That still doesn't explain the radio silence.'

It didn't, not completely, but Mila could understand that Mr Moorcroft might need some time to process the facts that had come to light.

He wouldn't stay with his wife after this, she thought. Nobody in their right mind would stand by the person who had abused their child in such a horrific way, and for such a protracted period of time.

Perhaps, if Mrs Moorcroft consented to have treatment, and if she was capable of managing and controlling her condition, then maybe, one day, she could have a relationship of some kind with her daughter again. Mila didn't think she even deserved that.

That was a matter for the future. The more pressing issue was not knowing where either David Moorcroft or his daughter were now.

Mila kept thinking about Billie Dexter too, about her courage and her determination and the fact that her reward was to be dumped in police custody, on her way back to South Wales, where she would face a number of serious charges.

It was all a mess, and Mila couldn't think of a way to make things right.

* * *

Later, Mila listened to the local news on the radio. The fire on the outskirts of Lorient was finally under control. There was a report about the evacuation of the hospital, an interview with its manager, a woman who spoke about the courage and dedication of the nurses and other staff who had facilitated the exodus.

Mila called Ceci, who answered, but only to say she and Ani were eating dinner. Carter was still out searching.

'There's nothing more you can do at the moment,' Ceci said to Mila. 'Try not to worry. I'm sure Carter will be in touch with some news soon.'

Mila felt itchy; anxious. She couldn't settle to anything. She decided to go for a swim, to burn up the adrenaline in her bloodstream.

The light was fading as she swam out towards the horizon.

As Mila pushed through the water, she thought of the body in the cave. Whoever it was had been there for a long time. Another few nights – however long it took for the authorities to get to it – wouldn't make much difference. The soul of that person wouldn't be any lonelier than it had already been for all the days and weeks and months when it had lain there, in the dark.

What if it is my Charlie? Sophie whispered.

Mila believed that it was. And if her hunch was confirmed, then life would be difficult for Ceci, Ani and herself. There would be an investigation and the family was bound to be the subject of gossip and speculation. Eventually things would get better, because they always did. But it might be a long time between now and then. There would be emotional mountains to climb, especially for Ani.

Mila swam back to the shore, letting the waves help her. The current

had pushed her further down the beach from the spot where she'd
entered the water, and she struggled to get out – she had to scrabble on
her hands and knees. When she managed to extricate herself, she
walked back through the gloaming and saw a man on the far arm of the
beach, the part that was submerged at high tide. His silhouette was
familiar: Mila realised that was because she'd seen him in a similar pose
earlier that same day.

It was Arnaud Girard, standing barefoot looking out to sea, unaware
that he was being observed.

Mila picked up her towel and wrapped it round herself.

She didn't need to speak to Arnaud to know that he was thinking
about the human remains in the cave too.

60

When Carter finally called, the sun had set and night had come in.

'Hi, Carter,' said Mila, skin tingling from a hot shower. 'Where've you been? What's happening? Have you found Briony?'

'No, but I spoke to one of the orderlies who helped look after her. The good news is, she saw a man helping Briony out of the hospital. The bad news is, she didn't recognise the man.'

'That doesn't help us then.'

'It does in a way. I've got a list of the staff who were on duty this morning. We need to contact each of the men in turn until we find whoever it was and where they took her.'

The previous unease had returned to Mila. A worrying thought was niggling at her. She was reluctant to put it into words.

'Where are you now, Carter?'

'In a village close to the hospital. It's still chaos. Some of the roads are going to be closed for days, they'll need resurfacing before they're fit for use. There might be more information on the local news.'

'Hold on...' Mila picked up the buttons and turned on the TV with the volume muted. As she did this, there was a ping on her laptop alerting her to an incoming email. She reached for it and pressed the mail icon. Berthaud jumped onto the counter and pressed her head into Mila's hand. The poor cat hadn't had much attention lately.

The incoming email was a response from Liz Rashidi. Mila glanced at it, and then back at the television screen, where people who lived in the area affected by the fire were being interviewed. The report cut to a picture of the outside of the hospital. The fire did not appear to have damaged the building, although everywhere was covered in a layer of ash.

'I've got the news on now,' Mila told Carter. 'They're outside the hospital. I'll turn the volume up.'

The reporter was telling viewers what Mila and Carter already knew: that all patients and staff had been urgently removed from the hospital. There was some footage of the evacuation taken on a mobile phone. The video was shaky but showed the panic as people scrambled to help others into cars. The more seriously ill came out of the hospital on trolleys and wheelchairs, some still attached to drips and monitoring equipment, and were loaded into the backs of ambulances.

'Can you see Briony?' Carter asked.

'Hold on...' Mila paused the image. Then she ran it forward, slowly, crouching in front of the TV with her reading glasses on her nose. It took her a while, moving the film forward frame by frame, but at last she spotted Briony Moorcroft, coming out of the hospital with a man. He had his arm around her and she was leaning into him for support. They were in the background, and for most of the two or three seconds that they were on the screen, Mila couldn't see the man's face. But then, just as they disappeared off the screen, the man turned.

And she recognised him.

It was David Moorcroft; Briony's father.

'Carter, it's her dad,' Mila said. 'Briony's father picked her up from the hospital.'

'You're sure?'

'Certain.'

'How could he have known where she was?'

'Ceci's message said Briony was in hospital. I guess he just phoned round until he found her.'

'Emmanuelle told me she'd flagged Briony as a vulnerable case.'

'But there was the fire and... Oh, Carter, it doesn't matter *how* Mr Moorcroft got to Briony. What matters is what we do next.'

'Is he driving the van?'

'I don't know. You've still got the key you took from Billie, haven't you?'

'Yeah, but Moorcroft is bound to have brought the spare.'

A text came through on Mila's phone. It was from Liz.

Sent email. Read ASAP.

'Carter, will you hold on a minute, there's an email I need to read, it's connected to the case.'

'Okay.'

Mila lay the phone down, and picked up her laptop.

Message from Liz Rashidi
Re: Briony Moorcroft

Hi Mila,

Regarding the Moorcroft family…

My colleagues and I have half-expected and fully dreaded the prospect of receiving an email like yours for some time. We didn't know what form it would take, but we were certain we would hear the name 'Moorcroft' again.

The Moorcroft cleaning service is not used by Llinas Powys Hospital, and our security systems are unparalleled, so I can categorically state that prescriptions aren't being taken from the hospital, neither is our system being manipulated.

But yes, you're right, Gwyneth Moorcroft did work here as a staff nurse for several years. When she joined, she was Gwyneth Swain, but she later met and married one of the hospital's doctors: David Moorcroft.

I'm guessing you aren't aware of David Moorcroft's history. He was a consultant oncologist but was struck off the medical register ten years ago after falsely diagnosing cancer in children. The Medical Practitioners Tribunal Service found that his motivation was greed: he'd been charging parents for tests and scans rather than referring them to the NHS (where the children could have been treated for free), but his colleague, Mr Rajiv Singh, the man who blew the whistle on Moorcroft, had always believed there was more to it than that. He cited Moorcroft's persistent dishonesty and the fact that he seemed almost obsessed with the details of illness. Mr Singh told the hearing that Moorcroft should never be allowed contact with sick children again.

I knew he'd set himself up in business running a cleaning agency, and I regularly check the Moorcroft's Maids website to make sure that man isn't getting anywhere near a hospital, cancer unit, children's medical facility or indeed anywhere where there are children.

I've had no dealings with Mrs Moorcroft for many years, but if you truly believe that Munchausen Syndrome by proxy is at play here, I recommend you urgently consider David Moorcroft as the culprit. He has a manipulative, controlling personality. His wife may have been administering the drugs, but I have no doubt she's been coerced into doing so.

Let me know what happens!

All my best,

Liz

'Oh God,' Mila whispered.

'What?' asked Carter. 'What is it?'

'I'm about to forward you an email. Read it, Carter, and then call me straight back.'

Mila counted to twenty, and then her phone rang again.

'Shit,' Carter said. 'Briony's with her father and he's the abuser.'

'That's what it looks like.'

'Hold on... I'm searching online. Okay. This is the *Guardian* twelve years ago.' Carter read: '"Doctor struck off for falsely diagnosing children with cancer." That's him, that's Moorcroft, there's a picture of him... and his wife's there too, and the child, Briony, she's in a pushchair with tubes coming out of her nose. Jesus, if he'd been misdiagnosing other people's children, did nobody think to question what he was doing to his own?'

'It's beyond comprehension!' Mila said.

'We need to find Briony and get her away from her father.'

'How?'

'I don't know. But Billie Dexter did it and she had a fraction of the resources we have. I'll be with you in fifteen minutes.'

* * *

Mila called Ceci, to let her know what had happened, and to ask her to keep Ani with her, no matter what. Logically, she knew Ani wasn't directly at risk from Mr Moorcroft, or any other source of danger, but she couldn't bear to take any chances.

After that, she went to wait for Carter outside the sea house gate, dressed in jeans, a sweater and tennis shoes. Her hair blew over her face. She looked at the sky above; perfectly clear and twinkling with stars. A shooting star bisected the sky, there and gone in a heartbeat.

An owl hooted from the branches of the trees.

The wind was gusting violently.

Please, thought Mila, *let it bring some rain.*

'Come on, Carter,' she murmured, and at that moment, sure enough, she felt, rather than heard, the rumble of the Harley-Davidson.

In another couple of minutes, Carter was with her, doing a fancy skid as he pulled up beside her, passing her his spare helmet and his spare leather jacket.

'Hop on,' he said.

'Have you got an actual plan, Carter?'

'We know they're in the van, which means they'll be heading for the ferry port.'

'Which one? St Malo, Roscoff, Cherbourg or Caen. That's four options, Carter, and they're hardly close together.'

'Yes, but they won't all have nightly crossings. You can check the schedules on the way.'

63

When Carter next spoke to Mila, it was via the motorcycle intercom. 'What do you reckon about the ferry crossings?' he asked.

'Caen to Portsmouth gives them the most options.'

'We'll go to Caen then.'

It was a risky strategy. If Mr Moorcroft had decided not to make the obvious choice, and headed, instead, for Roscoff, there'd be nothing Mila and Carter could do about it.

'Are the police looking out for the van?' Mila asked.

'They're on the case but the forces are stretched thin tonight because of the fires.'

'Okay.'

'There is still a possibility that they're not heading for the ferry ports at all,' said Carter. 'Moorcroft might have decided to fly back, or to go via a different route. This is a gamble.'

Mila tucked her phone back into her jacket, and prayed that luck would be on their side. They must be due some good fortune.

* * *

The next hours passed in a blur. She and Carter zipped through the countryside on the bike, taking the fastest roads. Mila couldn't see much in the dark, all she could do was lean against Carter's body and try to keep track of where they were.

From time to time, someone in a powerful car would stay with them for a while, the headlights illuminating the grain of the tarmac on the road around them, and trees and signposts would flash by like fence posts, and then the car would overtake, or turn off, and Mila's world would shrink back to darkness again.

Carter was playing the radio through the helmet intercom, and it was good to hear the music, although it was fighting with the roar of the engine. Soon even the radio became an annoyance. Mila was cold, despite the jacket. She was uncomfortable. They'd been driving for hours and she'd had enough. Every part of her body ached. She wanted to get off the bike. She was desperate for a hot drink. Just as she was beginning to think she couldn't bear another minute, Carter pulled off the road and onto the forecourt of one of the *aires de service*. He coasted around, ignoring the dedicated bike park area, and pulled up at the far end of the car park, with the nose of the bike facing towards a tall hedge.

Mila was hugely relieved. Her legs were so stiff, she struggled to dismount; Carter offered a hand to help her.

'Why are we stopping?' she asked, unfastening her helmet.

Carter nodded to a vehicle parked in darkness, separate from the other cars and vans in the service area. Mila peered through the gloom.

'Recognise it?' asked Carter.

It was the Moorcrofts' van, with a brand-new number plate hanging beneath the back door. Billie Dexter's clumsy over-painting meant the logo was still obscured.

The van looked as if it was empty.

Carter looked around him. 'They must've stopped for something to eat,' he said.

'Are we going to approach them?'

'No, we'll wait until they come out. If we can't get Briony safely out of the way, we'll call for back-up and follow at a distance. C'mon, let's go take a look.'

Carter and Mila held their helmets under their arms, and they walked towards the van, Carter using the torch on his phone to light their way. When they got close, he shone the light in the driver's window and then came round to the passenger side.

'Jeez,' he whispered.

Mila leaned forward, awkward in the leather jacket. But she saw what he had seen. Briony Moorcroft was in the passenger seat, which was tilted back. She was covered over with a blanket, tucked in like a child. She looked as if she was deeply asleep.

64

Carter knocked on the window with his knuckles. 'Come on, Briony, wake up.'

The girl didn't stir.

He banged on the window glass with the flat of his hand. Still there was no reaction.

'She's been drugged again,' said Mila.

'Shit.'

Carter patted his pockets and found the van's key. He opened the door and Briony slumped sideways. Mila caught her and pushed her back with difficulty, given that she was stymied by the stiff, fringed sleeves of the jacket she was wearing.

'She's out for the count,' Mila said.

'Bastard,' said Carter. 'He couldn't even wait to get her home to Wales.'

'Perhaps she didn't want to go with him,' suggested Mila. 'Perhaps she was fighting him and that's why he drugged her.'

'Or perhaps he's just a sick individual who gets a kick out of knocking out his daughter with drugs,' said Carter. 'A sick guy who's going to be back any minute. Excuse me, Mila.'

She moved out of the way and he leaned over the girl, trying to lift her head.

'Briony,' he said. 'Briony, wake up. Can you hear me? Can you say something, please, if you can hear me?'

She made a slight, groaning noise.

'There's no way she can walk,' said Mila. 'No way she can sit on the bike. She can't even open her eyes.'

'We'll have to take the van,' said Carter.

'What?'

'We'll take the van. Can you squeeze in here, next to Briony.'

Carter came round to the driver's side, opened the door, sat down and pushed back the seat to accommodate his long legs. Meanwhile, Mila awkwardly climbed into the passenger seat, pulling Briony almost onto her lap. She looked in the wing mirror.

'Carter, he's coming!'

David Moorcroft had exited the service station. He was carrying a coffee carton and eating a baguette sandwich. They had, perhaps, a minute before he reached them.

Mila pulled the door shut. Carter had dropped the key into the van's footwell.

'Carter, he's literally fifty metres away!'

'Okay, don't panic.'

'He's almost here!'

'I've found it.'

'We've got about twenty seconds.'

Carter slotted the key into the ignition and turned it.

The engine roared into life and he put the vehicle into reverse, slamming the gears. Mila's eyes were glued to the wing mirror, watching Mr Moorcroft's gait, waiting for him to realise what was happening.

Carter had backed out of the space and started to move forward again when the penny dropped. Briony's father stood stock-still for a minute. He was in the circle of light cast by one of the tall lamps dotted around the car park, and Mila could see the shock on his face, his mouth, fallen open. Then he shouted and dropped the coffee cup and what was left of the sandwich.

'He's coming, Carter,' Mila said. He was, lolloping towards them with dark stains all over the bottom parts of his trousers.

Carter put his foot down, and he turned the Moorcrofts' van and drove it down the ramp and back onto the highway, screeching the tyres as he accelerated.

Mila held Briony against her body, cradling her in her arms as if she were a child. In the wing mirror, she could see Mr Moorcroft running after them, flailing his arms. When he reached the ramp, he failed to notice the narrow hump that stretched across the top, designed to alert drivers that they were about to leave the service area, tripped and fell flat on his face.

Serves the bastard right, said Sophie.

'He doesn't know it's us,' said Carter. 'He doesn't know who's made off with his daughter. For all he knows, we could be anyone. You got your phone on you?'

'Yep.'

'Then call the police and let them know what's been going on.'

65

It was not long before dawn when the van pulled up outside the sea house.

Mila was feeling sick with tiredness. She slid out of the passenger door, and Carter picked up Briony, who was still unconscious. He carried her into the house; limp as a doll. Mila made an impromptu bed for her on the sofa and Carter said he'd sleep downstairs to keep an eye on her. Mila didn't argue with him; she wanted to be in her own bed. She fetched him a pillow and some blankets, then she went upstairs and collapsed. The laptop was still open, Liz's email still on the screen although the machine had switched to power-saving mode. The damp towel Mila had used earlier was spread over the drying rail, the swimsuit beside it on the floorboards. All these things seemed, to Mila, as if they belonged to a different life.

The sky in the slats between the shutters at the window was already glowing pale.

Mila felt as if she could sleep forever.

The soft mattress, the pillows, had never felt so good.

She closed her eyes and was asleep before the first drops of rain fell against the sea house window.

* * *

Carter woke Mila a couple of hours later with a coffee.

The rain had been and gone, but there was a freshness to the morning that had been lacking for weeks. The air smelled different too.

'How's Briony?' Mila asked.

'Still sleeping. Emmanuelle's on her way to check her over.'

'Good.'

'And I've spoken to Ceci. I told her what we've done.'

'What did she say?'

'She said: "Well done, Musketeers!"'

Mila smiled. She rolled over into the pillow. 'Can I go back to sleep for five more minutes?'

'No, you can't.'

* * *

Emmanuelle arrived at the sea house soon after. She embraced Carter and Mila, and went into the living room to examine Briony. She felt her pulse and shined a light into her eyes. Briony groaned, and moved her head, but she was a long way from consciousness.

Mila could imagine how claustrophobic it must feel to have one's energy and will suppressed by drugs; how nightmarish it must be to be unable to hold a coherent thought in one's mind because the mind had been chemically dulled.

Briony Moorcroft had been living a nightmare for years.

'Her father must have given her a massive dose of sedative,' said Emmanuelle.

'He probably wanted to make sure she'd be compliant until he got her back home,' said Carter.

'This isn't like giving your child a sleeping pill. It's playing God with her life.'

'Will she be all right?' asked Mila.

'At the very least, she's going to be dehydrated and have an awful hangover when she comes round. Poor thing.' Emmanuelle lay Briony's hand down on top of the covers. 'She needs to be in hospital, where we can set her up with some fluids to help flush out her system and keep a proper eye on her.'

'Okay,' said Carter. 'If you want to drive your car, Em, I'll bring Briony in the van and follow you.'

'That would work fine by me,' said Emmanuelle.

They smiled at one another. A tender smile.

Mila saw it and thought: *Oh!*

* * *

The Toussaints' staff were busy that day. Ceci finally got through to Mrs Moorcroft, who was staying with her sister in Caerphilly. She hadn't been answering her phone because her husband had told her she must not speak to anyone from Toussaints Agency. He'd told her they were wicked people and that he was instigating legal proceedings against the agency.

Gwyneth Moorcroft had sounded stunned, Ceci reported, when Ceci had explained about her husband's deception.

'She genuinely believes Briony is seriously ill,' she said. 'She's been told so many lies that she doesn't know how to recognise the truth any longer.'

'It will take time for her to assimilate all the information,' said Mila. 'She's going to need a good deal of support.'

Ceci had also spoken to Mrs Moorcroft's sister, Sylvia, who said she'd had deep reservations about David Moorcroft ever since Gwyneth first got involved with him. Her feelings against him had grown stronger after he was struck off the medical register. Sylvia wasn't as surprised by the turn of events as Ceci had expected her to be. She had listened carefully to everything Ceci told her and agreed to arrange some counselling for Gwyneth. She also knew a reliable solicitor and would get the ball rolling towards whatever the solicitor suggested was the best resolution for Briony.

Sylvia had convinced Ceci that Gwyneth's only crime was being in thrall to her husband.

'She said that Gwyneth Moorcroft has been manipulated by that man for so long that she doesn't know which way is up and which is down,' said Ceci. 'David Moorcroft is a trained doctor and, naturally, his wife believed that he loved his daughter, so she did exactly what he told her to do! She gave Briony the drugs because David said she needed them to keep her alive.'

'She didn't question his diagnoses, even after he was struck-off?'

'No, because he told her the tribunal was rigged against him and that the whole scandal was a conspiracy dreamed up by the elitist higher ranks of the NHS. He's deluded, obviously, and dangerous, but he is Briony's father and Gwyneth has only ever wanted the best for her daughter and couldn't comprehend that he would want anything different.'

It would be up to the police to decide whether any action would be taken against Gwyneth Moorcroft. Briony was old enough, and hopefully would soon be well enough, to make up her own mind about her mother.

David Moorcroft, meanwhile, had been in touch with his legal team. Ceci had a call from someone purporting to be from a firm of solicitors accusing Toussaints of all manner of professional violations. Ceci was not one to be cowed by someone speaking Oxford English in an educated accent. She referred the caller to David Moorcroft's professional disgrace, and explained that his daughter was currently in hospital under supervision because of a suspected overdose administered to her by her own father's hand. She explained that the police were going to be interviewing David Moorcroft as a matter of urgency with regards to the systematic abuse of his daughter, over a period spanning her entire lifetime. When the outcome of the criminal enquiry had been decided, then she would be happy to have a conversation with Mr Moorcroft's lawyer.

Carter spoke to his contacts within the UK police and explained about Billie Dexter, and how she'd been right in her conviction that Briony was being drugged by one of her parents. Billie, like the Toussaints' staff, had backed the wrong horse, but it was an easy mistake to make. He pointed out that without Billie's intervention Briony would still be effectively a prisoner in her own body and Gwyneth an unwitting partner in her abuse.

He volunteered to liaise between Mrs Moorcroft and Billie, to try to resolve their differences without further involving the authorities. Even if this was successful, and Mrs Moorcroft agreed to withdraw her complaints against Billie, it didn't mean Billie would be out of the woods. There were still a number of outstanding charges against her. Ffion Lloyd from the tennis club, for one, was not going to be appeased by an apology, but, with luck and support, Billie might be able to escape a custodial sentence this time.

Carter also spoke to Billie on the phone and said he would come to visit her as soon as it was feasible.

'I'd like to shake your hand,' he said.

Billie told him to fuck off.

66

Mila arranged to meet Ani at Jenny's café for brunch. She arrived half an hour early, and before Ani turned up, she filled Jenny and Marsela in on everything that had happened since they last met. She thanked Marsela for directing them to the sheep shed, gave her a Toussaints' card and asked her to let the agency know if any of her many contacts might need their services.

Ceci was resigned to the fact that Toussaints was going to have to foot the bill for Briony's second stay in hospital as well as the first, and dozens of other extras beside. The agency needed to work harder than ever to recoup its losses over this case and it would be useful if Mila could drum up some new business.

'Let's try and stick to heir-hunting and the suchlike for a couple of months,' Ceci had said. 'Lucrative work that won't put too many demands on our emotions.'

When Ani arrived at the café, she looked as tired as Mila felt. They both ordered hot chocolate for energy. Ani asked for a croque monsieur and Mila, who tried to go French most of the time, chose smashed avocado on toast with mushrooms and fried potatoes because her body craved the combination of vitamins and carbs.

After their meal, they bought ice creams – strawberry cheesecake for

Ani and lemon for Mila – from the ice cream shop, and they wandered over to the park and sat on the wall overlooking the crazy golf course, in the shade of the pine trees. Children were running round in the play-ground beside them and squirrels leapt through the branches. The birds seemed a little chirpier. The air was definitely a few degrees cooler.

'What is it?' asked Ani. She turned the cone in her hand to find the best part of the ice cream to lick.

'What's what?'

'Whatever it is you want to tell me.'

'How do you know I have something to tell you?'

'You've got that *I've-got-something-important-to-discuss-with-Ani* look on your face.'

'*Mon Dieu*,' said Mila, 'am I so transparent?'

'Yes,' said Ani. 'You are.'

So Mila told Ani the details of the boat trip out to the Quiberon peninsula. She explained about the jagged rocks that jutted so close to the surface, and the refuge pool that was only accessible at high tide, and how *Moonfleet* had been wedged in the rocks, perhaps deliberately, to make sure it didn't blow away in the storm, or perhaps it had been pushed there by the wind or the sea; either way, its occupants would have been trapped in that spot. She explained about the cave, and about how she and Arnaud Girard had climbed up the ladder and ventured into the interior; how, inside, they had found human remains.

'Was it my papa?'

'I don't know, darling.'

'You couldn't tell?'

'It was pitch black in the cave, Ani,' said Mila. 'We only had a tiny light; a pinprick. The only thing I saw clearly were the soles of the person's shoes.' She hesitated. 'I'm pretty sure they were a man's shoes. Trainers.'

'Oh,' said Ani. 'But in your heart, did you think it was Papa?'

Mila had thought about what she would say if her beloved niece asked her this question.

'Yes,' she said. 'In my heart, I thought it was.'

Ani nodded. Carefully, she nibbled around the edge of her cone, eating it down until there were only a couple of centimetres left, filled with pink ice cream. She put the whole lot into her mouth and crunched it.

Mila looked at her. 'Are you okay?'

'Yes,' said Ani.

'It's a big thing. It will take a little while for it to sink in, Ani. When it does, when you're ready to talk about it, you let me know, okay?'

Ani wiped her fingers on her bare thighs, pressing down into the tanned skin. 'Can we get a cold drink now please, Mila? I'm thirsty.'

67

The following week, Mila did not have to work at Toussaints. Carter and Ceci were both in the office, so there was no room for her, and anyway, she didn't feel like working.

It wasn't as if she didn't have plenty of alternative ways of occupying her time and she wanted to be available to Ani. She had been watching her niece closely over the past days, paying extra heed to her moods, and doing her best to look after her. Ani *seemed* to be fine, but she was quieter than usual, and more thoughtful. She had taken to sleeping beside Mila, in Mila's bed. Mila didn't mind this at all; it was reassuring to have Ani beside her and if her presence comforted Ani, even a little, then she was glad.

Taking a leaf out of her stepmother's book, Mila made a list of all the jobs that needed doing, and also other things that weren't tasks per se, but that required her attention. This included making sure she called Luke every evening, and her mother at least twice a week, whether she had anything to say to her, or not.

She opened a file on her laptop and started to plan Lydia's birthday. She would organise everything down to the last detail and then it would go swimmingly and Lydia would be happy and Mila wouldn't have to feel so guilty about her all the time.

In your dreams, said Sophie.

Mila spoke to her father, who said he would come over to Brittany for a visit.

'You're not coming to Maidenhead for Mum's birthday then?' Mila asked, defensively.

'I am, but I'll come and have a couple of days with you and my granddaughter first, if you're both agreeable to that suggestion, and you can fill me in on your concerns about Lydia and then we'll come up with a plan of action to help Lydia without Lydia getting offended.'

Mila found herself seduced by the way Patrick referred to Ani as his granddaughter. He had always treated both Sophie and Ani in exactly the same way as he treated blood members of his own family. Ani, of course, adored him.

'Ceci says I can stay with her, if that's easier for you,' Patrick continued.

'As long as you're not going to upset her.'

'Why would I upset her?'

'Oh Dad, I don't know. Maybe if she were to get wind of the fact that you've been spotted out and about by the *Daily Mail*'s online sidebar of shame with a certain actress with whom your name has previously been linked.'

'Deedee is a friend, Mila. Press speculation is bollocks, you know that.'

'I know, but I don't know if Ceci does. I've had a really stressful couple of weeks and I don't want any more drama.'

'No drama, I promise you. So, it's okay for me to book my Eurotunnel ticket?'

'Go ahead,' said Mila. 'It'll be lovely to see you.'

* * *

Mila finished emptying Charlie's wardrobe. When it was all done, she cleaned the entire interior with white vinegar, and then left the doors wide open for forty-eight hours which, according to the internet, was the most effective way to eliminate any musty smells.

She packed the old books that had been stacked beneath Charlie's underwear in plastic crates, and also the two wooden boxes of bric-a-brac that she'd collected around the house. These she carried out to the woodshed. The wood supply was greatly depleted, it being summer, so there was plenty of room to store them there until she'd decided what to do with them.

* * *

Mila went swimming every day; twice a day sometimes, depending on the tides. She felt better for it; each time, she could feel her muscles becoming stronger and she felt more alive afterwards.

One afternoon, when she was on the beach alone, she took a book with her, and after her swim, she lay on her towel reading, but it was an effort holding the book open above her face. The sun was shining in the most perfect way, so she felt warm, and healthy, but it wasn't so strong that she was worried about damaging her skin. She lay the book down, and put her dress over her face so she wouldn't burn, and she allowed herself to doze.

She was fast asleep when her father came onto the beach, stepping down, from the little path that led through the dunes. Ani was with him. Patrick had found his granddaughter alone at the sea house and she had said she would show him the way.

'There she is,' said Ani, pointing to Mila.

'There's who?' asked Mila, even in her sleepy state alert to her niece's voice. She pulled the fabric from her face and propped herself up on her elbow, covering her eyes with one hand. 'Dad?'

'Hello, number one and best daughter,' he said.

* * *

That evening, the various members of the Toussaints/Shepherd family, and some of their friends, came together for a meal in Moran-nez. Ceci had thought ahead, and booked a table at Le Croguervol – Ceci would have preferred Le Liège, but the party was too big for that restaurant to accommodate. In any case, Le Croguervol was a lively place, facing the seafront, more appealing to the younger contingent *and,* as Ani pointed out, they were less likely to be bitten to death by mosquitoes.

The whole front of the restaurant was made of panelled doors that could be pushed right back so that it was entirely open to the elements; there was a wide awning, and the waiters were young and cheerful.

Patrick, Mila, Ani, Ceci, Carter, Emmanuelle, Harry, Jenny, Melodie and Denis Sohar, Pernille, JP and Romeo sat around the tables, pushed together, on the terrace outside the restaurant, plastic gingham cloths clipped to the table legs. Candles burned in the necks of empty wine bottles; glasses were drained and filled; and bread was broken and passed around as the diners waited for their main meals to arrive.

Le Croguervol was a fish restaurant, like many of the most popular establishments in that part of Brittany. It also served pizza. The plates, when they came, contained fish cooked in cream, in wine, in garlic and herbs, or enormous hand-made pizzas with the thinnest of crusts, topped with oily tomato sauce and all manner of good things. Mila alternated her Margherita pizza with mouthfuls of a delicious salad, soaked in lemon juice and olive oil; hot, thin frites, and slices of herby vegan cheese.

There was music and chatter and laughter and the only awkward moment was when Solene Bolloré came out of the bar next door and saw Emmanuelle sitting beside Melodie – Emmanuelle and Melodie had been the closest of friends in the *Bande Sauvage*, but Solene had never liked Melodie. Nothing was said, but there was a tension as the three women exchanged brittle small talk. Then Solene's sister, who was with her, took her arm and told her they had to go, and the tension was abated.

Mila kept checking on Ani, but Ani was enjoying both the food and being in the warm glow of the spotlight of the joint attention of Patrick and Ceci. Her grandparents were competing for her affection and she was soaking it up. Mila, watching as always, thought Ceci seemed tired, but her father was in good form.

Patrick had intended to stay with Ceci, but that night he walked back to the sea house with Anaïs and Mila, and Mila said: 'You may as well stay here, Dad. You can have my bed.'

'I'll stay,' said Patrick, 'but only if you'll let me sleep on the sofa.'

Mila wasn't going to fight him over it.

'Put some music on,' he said. 'Proper music, not that modern sweary nonsense.'

He went into the kitchen to find a corkscrew and Mila and Ani dusted down the old music system with the turntable on top that hadn't been used since Sophie and Charlie disappeared. Mila remembered Charlie dancing in this very room a few years earlier, his fair hair jiggling as he hopped crazily, barefoot, holding a beer bottle by the neck in one hand, a cigarette between the fingers of the other. She thought of Sophie watching him, an expression on her face that was hard to read. Not approving. Not loving.

Oh come on, said Sophie, *all couples who live together piss one another off from time to time.*

But it wasn't that either, said Mila. *I couldn't work out what was wrong.*

Because nothing was wrong.

Mila wracked her memory, but couldn't remember *why* Sophie's behaviour had made her feel so uneasy that night.

'Let's have some Dave Brubeck,' said Patrick.

He put the record on, and for a few seconds there was only the sound of the needle jumping in the groove, then, as if at a distance, the first seductive jazz drumbeats began. Patrick passed Mila a glass of red wine and Ani lifted her hands above her head, and began to dance.

68

Dave Brubeck finished and Patrick pulled out another record: Erma Franklin. Ani sloped upstairs to chat to her friends online. Mila curled up on the armchair and watched her father.

The first track was 'Piece of My Heart'.

Patrick closed his eyes. 'Your mother and I danced to this the night you were conceived,' he said.

'Too much information,' said Mila. Then: 'I can't imagine Lydia dancing to this.'

'It was on a beach in Thailand,' said Patrick. 'It was a real hippy beach. There was a fine moon rising over the sea, making the water silver, and the palm trees were dipping towards the sand. There were shooting stars, and burning torches stuck in the sand. Music... drink... It was the most perfect evening.'

He was speaking with his actorly voice. The words and the tone painted a seductive picture.

'I never knew Mum had been to Thailand,' said Mila.

'Well, you're the living proof that she was there.'

'Wow.' Mila listened to the sublime voice of Erma Franklin for a moment, then said: 'She's never talked about it as far as I remember.'

She uncurled herself, and sat up, curious. 'But then, you never told me either. When did you and Mum go to Thailand?'

'We didn't. Well, not together. It's where we met. Has Lydia honestly never told you the story?'

'No.'

'And you never asked her the circumstances of your coming into being?'

'I asked her once, when I was about nine, but she just went pale and clammed up and I felt awful for upsetting her. I never mentioned it again.'

'She was ashamed,' said Patrick, 'of being pregnant out of wedlock.'

Mila frowned. 'I can imagine that when she told Grandma Constance she was expecting there would have been hell to pay.'

'Yep. Your maternal family was properly committed to old-fashioned values and old-fashioned humiliation.' Patrick sighed. 'I still feel bad about what happened to Lydia. Not that I regret you, darling, don't think that for a minute. But I didn't *mean* to ruin Lydia's life. As far as I was concerned, that night, *your* night, was just a beautiful night on a beautiful beach shared with a beautiful young woman.'

Mila was still struggling to think of her mother in that context. Full moon parties in Thailand brought to mind hedonistic young people with bare feet and colourful clothing: beads in their hair; piercings; fire dancers, friends drinking cocktails mixed in plastic buckets through straws. Not one of those things would have appealed to the Lydia who Mila knew.

'I was three years old when you and Mum got married, wasn't I?' she asked.

'Yes, darling.'

'So, what happened in between? You and she hooked up in Thailand and spent the rest of that summer travelling together?'

'No,' said Patrick. 'Your mother and I were together for just the one night on the beach. We slept in my cabin. It was magical. When I woke the next morning, Lydia was gone. Afterwards, when we were married, I asked her why she'd run away like that, and she said it was because...'

He paused. 'I'll tell you what she said, Mila, but please don't judge me for it.'

'I won't.'

'She said I'd taken advantage of her.'

'Oh!'

'She told me she didn't know what was going on. She thought someone must have spiked her drink,' said Patrick. 'It's possible, of course.' He looked up. 'But it wasn't me and, honestly, Mila, I didn't feel at the time that there was any advantage-taking going on. That night, Lydia was ebullient. She was happy and crazy and... and she didn't *seem* drunk. We didn't just dance, we talked. We talked for hours and hours and she seemed... fine. She was funny, rational, good company.' He fell silent for a moment. 'She kissed me first. She definitely made the first move. I thought she was the most amazing girl I'd ever met. She was bold, she was sexy, she was clever and hilarious. I thought we were soulmates.'

The woman Patrick was describing didn't sound, to Mila, anything like her mother.

'But you took each other's phone numbers?'

'We didn't have mobile phones back then. And we didn't take addresses or anything. I mean, I would've taken her details if she'd been there in the morning. I'd have asked her to stay with me so that we could travel together. But I never had that option. All I had of Lydia was her name and the memories of her, and the few snippets she'd told me about her life.'

'So how did you and she get back together?'

'It was three and a bit years later. I'd settled in London and I got a role in a TV crime drama series. My first gritty role.' He smiled. 'Lydia saw me on the television and sent me a photograph of you.'

'Really? That's how you found out about me? By photograph.'

'Yes.' He smiled. 'Hold on. Where's my jacket?'

'In the kitchen.'

Patrick got up and disappeared, returning a few moments later with his wallet in his hand. He opened it and took out a small picture, which he passed to Mila. It was an old-fashioned photograph, printed by Boots. It showed the toddler, Mila, wearing a pinafore dress with her hair cut very short, glowering into the camera. The photograph had been taken in the garden of the Maidenhead house.

'That's the picture Mum sent you?'

'Yes.'

'You kept it all this time?'

'Darling, of course I did. I mean, you were a bit of a shock, I won't pretend you weren't. But a nice one. The best shock ever. I got on the train at the first possible opportunity and came to visit you. Lydia was waiting at the station, and you were with her, a snotty little doll of a child, with rosy cheeks and...' He tailed off. 'It was love at first sight as far as I was concerned. You weren't as besotted as I was. You took a bit of winning over, but I got there in the end. I don't suppose you remember.'

Mila shook her head. 'No.'

'Well, you wouldn't. You were still a baby.'

'This is mind-blowing, Dad.'

'It's quite the story, isn't it! Perhaps I should have told you sooner, but by the time you were old enough to even begin to understand, things had started to go wrong between me and your mother and, to be honest, Mila, the right time never came.'

Erma Franklin was singing 'Son of a Preacher Man' now.

Mila asked: 'So, you and Mum resumed your romance in Maidenhead, did you?'

Patrick said nothing. A shadow had passed over his face.

'Oh God,' said Mila. 'You didn't want to get married, but she made you?'

'She didn't *make* me,' said Patrick. 'She delivered an ultimatum and how I reacted to that was my choice. It was difficult for her, Mila. She had so much to cope with. It was at that time that Constance was going completely – I know I shouldn't use this word – but *mad*. She was batshit crazy. And Lydia was trying to look after you and her mad mother in that great, gloomy mausoleum of a house. Her older sister had buggered off and left her in the lurch. She said she didn't need a boyfriend, she needed a husband. And you, she said, needed a full-time father, or else you'd be better off without one at all.'

'She threatened to cut you out of my life if you didn't marry her?'

'She was trying to do her best for you, Mila. Lydia wasn't the girl I remembered from Thailand, but she'd been through a lot in the intervening years. It was no wonder that she'd changed. I didn't want to marry her, no. But I wanted to do the decent thing and she needed to fight her corner; it was a fair enough bargain. There was no way on earth I was going to risk losing you. I wanted to be a father to you. I wanted to make up for the three years that I'd already missed. And I wanted to support Lydia. I thought, if I could make her happy, she might revert back to being the girl she used to be – at least the girl I *thought* she was.' He sighed. 'I did my best. I tried. I never did make her happy. But I can't have been all bad, because look at you! Look how well you turned out! Mila, I couldn't be more proud of you.'

Mila's eyes grew hot. She tried not to be affected by her father's occasional displays of love, but it was difficult not to be moved. When Lydia spoke of love, it was in order to weaponise the term: to make Mila bend to her will because Mila felt guilt or pity. Patrick's unconditional affection was unfamiliar. Mila did not know how she was supposed to react.

They squeezed hands and were quiet for a while, listening to the music. Patrick topped up their wine glasses.

'Darling, you're quiet this evening,' he said. 'What's the matter?'

'Nothing's the matter, Dad. But you know this body... the... the *person* we found in the cave.'

'Ceci filled me in on the details.'

Mila glanced towards the stairs. There was no movement from above, no sound or light to indicate that Ani was still awake. Still, she leaned forward before she next spoke so that Patrick would hear, but Ani, even if she was listening, would not. 'It's likely that it's Charlie.'

Patrick nodded. 'I realised it must be.'

'He was phobic about dentists,' Mila said. 'He had terrible teeth and he never had them seen to. Which means there'll be no dental records by which to identify him. He was adopted, so there's no easy access to blood relatives in the UK. They're going to have to take DNA from Ani and match it against that of the person in the cave.'

'To see if that person is Ani's father?'

'Yes.'

'I don't quite see what that has to do with us, Mila.'

A silence fell between the father and daughter. Mila turned the glass in her hands. She didn't know how to ask Patrick the question she needed to ask.

'Are you wondering if I'm sure that I'm your father?' Patrick asked.

Mila stared into her glass. 'I've always thought that you and Lydia seemed an unlikely couple. The story you've just told me explains much of it but... I don't know. We don't look much alike, Dad, do we?'

Patrick smiled. 'I think there are certain similarities. We both like our coffee black and our wine white.'

'I'm not sure that proves anything.'

Patrick reached across to squeeze Mila's shoulder.

'Would it matter very much to you if I wasn't your genetic father?'

Mila considered for a moment, then said: 'I don't know. I'd like to think it wouldn't change anything but I don't know, Dad. Emotions are funny things. They don't always do what you expect them to do.' She thought some more. 'Deep down, it wouldn't change how I feel about you. But I think I'd be superficially upset.' She glanced at him. 'Why did you ask that question?'

Patrick stared into his drink.

'Oh my God,' Mila said. 'You took a test already, didn't you?'

'Forgive me, darling, but yes. Yes, I did.'

'To check that I was your kid?'

'It wasn't my idea. My father was rewriting his will after Lydia and I were married and he insisted on it.'

'Does Mum know?'

'Yes.'

'Wow.'

Patrick cleared his throat. 'I, err... I didn't tell her before I took the test, I told her after.'

'I bet that went down well.'

'It wasn't my finest moment.'

Mila smiled. Then she looked up, and directly at Patrick. 'And what did the test say? Are you my blood father?'

Patrick took a handkerchief out of his pocket and carefully wiped the corner of his eye. 'Yes, darling,' he said. 'Yes, I am.'

69

TWO WEEKS LATER

Luke drove Mila along the M4, over the Severn Bridge and into Wales. They passed Cardiff and then took the junction that led them towards the coast, and Carnarth.

Luke had taken Friday and Monday off work so that he and Mila could spend the long weekend together. Lydia's birthday celebrations were scheduled to take place on the Saturday. Luke had agreed to go to Maidenhead with Mila. Patrick was going to meet them there and had organised rooms in a nice hotel on the river for Friday night – Patrick's treat.

They were going to stay at Lydia's house on the Saturday. 'We have to, Luke!' Mila had protested when he'd objected to that part of the plan. 'We can't let her be alone on the night of her seventieth birthday and she won't stay in a hotel.'

It was only the one night when all was said and done. They could both put up with the discomfort of the Maidenhead house – the musty bedding and the rattling plumbing – for one night.

For the Sunday, Luke had booked a room in an old pub in Marlborough, so Mila and he could spend Monday walking the Wiltshire countryside. That was something to look forward to.

Patrick had exclaimed, 'Over my dead body!' when Lydia had said that she'd like her birthday dinner to be at The Rookery. He'd arranged, instead, for them to go to a gastropub in Marlow run by someone who had been a runner-up on *MasterChef* a couple of years previously and who Patrick said was rated highly by those in the know. Lydia would hate it, no doubt. She'd complain that the food was too fancy at the time, and afterwards she'd say she had heartburn and couldn't sleep. Although she wouldn't come out and say it in so many words, the inference would be that Patrick's insistence on not eating at The Rookery was to blame for her suffering.

Mila made a mental note to ask her father about Lydia's assertion that they used to go to The Rookery when they were courting. She suspected that this was a misdirection of her mother's, if not an outright lie. Perhaps they'd been there once. Perhaps it was over some dismal meal there that they had the 'ultimatum' conversation that Patrick had mentioned. And anyway, she now knew that 'courting' did not, in this context, signify love's young dream, as she had previously imagined, but a far more complex relationship; a contractual one, in fact.

A marriage that had only happened because of her, Mila; that blissfully ignorant, runny-nosed toddler.

It rained the whole way from Bristol to Carnarth; heavy, relentless rain that made motorway driving nightmarish and meant the windscreen wipers on Luke's car were working overtime. Lorries sent up great clouds of spray and Mila felt claustrophobic. It wasn't a straight section of motorway, it curved and dipped and rose. Luke, like Carter, was a fast driver. Mila tried to relax. At least she was inside a car, not on the back of a motorbike.

'What are you going to say to Mrs Moorcroft?' Luke asked.

'I don't know,' said Mila. 'I just want to make sure that she and Briony are all right.'

She had spent many hours thinking about Briony and Mrs Moorcroft. She had hoped they were untangling the knots of the lies in which they'd been imprisoned for so many years. Every time she saw a small, white van, she was reminded of the night when she and Carter rescued Briony.

Every time she saw a gnome in someone's back garden, she thought of Billie.

* * *

The rain had eased a little by the time they came into Carnarth, and had all but stopped when Luke turned the car into the estate where the Moorcrofts lived.

'That one,' said Mila, pointing, to their house. This time, although the BMW with the personalised plates and the Moorcrofts' Maid Services van were absent, a beaten-up old Ford was on the drive. A *For Sale* board had been hammered into the patch of soil beside the fake lawn.

'Are you coming in with me?' Mila asked Luke, as she undid her seat belt.

'No, thanks,' he said. 'I'll wait here. I'll listen to the cricket on the radio, if there's anywhere that hasn't been rained off.'

Although Mila was profoundly grateful for the lift, she was relieved to be going inside alone. She climbed out of the car, holding the flowers she'd ordered and collected from the reliable shop in Totterdown before they left Bristol, and walked up the drive to ring the doorbell. She knew she was being videoed, which made her feel awkward. But she only had to wait a moment before the door was opened.

Mila had been expecting to see Gwyneth Moorcroft. Instead, she looked up into the face of Billie Dexter.

'Oh!' said Mila. 'Hi!'

Billie scowled. 'You,' she grunted, but she held the door wide so that Mila and the flowers could go in.

The house wasn't as tidy as it had been last time. Boots cluttered the hallway; a coat lay over the back of the chair; a half-eaten dog chew was on the rug. Mila followed Billie into the living room. In the middle of the room was a rowing machine, which took up most of the available space; the furniture had been pushed back to accommodate it.

Briony Moorcroft, wearing a Lycra leotard and shorts, was using the machine, moving backwards and forwards on the sprung seat. The dog was lying beside her and he wagged the end of his tail when Billie came into the room.

The exercise was making a difference to Briony. Already, her arms had some muscle definition. There were roses in her cheeks and her eyes were brighter.

'You're looking good,' Mila told her.

'She's doing great,' said Billie, proudly. 'We'll have her running marathons soon.'

'Ha, ha!' said Briony.

The door at the other side of the room opened and Gwyneth Moorcroft stood there, in a slouchy, velour tracksuit, with her hair loose around her shoulders.

'Hello, Mila,' she said with more warmth than Mila had been expecting.

'Hi,' said Mila. She leaned across the machine and handed over the flowers. 'These are for you.'

'How kind! You didn't need to bring me anything; it was a nice enough surprise that you were dropping in, wasn't it, girls?'

'Not really,' said Billie.

'Not at all,' said Briony.

'Don't mind them, Mila,' said Mrs Moorcroft. 'Come through into the kitchen, I'll put the kettle on.'

The kitchen was untidy too, but not dirty. It felt, to Mila, more homely; normal. The two younger women had clearly got into the habit of helping themselves to snacks and drinks, but neither, it seemed, enjoyed loading the dishwasher.

Still evolving, said Sophie.

'You preferred coffee, didn't you?' said Mrs Moorcroft.

'That's good of you to remember.'

'I was trained to remember details like that. My husband used to get cross if I got things wrong.' She filled the kettle and plugged it in.

'How are things?' asked Mila.

'So-so.'

'It must have been a hard time for you.'

'It has been,' said Gwyneth Moorcroft. 'Some people... well, when they found out that Briony wasn't really ill, they blamed me. Of course, they did. Because in the past, you know, when they used to ask how Briony was, I'd go into great detail about her illnesses and her medication and...' she trailed off. 'Some of the neighbours have been really off with me. They said I should give back the money that was raised for Briony's holidays, and for the modifications to the house. And they're right. I should give it back, and I will, as soon as the divorce is settled. Once the house is sold, and I know how much money I have, I'll put things right. I'll give back what I can, and I'll fundraise for the rest. I don't want anyone to be out of pocket on account of us.'

'What about your husband?'

'He's getting treatment. He went voluntarily, sectioned himself. I could be cynical and say he's doing that to avoid facing up to his crimes, but maybe that's unkind. Maybe it's for the best.' She pushed her hair back. 'I just don't want him to ever have the opportunity to do to anyone else what he did to Briony.'

'He abused you too,' said Mila gently.

Mrs Moorcroft shook her head. 'I should've been stronger.'

'No victim,' said Mila, 'should blame themselves.'

Gwyneth Moorcroft made the coffee, and, from a plastic container, produced a Co-op coffee and walnut cake. She cut two slices, put them on plates, and passed one of the plates to Mila.

They ate in the kitchen, standing up, with their mugs on the counter.

'Does Billie come round here often?' Mila asked.

'She's living here,' said Mrs Moorcroft, and then, in response to Mila's surprised expression: 'It made sense. We have the room and she had nowhere to go. My sister, Sylvia, she's been very good. She's got this lawyer friend of hers working for all of us: me, Briony and Billie, trying to sort out our messes. Billie might have to go back to prison for a short spell, but hopefully they'll be lenient, now her circumstances have changed. I've told her she can stay with us as long as she likes. She's part of the family as far as I'm concerned.' She smiled. 'She's a good girl. She has a good heart. Briony recognised that. I didn't.'

'And does Briony have any plans?'

'She does actually. She's thinking of applying to university. Who'd have thought that Briony would ever be well enough to go away and take a degree. And Billie too! She's a bright girl, Billie, you know! The only problem with her is, that up to now, nobody's given her a chance.'

70

SATURDAY AFTERNOON

Mila had a text from Carter.

Human remains removed from cave and taken for examination. Also diving gear.

What diving gear? Mila replied.

Found in cave.

Mila didn't think a response was necessary, so she put her phone in her pocket and continued to walk down the garden of Lydia Shepherd's house, to the water's edge.

Because of all the rain, the river water was brown and soupy. It was running high; a whole section of sloping bank that had been accessible on Mila's last visit had disappeared now beneath the torrent. The water swirled and rushed; a plastic bottle, on its surface, spinning downstream at warp speed.

What was left of the old boathouse was leaning over at a dangerous angle. It wouldn't take much, thought Mila, for the whole thing to collapse into the water. And then what? The wood would fall apart and be washed downstream towards London. And either it would get stuck in the Thames Barrier or it would carry on, and perhaps it would float right through the capital city, past the banks and the tower blocks and the hotels, and the palace, and the cathedral and under the bridges. It might find its way out to sea.

And then... then the world would be its oyster.

It could end up in the Bay of Biscay, thrown about by the infamous storms, or it might travel further, finishing its journey on some beach in Western Australia, thousands of miles from where it started, because that was how life worked. You started off somewhere, and you were moved about, partly of your own volition, but mainly by forces beyond your control. If you were lucky, and courageous, like Billie Dexter, you ended up somewhere better than where you started. If you were unlucky, like the person in the cave, or like Sophie, you didn't.

Mila sighed. The air was humid; heavy and close. The sky was low, grey and threatening. She didn't want to go too close to the water. She was afraid of slipping into it, afraid of inhaling the toxic soup discharged from the storm drains into the river, and afraid of having another flash-back. She didn't want to see Sophie's dead body swirling in that brown mass. She'd had enough of grief; of searching for the missing.

Of finding them.

Go inside, Sophie told her. *Go and be with the others. Lighten up. Have another glass of wine.*

I miss you, Sophie, Mila told her.

I know you do, said Sophie.

Mila turned from the water and headed back up to the house, to her family.

She couldn't wait to return to Morannez.

ACKNOWLEDGEMENTS

It takes a team to make a book. In my case, it takes an incredibly patient team of brilliant editors. So the biggest thanks as always go to Sarah Ritherdon, Jade Craddock and Rose Fox. You are the absolute best.

Enormous thanks too to the whole Boldwood team, especially Amanda, Claire and Nia, but everyone else involved in producing, designing, marketing, distributing and promoting my books, including the audio and foreign language versions. I am so proud and privileged to be part of #TeamBoldwood and appreciate the hard work, skill and talent of everyone connected with this fabulous publishing team.

Thank you to Estelle Taylor who has been a brilliant Welsh language consultant for this book, and special thanks also to Alice Twaite, who helped with the French for *The Lost Notebook* and this book, and who I omitted to credit last time. Sorry Alice and merci.

Massive thanks as always to my wonderful agent, Marianne Gunn O'Connor, and to Pat and everyone connected with selling, promoting and producing the foreign language versions of my books.

Thank you to all the authors most of whom I've never met in person, but all of whom I consider friends. Thank you to the librarians, book bloggers, sellers, promoters, enthusiasts and influencers. Thank you to RNA. Thank you to every person who's read any of my books and to readers, everywhere. Thank you to everyone, involved in any way, with the publishing industry. Thank you to my friends in person, on Facebook and Twitter who help make writing fun.

This book is the second to be set in Brittany. I have combined fictional and real-life locations, and have been writing largely from memory. I've tried to stay true to the spirit of Finistère, one of my favourite places on earth, although I have taken a few liberties with the geography of the region. Thank you to the people of Brittany for giving me such wonderful inspiration.

BOOK CLUB QUESTIONS

1. What lies do you think the title is referencing?
2. From the very first line, the weather is mentioned. What role does the heatwave play in this story?
3. What are your impressions of Lydia? Do you like her? Do you feel sorry for her?
4. How do the descriptions of Lydia's house, the restaurant and the home where Constance lives make you feel? Do you think Mila is projecting her own discomfort onto the reader?
5. What do you think of Mila's fiancé, Luke Hogg? Do you believe Mila and Luke really do have a future together?
6. How do you feel about Mr and Mrs Moorcroft? Did you have your suspicions about their version of events from when you first met them, or was the truth more of a slow-burn?
7. Who do you think is the stronger character, Billie Dexter or Briony Moorcroft?
8. The story of Billie and Briony is driven by their characters, but also by events beyond their control. Which aspect do you feel is more important to their story?
9. What are your impressions of Billie? Did they change as the book progressed?

10. The factitious disorder Munchausen Syndrome by proxy is important to the plot of this book. Have you encountered any real-life cases of this condition or read about them? Do you feel it is accurately portrayed in *The Summer of Lies*.

11. As well as the main story about Billie and Briony, the mystery of what happened to Sophie and Charlie is bubbling away in the background of this book. Do you think this device works?

12. As a reader, how do you feel about the focus of the book moving between these two different plotlines? Do you feel more strongly about one plot, and if so, which one, and why?

13. Although Sophie has been dead for two years, she is very present as a character in *The Summer of Lies*. Why do you think it's so important to Mila that she keeps Sophie 'alive' by talking to her in the way that she does?

14. The theme of good mothers runs through this book. Who, in your opinion, is a good mother in this story, and who isn't?

15. What are your theories about the body in the cave? Who do you think it is, and how do you think he got there?

16. The author has cited the influence of Daphne du Maurier's work on her writing. Can you spot any homages to *Rebecca*, in particular, in *The Summer of Lies*?

ABOUT THE AUTHOR

Louise Douglas is an RNA award winner and the bestselling author of several brilliantly reviewed novels. These include the number one bestseller *The Lost Notebook*, and the *The Secrets Between Us* which was a Richard and Judy Book Club pick. She lives in the West Country.

Sign up to Louise Douglas' mailing list here for news, competitions and updates on future books.

Follow Louise on social media:

facebook.com/Louise-Douglas-Author-340228039335215
x.com/louisedouglas3
bookbub.com/authors/louise-douglas

ALSO BY LOUISE DOUGLAS

The House by the Sea

In Her Shadow

Your Beautiful Lies

The Secrets Between Us

The Secret by the Lake

The Scarlet Dress

The Love of My Life

Missing You

The Room in the Attic

The Lost Notebook

The Secret of Villa Alba

The Summer of Lies

Boldwood

Boldwood Books is an award-winning fiction publishing company seeking out the best stories from around the world.

Find out more at www.boldwoodbooks.com

Join our reader community for brilliant books, competitions and offers!

Follow us
@BoldwoodBooks
@TheBoldBookClub

Sign up to our weekly
deals newsletter

https://bit.ly/BoldwoodBNewsletter